All the Way Around the Sun

XIXI TIAN

Quill Tree Books
An Imprint of HarperCollinsPublishers

HarperCollins Children's Books, a division of HarperCollins Publishers,
195 Broadway, New York, NY 10007

HarperCollins Publishers, Macken House, 39/40 Mayor Street Upper, Dublin 1,
D01 C9W8, Ireland

Quill Tree Books is an imprint of HarperCollins Publishers.

All the Way Around the Sun

harpercollins.com

Library of Congress Control Number: 2025933582
ISBN 978-0-06-308607-4

Typography by Jessie Gang
25 26 27 28 29 LBC 5 4 3 2 1
FIRST EDITION

For my grandparents;

and for Da Ji Cun, which lives only in memory,

and now, the pages of this book

one

THE BEGINNING

It's strange to think about how, for me, there is no time before you, but there will be, after. When I came into this world, you were already here, two years ahead of me. I guess that's what makes it hard to get used to. I guess I'm still getting used to it, even now.

The day you leave for college, we drop you off at the airport. Mama and Baba buy you a one-way ticket to Boston. We'd never bought a one-way ticket anywhere until then. The ticket sticks out to me the most, the idea that we couldn't plan for when you'd come back. You are flying into the wider world, and we are letting go of the tether, hoping that you will return on your own. That you won't get lost in space.

Looking between you and our parents is like two sides of a looking glass. Mama and Baba are teary. But even though you are trying to seem sad too, I can see that you are actually suppressing excitement.

I wonder what I look like.

You give us each a hug outside the security checkpoint. I've never seen Baba cry before, but his face leaves damp patches on your shoulder. I mainly just feel curiously detached, as if my body hasn't quite figured out what's going on yet.

"Enjoy being an only child," you whisper, teasing.

"I've been waiting all my life," I retort.

You hug me tight for an instant, and then it's over. You walk toward the security entrance. Right before you turn the corner, you look back for a moment and flash us a grin. You disappear.

My entire life, I've felt as though you were walking ahead and I was following you. When we were young, I remember Nai Nai shouting after you wherever you went, "Deng deng mei mei, wait for your sister!" Me, toddling after. Seeing your back while you headed somewhere else was nothing different for me.

What's different is that this time, no one asks you to wait. You are really leaving me behind.

I watch you go and know that nothing will ever be the same for me again.

The beginning of life without you.

If we had known then that you wouldn't return, we would have never let you go. We would've forced you into the car and driven all the way back downstate.

We would've kept you here.

We would've made you stay.

two

I WAS GETTING tired of starting over.

The past year had been full of figuring out how to adjust to our new reality in different ways, but this was the biggest change yet.

I wanted to get on a plane and fly back to the only house I'd known in the United States, back in Mount Pierce, Illinois. Failing that, I wanted to go back to sleep for another three hours.

But in this, like most things, I had no choice.

My alarm clock was ringing. It was morning. I was in San Diego, California. I needed to get to school—my new school—so I could finish out my second semester of senior year, in this place where I had nothing and knew nobody.

Well, not nobody.

My head throbbed. I had a hundred thousand worries here. Almost everything ranked higher than that particular problem.

It was seventy-five degrees outside, and we had a palm tree in our new backyard. Two facts that I could not process, given that it was also January. Baba had said when we moved here that it would give us the mood boost we needed, as though all we had been missing was a little bit of sunshine. As though we had just been suffering from an acute case of seasonal affective disorder.

If only it were that easy. I would've suggested that Baba simply go out and buy us some SAD lamps instead of finding a job on the other side of the country and uprooting what was left of our lives.

The golden sunlight filtered into my bedroom like a mockery. My window was open. Winter wasn't supposed to be like this. It just didn't feel right.

Of course, nothing had felt right since Sam had died, so maybe it didn't matter.

I put on the first clothes I could get my hands on at the top of my unpacked boxes.

When I got downstairs, Mama was waiting with a fresh steamed bun for breakfast in the kitchen. Baba must have already left for his new job at the cybersecurity company headquartered here.

She raised her eyebrows. "You will wear that to your first day of school here?"

I looked down. I was wearing a pair of gray sweatpants and a yellow T-shirt from being on my old school's newspaper staff.

The shirt had been washed so many times that the cheap iron-on lettering was crumbling off.

Mama spoke Chinese to me, and I answered, always, in English. It was the way it had been since Sam and I moved to the United States to join them in Illinois, and we started going to school there.

"It's fine," I said. "The other clothes smell like travel. I have to do laundry."

"It's important to make a good first impression as a new student. The teachers don't know you yet." She paused. Her worry pumped through the air in the room. "I still don't understand why they did not put you in the advanced classes, like you were at home."

I noticed that *home* slipped into her phrasing too easily. I was slightly heartened that she, too, still felt as though this were not home yet.

"In Illinois," she corrected. She looked heavily concerned, an expression I was too familiar with over the past couple of months. There was no detail of my life that was too minor not to fret about, no facet of my future she couldn't polish over and over in her careful hands. After all, it was only me she had left to mold. I had to fill the place of two.

Under her scintillating attention, I was suffocating. I had to get out of here.

"I don't know. I will work it out with the school counselors. I'm sure it was just a mistake with the transcript or something when I had it transferred over."

Her forehead relaxed. "Yes, that would be good. I know you will take care of it. You are good with these things."

I took the bun and wolfed it down in two bites, even though I wasn't hungry at all.

"Are you nervous?" she asked, a sliver of her worry creeping back in.

"No," I said automatically. "Don't worry about me, Mama. I will be okay. It's just a new school. I'll make the adjustment."

I was so used to lying to her. It came out easy. Like a bird flying, or a tree shedding its leaves in the fall. I lied like it was all I knew how to do.

Weston High School was going to be different. The social hierarchy, the teachers, the curriculum. I knew all that. I was going from a lowly ranked public school with a bare smattering of AP classes to one of the most highly ranked public high schools in the state, with a standout science program, access to college courses at the university, a complete suite of AP and IB classes, two high-tech labs, and a student body that regularly fed to the Ivy League every year.

Yet for some reason, the thing that I couldn't get over was that Weston had outdoor hallways. I had never seen anything like that before. The corridors had an awning over top but were open-air. They crisscrossed through a large square courtyard.

And the courtyard had orange trees. Seriously, orange trees. I felt as though I had moved to another country, not another state.

Besides that, it meant that a significant portion of the student body could see me walking down the hallway as I headed toward my first class, in my sweats and old T-shirt. I was new, I wasn't dressed like everyone else, and I looked ridiculous.

People stared.

I tried to ignore them. At the same time, I wanted to stare too. Back home, I had been one of two Asians in our small high school. The other kid was a third-generation Vietnamese guy, while I spent the first eight years of my life in China. To Mount Pierce's student population, though, we were basically the same.

Here, it was like I had moved back to Asia. If I had to guess, two-thirds of the student population were some kind of Asian. But it wasn't like being in China. These people were all very American in the way they dressed and the way they looked. I was surrounded by tanned skin, straight white smiles, and glossy hair. The girls had perfect eyeliner that I'd never been able to master. Mine always seemed too thick or too thin, and the flick at the end was never at the correct angle. A lot of girls had dyed hair that started off dark at the roots but lightened to a smooth caramel at the ends.

My flat black hair seemed so boring and unfashionable in comparison.

Behind me, I caught snatches of people speaking Chinese. I turned around, startled. Two girls almost ran into me.

"Watch where you're going," one said in perfect English.

They were like me, completely bilingual. Yet they were flipping back and forth in public, as though it were nothing. I never spoke Chinese with anyone except my family.

The girl who had spoken watched me expectantly, as if waiting for an apology. I wanted to say something to her. I wanted to tell her that I was like them. It would've been silly, but it was all I could think about.

In the moment, though, I couldn't summon anything to say in either language. I could see their eyes traveling up and down, taking in what I was wearing.

Before I could say a word, they shrugged and brushed past me, continuing to babble in Chinese about some guy in their AP Chem class.

I stood there for a minute as people rushed around me. I gathered myself, shrugged my backpack on my shoulder, and resumed my path toward Wing C, where my first class was waiting.

I wondered how I was going to navigate this place, so utterly different from anywhere I'd lived before. My life had been uprooted once, when I moved from my grandmother's small village outside Xi'An, China, to the utter center of the Midwest in Mount Pierce, Illinois. And now, it was being uprooted again. It hadn't occurred to me that this change might be just as big as the first one.

I sat in the counselor's office during my lunch period, nervously tapping my fingers against my thigh.

"Let me pull up your current schedule," the woman behind

the desk said. She was youngish. Maybe in her mid-twenties. Her brown hair was pulled back in a neat ponytail, and she had bright red glasses. "Sorry, the internet is a bit slow today."

I scanned the walls of her cramped office. I tried to create a plan for what I was going to say to advocate for myself. The Stella of a year ago would've written bullet points in advance. But the Stella of a year ago also wouldn't be in this predicament in the first place.

"You're enrolled in all standard curriculum for a senior in the state of California, except that we allowed you to transfer over to the AP Literature class here."

"Yes," I said. "But I have my transcript from Mount Pierce, and I was in three other AP classes." I was in all the AP classes that Mount Pierce offered. I handed over the piece of paper to her.

She scanned the sheet. "Right. AP Bio, AP Calculus, and AP European History. I remember." She hesitated. "Ms. Chen, our curriculum here is rigorous, perhaps even more rigorous than what you're used to. And your grades the first semester in those courses . . . they aren't what we'd expect for someone continuing on that track here. Even if you were a current student, we would've been having serious discussions around whether you should consider easing up."

She slid the paper back across the desk. I could see the grades popping back out at me in bold. C- in AP Bio. D in AP Calculus. C+ in AP European History. A- in AP Literature, the one class I'd qualified to keep here.

My parents hadn't seen these grades. I had quietly ferreted away the copy before we moved and vaguely blamed it on address problems when they didn't receive anything in the mail.

"I'm sorry. I cannot justify slotting you into those courses here. I would be setting you up for failure, when it will already be difficult to jump into a class halfway through. Second semester is going to go so quickly. There is no time for catch-up." She tilted her head, not without sympathy.

Seeing the letter grades in front of me felt freshly humiliating. I had never been assigned anything like them in my life, not even when I had first moved to the United States and didn't speak a lick of English. I wasn't always straight A's, like Sam, but I certainly had never sniffed a D before.

"I had extenuating circumstances," I said.

Her eyes widened. "I see. What might they be? I see you were a good student for much of your high school career. But then, last year was the first year you started taking AP classes. It can be a big adjustment."

I couldn't look at her. I stared at the transcript sitting between us. There wasn't any kind of contextual explanation for your GPA ever on your transcript. It was just a bunch of letters, just your high school achievement boiled down to a single decimal number. It wasn't as though there could be an asterisk appended to my senior year, indicating that my brother had died. If I wanted people to know that, I would have to tell them.

I realized that this was the beginning of it all.

I would have to tell this woman, whose name I couldn't even

remember, whom I just met minutes ago. I'd have to write it down in the Common Application so I could tell colleges, probably in response to one of the inane essay prompts like *Recount a time when you faced a challenge, setback, or failure; how did it affect you and what did you learn from the experience?* Whenever I explained my transcript, I'd have to do it within the structure of that crude framing—something that happened to me and what I learned from it. It felt infantilizing and cruel to assume that there was anything that could be learned from Sam's death, and it also seemed unbearably crass to use it as a shield for my academic performance.

The woman was waiting for me to respond. I couldn't.

"It was nothing," I said finally, my throat so dry I could choke.

She closed her laptop. "It's fine. It'll be less stressful this way. You'll see."

"How was your first day?" Baba asked at dinner.

We were eating simply because we hadn't fully unpacked everything yet. Mama had made one dish of tomatoes and eggs and a pot of rice. The rest of the pans were still in boxes.

The house was bare, uncomfortably bare. Everything around us, from the cardboard to the blank walls, reminded me that we were no longer home. I would be here for eight months before college—if that happened—and then I'd be gone. Not enough time, in my opinion, to ever adjust to this place.

In the room between mine and my parents', Sam's things sat

in boxes stacked high to the ceiling. I knew they would be the last to be opened. We all seemed to walk more quickly past that doorway, until finally, someone had shut it so we wouldn't have to see the everlasting reminder of unfinished business.

"Fine," I said.

"Everyone nice?" Mama asked.

I nodded, although I did not talk to anybody, other than in passing and to introduce myself in each of my seven classes. Nobody was mean, but neither was anyone interested in getting to know me. It seemed that I barely existed. That was okay, though. It was what I expected.

"Good, good," Baba said. Everything was going according to plan. "Did you see Alan today?"

I shook my head. He was the one person at Weston I knew, and our families went way back.

"It's a big school," I said, not wanting to put any significance on whether I'd seen him or not.

Quickly, I changed the subject before they could pry further. "How was your job?"

"Great," Baba replied. "They have food trucks in the parking lot for lunch. Can you imagine? Food trucks, every day." He shook his head, like this was an unbelievable extravagance. Toto, we were definitely not in Kansas anymore. I thought about telling him about the outdoor hallways and orange trees, but we were not in the business, ever, of sharing much about our lives. For years, I didn't even know what my father did. I always said he was a systems analyst, but I wasn't really sure what it meant, and he never bothered to tell me. Baba was efficient in his actions and his words. He elicited exactly what information he wanted and never anything more.

Mama worked as a program manager, but she was still interviewing for jobs. All the more time for her to hover. I needed her to be gainfully employed again, and soon.

"Did you fix your class schedule?" Mama asked.

"I'm working on it. It's going to take a couple of days." I wasn't sure what I was going to tell her when my schedule stayed the same through the rest of the semester. But I would buy myself some more time to figure it out.

She frowned. "You have to fix it quickly. You don't want to miss too much time out of your classes. You'll fall behind. Especially at a new school. You want to end high school on a strong note. Besides, you have so much to do with college applications. It's a lot." She was sharp, apprehensive.

I absorbed her anxiety like a sponge. "I know, Mama."

Baba cleared his throat. "We have been discussing, and your mother and I—"

My chest constricted, suddenly fearful of what they might say next.

"—decided it might be a good idea to do some college visits this month in California. You'll qualify for in-state tuition since we'll be California residents, and there are some very good schools here."

I put down my chopsticks. This was not what I was expecting. I tried to draw out how I felt about it. Not good.

"In the next few weeks, before applications are due. I know you are still working on them. Maybe this will give you the inspiration you need. What do you think?"

It was clear that this was now going to be my parents' North Star, getting me into the right college. I was no Sam, of course. With him, going to an Ivy was a given. For me, the expectations were a little closer to earth, but I knew they were still thinking a UCLA, maybe. A Berkeley.

They believed that getting my applications finished was a simple matter of dedicating time and effort. I hadn't told them the truth. In the past month, as the deadline approached, I'd realized I had a more complicated problem than I could describe.

I was afraid of going to college.

For many people, it was a normal rite of passage. The next step toward independence and adulthood. But eight months ago, my brother had died in his dorm room at Harvard. It would be ridiculous to think that we would all just come out of that unscathed. Yet my family was desperate to try.

The idea of going to college made me ill, filled me with this uncontained fear, no matter how much I tried to reason with myself. I was mostly dealing with the problem by putting it off, thinking maybe it would just go away by itself. Time was the great healer, but I was running out of it. The application deadline for the UCs was in under a month.

"It will take some days away from school," Mama said. "But this is so important, you know." Her throat seemed to quaver. "We worry about you, after everything that has happened."

Baba threaded his hands together on the table, a position I knew to mean he was about to say something serious. "There are moments in your life that are critical and shape the future direction. College is the most consequential decision so far for you. Without it, you cannot succeed in this country. You cannot make a life for yourself. That's why we worry for you. Do not lose focus. We need to know that you are still on the right track. We are thinking this trip will help you."

They were both looking at me with a mixture of hopefulness and uncertainty.

I could hardly stand their expressions. The expectation laden in their eyebrows. The desperation pulling at their cheeks.

But it was easy to make their troubles slide away. It was a gracious power, and I exercised it generously. I could always say the right things, put forward the words they wanted to hear, and they would fade back into a numb comfort.

I shaped my face into an imitation of a smile. "Okay," I said. "That sounds like a good idea."

Their faces gleamed back at mine, two worthy mirrors.

three

Sometime in the middle of my second week, I sat in US Government, my eyes on the sweeping second hand of the clock over the door, my mind wandering to a different plane.

Given the state of my grades this year so far, I should've been more focused on what was going on in the class, but I couldn't make my brain do much of anything these days. Soon, we'd be going on a road trip through California to see a series of colleges that I might never be attending, if I couldn't get over my mental block.

I pushed the thought away.

"Okay," the teacher said. His name was Mr. Starnes. He was tall, mildly balding, and gangly; a perfect prototype of a US Government teacher. "You're going to need to pair up for the next project, because we will be doing debates."

I straightened up and scanned the room. People were already

making eye contact with one another and scooting close to each other. I hated this. It was like picking teams in gym. I was at a massive disadvantage.

Predictably, I watched as everyone else grabbed a person right away. I was left looking to my left and right and seeing no leftovers.

"Anybody not paired up?" asked Mr. Starnes. "Ah, yes, Stella. Morgan over there needs a partner as well. Why don't you move over and join her?"

I grabbed my bag and trudged across the room to the empty seat next to hers. I recalled that her last name was Park, so she must be Korean. She had straight-across bangs and an under-streak of blue.

"Hi. Sorry you have to be stuck with the new girl," I said, trying to break the ice with a little self-deprecation.

She shrugged and summoned up a huge sigh, as though she had, indeed, drawn the short straw. I felt chastened.

"Where are you from again?" she asked.

My defensiveness kicked in, having gotten that question from a countless parade of people in my life, ranging from curious to hostile. "China," I responded, shortcutting to the answer I assumed she wanted.

"No, no," she said impatiently. "I meant where did you move from. I forgot what Mr. Starnes said when you joined."

"Oh. Illinois."

"Like, Chicago?"

"No. Mount Pierce."

"Where is that?"

"It's downstate."

She wrinkled her nose. "What did they have there?"

I didn't know what to say. There were no identifiable landmarks, other than the midsize telecommunications company Baba had worked at. "Corn, I guess. It was small."

She frowned, as though she couldn't contemplate such a place. "I didn't know there were any Asians there."

It was my turn to shrug. "There weren't that many."

"Weird," she said. I couldn't decide whether her statement was a pronouncement on me, Mount Pierce, or my place in it. I felt oddly protective of my home. For all its flaws and my rocky start there, it was still unquestionably a big part of me. I hadn't ever expected to move somewhere that would look down on it.

My locker was on the opposite side of the school from my last class of the day. As I walked down the long, beautiful outdoor path to the building on the other side, peering at groups of students chattering along the stretch, I wondered if I would ever make any connections here. It was brutal to move during the final semester of senior year. While I couldn't blame Baba for wanting to start over somewhere away from all the memories, it was impossible for me to extinguish the small flame of resentment I held against him.

I wanted to feel the familiar. I didn't need sunshine and citrus. Beaches weren't as appealing with no one to go with. I wanted gray skies and movie theaters with my friends. I even missed the icy winter blasts I would've been braving to the parking lot every day at this time of year.

I opened the double doors into the building and turned the corner. There, right down the hallway, unmistakable as day, was Alan Zhao.

It had been four years since we'd last crossed paths, but I still recognized him. He was tall now, taller than the two Asian guys he was walking with. He had rectangular black glasses, a straight nose, and a neat haircut, revealing a high forehead. He was tanner than I remembered, maybe a consequence of becoming a California transplant. He looked relaxed and happy. He was chuckling with his friends.

A few things happened in quick succession.

His eyes caught mine.

I felt a hard swoop in my stomach.

I immediately turned toward the closest wall to face a bulletin board of student extracurricular activity announcements.

I hadn't prepared for this moment. For some reason, having not seen him thus far made me believe that maybe I just wouldn't see him at all. It was a big school. As I understood it from my parents, he was a fantastic student, so he was probably in all those advanced classes the counselor refused to bump me into.

Hearing his voice behind me now, it was clear what an unrealistic assumption that was. There was no way I wouldn't run into him, sooner or later.

He had seen me, for sure.

I held my breath, bracing for him to call out to me or tap me on the shoulder. But it never came. I heard his laughter as he passed me by. Within a minute, his voice had disappeared. He was gone.

Embarrassment filled me to the brim, then a simmering anger. I couldn't believe my first reaction was to hide, as though *I* were the one who had something to be ashamed of. It turned out, although he had grown up and much about him had changed, the one constant was still that he wouldn't be caught dead around me.

I was about to turn back to my locker when one of the flyers on the bulletin board grabbed my attention. The school newspaper was looking for more writers this semester. There was an email contact if you wanted information. I pivoted away without allowing myself to linger. If I couldn't get my grades up this semester, I couldn't get distracted with extracurriculars. I had to keep my focus.

I packed my things and headed out into the winter sun, trying to shake Alan's face, the snapshot of his smile just before my eyes slid away.

I splayed across my bed. My laptop was open in front of me to the Common Application.

All I had left to do was just write a personal essay and hit Submit. I could write about anything. It didn't even have to be particularly good. I could generate a couple of paragraphs of bland garbage and call it a day. But I had reached this point two months ago and still hadn't gotten any further.

I kept thinking about what it was like when Sam applied for college. A whole different situation. We had gone on an entire college tour up and down the Eastern Seaboard. I remembered Sam's energy back then, his repressed excitement. Even though he was quiet, I could see the shine in his eyes.

I watched him, jealous and itchy that I would have to wait another two years for my turn. College would be a whole new world. He knew he was going to be free. That's what we thought.

Now I sat in my new room, in the same life stage as he once was. The screen was too bright. The air was too warm. My clothes scratched at my skin from the new detergent Mama bought, different from what we used in Illinois. Even the small things had to be all wrong.

I opened the window and then closed it again. I tried to meditate using an app I downloaded. Nothing was working. Whenever I pulled up the tab on my browser for the Common App, my anxiety spiked. My heart went at an unnatural gallop. My palms went suddenly damp.

A medical condition, maybe. I could ask my parents to take me to a doctor, get it checked out. Something was deeply wrong with me. The idea of going to college, going away from home, like Sam did, made me physically ill. This was not normal. I knew that. It was debilitating enough, enormous enough, that I was not sure I could fix it by myself, much less in the span of the few weeks I had left before applications were due.

But I couldn't bring it up with my parents.

For the past six months, I'd developed acute insomnia, where I couldn't fall asleep for hours. At first, I'd tried just lying still with my eyes closed and blanking my mind—the standard advice. I tried counting sheep. I tried spinning up stories to lull myself into slumber. I tried reading boring books before returning to bed. I couldn't beat it. Eventually, I gave up and just started scrolling on my phone, even though screen time supposedly made it worse.

You could tell by the circles under my eyes after a week of really bad insomnia. I could see it in the mirror when I brushed my teeth in the morning.

Mama and Baba never said a thing.

Such was the precarious state of our equilibrium, after Sam. We didn't ask too much of each other. I didn't ask them about the throaty hacking sounds I heard from their room in the middle of the night. They didn't ask about why I couldn't sleep.

How could I introduce my existential fear of college to them, if we couldn't even talk about something as concrete as insomnia?

I closed my laptop after an hour, my cursor still in its blinking position on a blank page. My bones ached. I felt exhausted, although I knew I was doomed for another night of staring at the ceiling.

There was a knock at my door.

"Liang Liang?" Mama said. "Can we come in?"

I sat up and instinctively attempted to straighten up my bed. "Yeah. What's up?"

My parents both stepped inside, their hands folded. I felt taut as a bowstring. Somehow, I knew before they even said anything that something was wrong.

"There's been a bit of a change in plans," Baba said. His face was pained, but he was trying to draw it into a gargoyle optimism that looked far worse than the alternative. "Something has come up in China. Your mama and I have bought tickets to return in two weeks."

"In two weeks?"

They nodded.

Without you was the unspoken part.

My parents watched me carefully. The bed beneath me felt like water. I was floating unsteadily, across the deep blue. A lake, or the Pacific Ocean. Waiting to be pulled out; waiting to drown.

four
FROGS

The yellow dirt of the summer comes thick and dusty each year to Da Ji Cun. I squat to tie my shoelaces in front of Nai Nai's house. My sneakers are coated.

You come clomping after me through the front doorway. We're both wearing tank tops and shorts, but even so, we're sweating. It's still morning. Summer in the middle of China is so hot that everything wilts. The hazy sky spreads all around like a whiteout, so bright that you can't look up without squinting into tears. The ground is coated with fuzzy pink mimosa flowers from the tree next to Nai Nai's door. When we go on the roof, the branches are close enough that we can reach out and gather them for tea.

You have a big bucket swinging in your right hand. "Let's go catch some frogs," you say, your face splitting with a grin.

Nai Nai's house is at the end of Da Ji Cun, which means the village of big joy. I learned the words for it in English only this past year. Village of Big Joy sounds clunky on my tongue, like most of the new words I'm learning in school. In front of the house, there's a small circular pond with steep banks like the sides of a whirlpool. Nai Nai told us not to get close because the water is deep and a boy had drowned in it before.

Da Ji Cun is outside Xi'An, after the pavement grounds into packed yellow earth. Follow the road for forty-five minutes, until you begin to doze off and the outer suburbs give way to low fields of wheat, the road edged with rows of dusty ash trees.

The village is surrounded by an old brick wall with its name in faded paint. It consists of three dirt roads in parallel. The houses are built right against each other, sharing cement walls on either side, easy for shouting over the top and passing across meals. Each house has a front room with a sitting area and kitchen, a back area with bedrooms, and a courtyard in the middle open to the sky, with stairs leading up to a second level. Nai Nai's courtyard is full of roses and grapevines. In the most frigid winter nights, we used to huddle in Nai Nai's hard bed, warmed by the coal furnace underneath.

But now we live in America with Mama and Baba, and so we only come back in the summertime. When I'm here, it's easy to forget that this is not home anymore.

The other kids in the village join us. We're a ragtag pack, feral and loud, ranging from four to eleven. School has finally let out in the village, and they're as ready to wreak havoc as we are.

"What do you learn in American school?" Lixin asks me. He's a year younger than me. He's got a streak of dirt in his hair and has big round eyes. He's a runt, but the villagers say he's got the best eyes in town. "Do you eat pizza and hamburgers every day?"

I shrug as we trek out of the village onto the dirt road, under the trees. I don't like talking about life in America. The others are endlessly curious. You have a lot to say, but I never do. It reminds me that in three weeks, we have to go back.

Although you're not the oldest, you lead the way. Maybe because Nai Nai is the eldest in the village and you are her prized grandson, or simply because you're the special kid from America. We all fall in line.

I skip to the front of the group to walk side by side with you. "Where are you taking us?"

You shake your head, smiling. I'm annoyed but giddy. You usually don't keep secrets. It must be a really good one.

We walk for twenty minutes, which feels like hours in the sweltering temperature. I am panting by the time you stop abruptly. We've passed at least three different fields. It's the farthest I've ever gone out without an adult. I glance behind me, and Da Ji Cun is a tiny dot far away. The air shimmers with heat. I stick my tongue out like an animal to see if I will cool down faster.

"Listen," you say, your hand cupping your ear.

We stand stock-still. We hear it all at once. The sound of running water.

You scramble down the side of the road, sloping toward the line between two fields. And I see it. A tiny creek, cutting the two properties in half. In a flash, we're all in the gully, our shoes squelching with mud, our ankles wet.

We don't have to look very hard. Frogs begin leaping out of the water, out of the grass. We're surrounded by frogs, bouncing all around us, croaking in a ribbity chorus. They're different colors on a spectrum of brown to yellow to bright green.

We fill our bucket with a shallow amount of water from the creek and then load it up with frogs. Some of them leap out, but we cover the top with a lid with holes.

Soon enough, we've gotten our prize and climb out back onto the road. Dirty, hot, and supremely satisfied.

"A pet frog," I keep saying over and over again.

Mama and Baba never let us have any pets.

I hold hands and sing on the way back with a girl nicknamed Gou Gou, for little dog. Her hair sticks up in pigtails and she's wilder than any boy.

Gou Gou's mother stands at the head of the road. She is out of work this summer, souring slowly at home. She's a stout woman with big hands and a wide face. She's wearing a dress with a faded floral pattern, inevitably coated in dust, and scowling up a storm. "Gou Gou!" she shrieks. "Where have you been? I'm going to kill you."

Gou Gou squeals and whispers in my ear, "I stayed out all last night and hid on the roof. She never found me."

Gou Gou's mother makes to rush toward us, her hands on her hips. "Give me your ear, you little devil." Her Chinese has a strong local accent, earthy and brash. The adults in the village don't speak Mandarin well, because most of them never went past high school. The kids can switch back and forth because the teachers now are required to teach in the Mandarin dialect—or Beijing dialect, as we call it in Chinese—even out in the countryside.

You and I used to speak the local dialect perfectly, but now that we live in America full-time, the village children switch to Mandarin when they speak to us, as though we are no longer from here.

"Run!" one of the boys shouts gleefully, and we all scatter before Gou Gou's mother's rage.

At high noon, we take the bucket into the courtyard and gingerly set it down under the shade of the grape trellis. Inside, Nai Nai has dressed cold noodles with spicy chili oil, black vinegar, soy sauce, cucumbers, spongy wheat gluten, cilantro, and bean sprouts. You add an extra dribble of the hot oil to your portion. We slurp our lunch happily, faces smeared with oil and sauce. Cold noodles are perfect for a hot day.

There is no air-conditioning here, and the electricity stops working during the day, siphoned off to the city for use, so we don't even have fans. The midafternoon is too hot to breathe. Nai Nai goes into the back room to take a nap. You and I lie on the cool tile floor, pressing our cheeks one way and then the other for relief. When we get bored of doing that, we creep into the garden quietly to check on the frogs. They must be warm too. They bob in the water, legs bending and extending slowly. They've quieted down and stare out with glazed eyes.

Evening comes. Nai Nai is in the kitchen, prepping dinner. She pulls aside the curtain to the courtyard, her hands covered in flour. "Let's clean up. You two are filthy."

You take the bathroom, which has a showerhead and a sloped floor where the water drains away. Nai Nai and I bathe in the courtyard, where she fills two big tureens with water. The cool water feels wonderful as it evaporates off my skin. Nai Nai rubs a citrusy-smelling shampoo into my hair.

"Dirt everywhere," she scolds.

I throw my head back and take in the sun-streaked sky, as pink as the mimosa flowers. Nothing is better than an outdoor bath. I hate washing up in our new bathroom at Mama and Baba's house. Tiled and sterile and nothing to see when you look up.

"Next time we take a bath, the frogs can be with us," I say.

"Mm," she hums noncommittally. She hands me a rough-textured towel so I can dry off.

I shake my hair so it flings droplets of water everywhere.

Nai Nai laughs. "Silly girl." She asks me to get rid of the dirty water while she sets the table.

I pour the water into the garden. It seeps into the rich black earth.

We eat ravenously at the dinner table.

"I'm thinking about the frogs," Nai Nai says carefully when we're almost done. "Don't you think they would be happier if you let them go into the pond?"

My head jerks up from my bowl. "They're our pets," I protest. I look to you.

You shake your head. "Do we have to?" you ask.

"You don't *have* to," Nai Nai says. "It's your choice. But maybe the frogs miss their home. Maybe they don't think it's fair for you to have taken them somewhere new where they don't know anybody." Nai Nai never raises her voice, not like our parents. She never scolds or disciplines. Instead, she provides commentary, but with enough suggestive flavor so that you feel her disappointment deep into the soles of your feet.

You look at me, upset. My face flushes red in shame.

"We didn't mean to," I say.

"I know," she says gently. "But you can let them go back."

I glance to you for direction. In everything, I always still defer to you, the one who knows best, the one who speaks for both of us.

Your face wrestles with the decision, but in the end, your sense of responsibility wins out. "Okay," you say at last. "But can we wait a little bit after dinner?"

Nai Nai nods.

We go into the courtyard to check on the frogs as Nai Nai cleans up. They are quiet and watchful, as if they know they are close to freedom. I take one finger and slowly stroke the top of one frog's slimy head. Its eyes blink. It opens its mouth and croaks.

"Be good, froggy," I tell it.

After it gets fully dark, we take the bucket outside and Nai Nai follows us. The moon shines in an almost full coin. Against the horizon, the artificial city lights glow in the distance, giving the deep teal-blue sky a pale-colored rind, like the edge of a watermelon.

The pond is completely still. We stand at the road, right before the banks begin to slope toward the water.

"We can let them go here," Nai Nai says. "Frogs will always find water."

"Are you sure?" I ask, looking up at her.

"I'm sure," she says. "They'll be just fine."

You pour the water out carefully. For a moment, the frogs seem stunned, but then one of them croaks and they all start hopping madly down the banks. They hit the water with bright moonlit ripples and disappear. I watch the lagging frogs leap around until all of them are gone. The bucket is empty, and the night is quiet.

I feel sad.

"Nai Nai," I say, "how come the frogs get to stay here at home but we have to leave? I want to stay too."

A flash of surprise flickers across her face before she quashes it. "America is your home now, mei mei. With Baba and Mama."

In three weeks, we will have to get on a plane back to Illinois. The next time we come back, everything will be different.

We stay outside until the song of the cicadas makes us sleepy.

We hold hands in the time before childhood ends.

I DIDN'T KNOW much about Alan these days and what he was like.

From my parents, I knew he was a model student. Straight A's. Bound for a top-tier school. Debate team. Two-sport athlete—cross-country and tennis. Mama and Baba spoke of him with a tone of subdued admiration. He'd taken to California like a flower to the sun. I wasn't surprised, of course.

From Morgan Park, I knew that he was well-liked. Popular. She knew his name instantly when I brought it up, which was enough indication, given the school had two thousand people. She'd looked at me with surprise when I'd mentioned it.

"You're friends with him?" she had asked in a tone that felt borderline insulting if you read into it at all.

"Not friends, really." I struggled with trying to figure out how to describe what we were. "We used to know each other," I said at last, which was the only thing that felt remotely accurate.

"Years ago. Back in Illinois."

"He's from Illinois too?" Her finely penciled eyebrows almost disappeared into her bangs. "Since when?"

"Since always?" I scanned for signs of recognition and found none. "He went to my school for two years before moving here."

She shrugged. "He always said he came from Shanghai."

"He did. But that was before."

"Huh. Maybe he doesn't like to talk about it."

"Maybe," I'd replied.

So that was the only other thing I knew about him. That he'd disappeared a chunk of his past—all the parts that included me—once he'd come out here.

Besides all that, he was a stranger to me. But he wouldn't be for long.

We were parked in the driveway of Alan's house early on a Saturday morning. Salmon-colored stucco siding, a two-car garage, and the distinctive Spanish red-tiled roof that was so popular in this area.

Baba killed the engine in the driveway and turned to look at me. "Ready?" he said brightly, as if I were about to embark on the adventure of a lifetime.

They had laid it out methodically, piece by piece, that night they came into my room to tell me something had come up. My cousin in China was getting married. My cousin's father traveled frequently for work, and his mother—Baba's sister—had slipped down the stairs and broken her leg. Baba was the eldest man remaining in the family, and thus, had a responsibility to help finish up the arrangements for the wedding while his sister was immobile. Nai Nai was frail and in no position to have the stress put upon her. They would be there for two weeks. They would come back.

I couldn't go with them.

"But we haven't forgotten about the college visits. I know you were excited about them," Mama had said.

They had called up their friends, and it turned out Alan was planning a trip up the coast to visit the major schools too. He would be happy to take me. They had already scheduled out where we would stay. Two stops with our parents' family friends, so we'd have appropriate supervision, of course, and then the final stop in Palo Alto as part of a formal "overnight with student ambassadors," where we'd both already been registered.

"We would go with you if we could. You understand," Mama had told me, almost as an afterthought.

How could I say no? It was already locked. All I was doing was providing the rubber stamp so my parents could feel like we had come together to agree. But I didn't feel like I had any choice.

Sitting there on the cusp of this plan, the reality of the situation was bearing down on me. The pull of my anxiety became urgent.

I finally managed a real protest. "Do I have to do this?" I asked.

Mama turned around in her seat. "What's wrong?"

"Why can't I go with you to China?" I sounded timid and

pathetic, even to myself.

"Come on," she replied. "What are you nervous about? Alan is nice. You remember him. You used to get along so great."

"It's not that," I said, although it was that, somewhat.

"What, then?" Her eyes probed me. "Tell me."

It was silly. But I had always imagined that we would go on the trip together, like we had done with Sam, way back when. Shouldn't they have wanted to come with me? Shouldn't this have been more important than Xiao Xiao's wedding?

Before I could say anything, the front door to Alan's house swung open.

"Xiao Chen!" Uncle Zhao shouted, barreling down the front walk toward us, hands extended.

Mama's expression snapped back from curious to composed, and I knew the time to put my foot down was over.

Baba emerged from the car, his face split in jovial enthusiasm. The two men embraced heartily. Uncle Zhao, lanky and balding; Baba shorter, but with his silver hair intact. Seeing them together again reminded me of that first summer, the smoky barbecues in our old backyard, when the Zhao family had first moved to Mount Pierce. The smell of cigarettes from our fathers permeating long into the grassy night air, while Alan and I gleefully collected fireflies and mosquito bites.

I blinked away the sharp memory, catching me off guard with its potency.

Auntie Li followed on her husband's heels. "Grew taller," she said to me in Chinese, the ultimate compliment, patting me on the head as if I were a poodle. "Quick, quick, come inside."

Although we had moved several weeks ago, this was the first time we had seen the Zhao family. Like Alan with me, they had kept their distance, letting us settle in slowly. I often wondered with situations like ours, if people could sense some kind of aura that drove them away. It had felt like that back home. The unbearable faces of even the people at school who knew me, once they found out what happened to my brother.

Tragedy was a repellent to others. It forced you to be alone.

We went inside and took off our shoes. "Thank you for supporting us during this time," Mama said.

"Of course, of course. We are so happy Alan can help," said Auntie Li, waving her hand modestly to indicate that this was nothing.

"Where is he?" Mama asked, looking around as though he might be hiding behind a corner somewhere.

"Still sleeping. He had an event last night, but he'll be up soon. I thought he could use the extra sleep, since he's driving today."

I lingered briefly while the adults pattered into the kitchen. I could smell tea brewing and pork buns heating in the steamer. Against the wall, a big cabinet with clear glass doors sat across the way, and it was jam-packed with trophies and medals. All from Alan for chess, tennis, and various other extracurricular activities. A floor-to-ceiling bookshelf featured a lot of sci-fi and fantasy novels. The wall against the staircase was lined with photos of the family.

This house felt so lived in. The contrast of it to our house. It all seemed like a knife, further twisting in my belly. I turned away.

"Have some breakfast, Liang Liang," Auntie Li called from the other room.

I went in. All the adults were assembled around the table watching me. They hadn't sat down. I felt shy. I wasn't sure if I was supposed to take a seat or not, so I stayed standing.

"How is the adjustment to the new school?" Auntie Li asked.

"It's fine," I said automatically, picking up a bun from the table.

"Yes, I hope Alan is making a good introduction for you."

"Mm." I tried to be politely noncommittal. I couldn't throw her son under the bus right in front of her. "I'm finding my way."

"We are happy you're here. Closer to friends is better," said Auntie Li. "It's been so long since we've seen you. We have many things to catch up on."

"Yes, yes," Mama agreed readily.

"So much has happened," Baba said.

Mama gave him a sharp look, her eyes widening with dismay.

I was chewing, and suddenly, I found it difficult to swallow. The discomfort around the table was immediate and palpable.

"We know it must be hard," Uncle Zhao offered.

There was a painful silence. None of us seemed capable of looking at each other. I stared at the design on my plate. Delicate pink flowers.

"We're so sorry for your loss," Auntie Li said. "We are always here for you, if you need it."

This, I guessed, was what it would've been like to have a funeral for Sam. The endless condolences as we stood in a line. Would it have been better? Instead, my parents had decided to cremate his remains and hold no memorial. Everything we did, we did in private. It spared us the raw exposure to others and allowed us to hide our secret guilts.

Baba's face looked like a jigsaw puzzle; the portrait of a man who had not figured out how to put himself back together yet.

It was Mama who laid her hand on his forearm. "We should go," she said to our hosts. "Thank you so much for all of this."

Baba seemed to shake himself back into place. "Go?"

"Yes," she replied firmly. "We have to finish preparing our things. Our flight is in only a few hours. And we should get there early to deal with the international terminal."

A lie, but only I knew. Their flight was closer to evening. And they had already packed everything the night before.

She gave him a significant look. He seemed to understand.

"Stay," Auntie Li said weakly. "There's all this food."

"You are too generous. You are already offering us so much help with our daughter. Please," Mama said. "We will find another time to stay longer."

They were shuffling out, backing away, as they spoke, and it was clear that the escape was underway. We were powerless to stop them. Me, most of all.

We moved out of the house in a slow retreat, a reluctant herd. Until we were gathered by my parents' car. To my great shock, it was time to say goodbye. It was happening too fast. They were leaving me alone. My family would be all together on the other side of the ocean. Everyone together, except for me. I was being horribly, horribly abandoned.

Baba opened his arms to me and pulled me close. He smelled like ginger and five spice. I suddenly felt quite afraid.

"Take me with you," I whispered urgently. My voice quivered. "I want to hui jia. I want to see Nai Nai."

He let go before I did. I thought I saw a glint of wetness in his eye. A glimmer of regret. He seemed to want to say something, but nothing came out.

Mama cut in with her embrace next. It was short and efficient.

"You will be okay?" she asked. She phrased it as a question, but I could see that she was looking for reassurance. Her eyes were searching, her face taut.

I looked back and forth between her and Baba. I was used to this now after Sam died. They wanted to know that I wasn't going to fall apart on them. That I could handle it all.

They needed to know.

Every time, I thought about telling them that I couldn't actually do it. I thought about telling them that we were messed up. *I* was messed up. None of us knew how to move forward without Sam. I wanted to tell them about my lingering guilt. The secret I carried to Sam's grave, up to now. But every time, I studied them and knew that if I opened a crack in the fortress we had built around ourselves, we would crumble into nothing.

So, of course, I said what they wanted to hear. "I'll be fine. Don't worry about me." *Fine* rang strangely in my ear, such an odd word. I had said it so many times that it had lost all meaning.

Mama hugged me again, tighter this time. "Thank you," she whispered into my ear. "You're my brave girl. We'll talk soon, when we get to China. I promise."

It occurred to me that I had the answer to my question I didn't get around to asking. My parents didn't *want* to do any college visits with me. They had taken the first possible excuse to leave.

Maybe it hurt too much to be reminded of before. Or it scared them to think of where I'd be going, after Sam never came back. But I was scared too, and yet, it didn't seem to matter.

I watched them pile into the car and wave from behind tinted windows.

They drove away without looking back.

THE LAST TIME I saw Alan, I still had braces and he was a foot shorter. Now we were stuck together in a small silver sedan for the next three and a half hours until we reached Los Angeles. He would be my companion for the next week.

"You can call us if you need anything," Auntie Li said through the driver's side window to her son. "Drive safe, please."

"I will, Mom," he said.

I considered him in side profile. Close up and in detail, since I was not hiding from him in a school hallway. I could see that he did still resemble the boy I remembered. His voice had, of course, deepened. His slight British pronunciation from international school in Shanghai had flattened out. His skin had cleared up. His shoulders had broadened, although he was on the thinner side.

I didn't know how to feel about him. Thinking about how we'd left things back then still made me angry, but in the same way an ember in a dying fire glowed: a dull red, unless you deliberately blew on it. We were children, and now we were grown. I was ready to let it go. Yet I knew that, back in the hallway, he saw me and pretended like he didn't. And Morgan had told me he omitted his entire time in Mount Pierce from the history of his life. Just excised it right out, like removing a clip from a video. What was I to make of that?

He glanced at me sidelong, as we backed out of the driveway and hit the road for real. I took a deep breath and pressed my lips together, not knowing exactly how to break the silence now that we were alone and no longer doing parentally mandated small talk at the breakfast table. None of the stuff we had said before counted. I had already forgotten it all.

This was where it was going to start.

He went first. "Long time no see, I guess," he said mildly.

I almost laughed. Talking to him should've made me think of the last time we spoke to each other in Illinois, but instead, it made me think of the first time. The way his eyes brightened when he saw me, the only other Chinese kid he had met since moving to America. His opening joke.

"Indeed."

He was trying to crack the ice, but I was cautious. My heart was still a fist. It would not open so easily for him again.

"Your English has gotten better," he said.

"Same to you."

"We are both American now." He looked at me quickly with a grin.

I offered a polite smile back, revealing nothing. I thought he might switch to Chinese to see how I'd respond, but he didn't, to my relief. It had become a language of closeness and intimacy for me, something he and I no longer shared.

There was an extended silence as we passed several stoplights. I looked out the window. The sun, still unreal to me. The palm trees, like paradise. What kind of place was this, anyway?

"Can I tell you something? I was kind of worried about seeing you, to be honest."

I glanced sharply at him.

"I thought you might still be mad at me. Even after all this time. Is that silly?"

He was testing me. He was making light of everything, to make me the petty one if I weren't willing to laugh with him. I resented it. He was always like this. The kind of person who couldn't bear having someone be mad at him, even if he were at fault.

"Why would I be mad at you?" I asked, playing innocent. Yes, Alan, I thought. Explain it to me. Explain why you were so bent on acting like I didn't exist, only to pretend to be my friend again now. If he was going to poke at me, I was going to make him say it out loud.

He shook his head, retreating. "It was so long ago, I know. We were so young and naive. I hadn't even seen fireflies before in Shanghai, and I thought they were made up, like fairies or something." He was practically blabbering to himself now, his words speeding up as though they had somewhere to go in a hurry. "It's hard to believe how far we've come from when we first moved to the States. I feel so different now. I feel like every place you go makes you a new person. Do you feel like that too?"

He was nervous, I realized. It gave me a slight surge knowing this, a mild power trip. It seemed impossible that anyone could dent his confidence, but something about me did.

"Hey, Alan?" I said, interrupting his chatter.

He stopped immediately. "Yeah?"

"I'm kind of tired. Do you mind if I take a nap while you're driving?" It was basic courtesy to stay awake as a passenger and keep the driver company, but I didn't think he deserved that particular courtesy. At least not right now. He was right in one way. I was a different person from when he used to know me.

"Okay. Sure. No worries." He sounded disappointed. "Do you want me to put on music or something? What do you like to listen to?"

I shrugged. "Driver's choice. I don't care." I pushed my right shoulder into the leather seat and faced the other direction. Eyes open because I wouldn't actually sleep. I waited a long time for the radio to come on, but it never did. We drove in silence, me facing one way, him facing another.

When our parents introduced him to me and Sam, I was nine. The adults left the kids to play in the basement while they cooked and gossiped upstairs. We defaulted to speaking Chinese with Alan.

We had never met this kid before, but he brimmed with confidence, as though we were already close friends rather than total strangers. He brandished a pack of cards out of his pocket right away and asked if we wanted to see a magic trick.

"I need someone to be my assistant," he said grandly.

I was standing partly behind Sam, skeptical already of this boy's bright energy. I wasn't used to new kids coming on this strong, and it had been a long time since I'd made a friend. I hardly remembered how.

He pointed at me. "How about you?"

"Me?" I didn't move. "What do I need to do?"

"It's easy. You just have to pick a card. And I'll read your mind." He was so theatrical.

I looked at Sam. At two years older, he was less intrigued by this setup. He was losing interest in hanging out with his kid sister by the day and thought everything I liked was childish. He rolled his eyes, which made me a bit more determined.

"Okay."

Alan fanned out the cards face down. "Pick one and look at it. Don't show me."

I slid one out from among the lineup. Six of spades.

"Remember it?" he asked.

I nodded.

"Put it back."

I complied.

He shuffled the cards once, twice, three times. "Now I'm going to pick the card that you looked at."

I watched him, fascinated, as he carefully thumbed through the deck. After a few seconds, he triumphantly pulled out the six of spades. "Was that your card?"

I clapped, thrilled at this incredible sorcery. "How did you do that?"

He bowed. "A magician never reveals his secret."

Sam's eyes were sharper than mine. "Come on," he said loudly. "Are you serious?" At first, I thought he was also impressed, but his face was twisted into a frown. "You just flipped the last card in the deck upside down and then had Stella put the card in the other way so it would be the only card facing up after your shuffle. Stella, you didn't see that?"

He always noticed things when I didn't, or was able to discern how to solve a problem when I couldn't. He was sharp-eyed and logical. The scientist. I was always the one who wanted to believe in miracles.

"Was that the trick?" I asked Alan.

He colored slightly but kept his composure. "I'll never tell." He winked at me. "You want me to show you another one?"

Sam scoffed. "This is juvenile. I'm going to play video games." He stalked off upstairs, leaving the two of us.

"Sorry," I said, feeling responsible for my brother exiting so rudely. "He just thinks I'm boring and pathetic. It's not you."

Alan shrugged. "It's okay. He doesn't want to be friends with me. I can be friends with you." He said it as though it were a forgone conclusion rather than something I had any say in. "I know more card games for two people than three." He grinned cheekily, having already rebounded from my brother's rejection. "Maybe the trick was to get him to ditch us all along, so I'd have the right number of players. He didn't figure it out."

I laughed in surprise, which seemed to please him. It felt nice to be chosen.

That was how it started. The way we connected was easy. I barely had to do anything at all.

Alan was the kind of boy who loved introductions and finding a way into your heart. He was like sunshine in summer. You couldn't deny him. All you could do was bask in his glow.

After two hours of driving, we stopped to refresh, stretch our legs, and eat something.

He tapped my shoulder blade lightly. "Wake up," he said. "Noodle soup okay?"

My belly, as though responding on cue, growled.

He chuckled. "I'll take that as a yes."

I followed him into a dumpy-looking building in a strip mall. His rangy stride was still the same, shaped by a slight slouch. He had clearly been to this place before. There were several different booths inside, offering lit-up menus on display. Like a shabby food court. All the options offered different types of noodle soup. Roast duck, red-braised beef, pickled vegetables with pork, seafood. We both ordered and got our bowls within five minutes.

I was ready to be skeptical about the presentation, but the first scalding spoonful wiped away any doubt. It was delicious. Back home, I wouldn't have been able to get food like this unless we drove two and a half hours up to Chicago.

"Good, right?" Alan said. "We always used to stop here on the way to LA. There's a great boba shop two doors down we can hit up before we get on the road again, too."

He slurped loudly. It was immediately noticeable to me. I had spent so long adjusting my table habits when I moved here to eat more quietly, after one of the kids at school mocked me for eating with my mouth open. I still watched my manners scrupulously while eating in public. I'd probably always be self-conscious about it.

"I'm sure it must've been hard to move in the middle of senior year," he said, apparently determined to fill the empty space with or without my help. "But I think you'll like it. The food is way better, for one. And the weather. This is a pretty good place to end up, whatever you're leaving behind." He ended the sentence with an upward lilt, like he was cracking the door open to a question.

I *was* leaving things behind, although less than I would've a year ago. It turned out relationships needed nurturing. I hadn't been the best at that over the past semester.

I couldn't admit this to Alan, especially now, but the worst part of moving had been realizing that by the end, I didn't have anyone, really, to say goodbye to. The embarrassment still clung to me like an invisible cobweb. At least no one here would have to know about that.

My eyes traveled up from my bowl, and I found him staring

at me. Instantly, I recognized that look on his face, the one that preceded every time someone was about to give condolences for the terrible tragedy that befell my family, followed by the light curiosity around how my brother had passed, since my parents had been so tight-lipped about it.

"You know, I'm sorry about Sam," he said.

My insides clenched automatically. It used to be something I just managed to suffer through quietly each time I had to go through it. It was more about making the other person feel like they had done the right thing; after all, it wasn't like hearing their sorrys actually made *me* feel any better. It was merely a performative ritual that we all did for the sake of upholding societal norms around grief. Both of us, following a prewritten script. But the more time had passed, the more I hated it. Sometimes, I wanted to do something dramatic in response—throw a fit, run away, be honest about how little their words meant to me.

I thought about doing that now, letting out all the ugliness I kept inside. But Alan's eyes were deep and sincere.

Whatever I was going to say evaporated. There was a difference between him and those other people.

He had known Sam. Same as he had once known me. That was worth something, at least, even if it was a long time ago. I held a small, precious fistful of gratitude for it. The world was filled with people who did not know him, and now they never would.

"Thanks," I said. "What did your parents say about what happened to him?"

"Nothing, really. That he died in his dorm room. They said your parents didn't say why. They guessed it was an undiscovered health condition. Complete shock."

I didn't know whether to be relieved or disappointed that my parents were still keeping it to themselves.

"You don't have to tell me what happened. It doesn't really matter anyway, because at the end of the day, he's gone, right?" he said.

I took a sip of tea, its bitterness rolling around my tongue. "Can we not talk about this?"

He blinked. "Yeah, of course. I didn't mean to pry."

"It's just, like, I don't really even know you very well anymore, and I got forced into this trip out of nowhere, and I'm not going to get into the deep stuff with you in the first two hours, you know." An understatement, to be sure. I hadn't gotten into *the deep stuff* with anyone before, not even my own parents.

He blushed, and I felt kind of bad. I had sounded sharper than I meant to. I thought maybe I had shut him up for good, but he wasn't one to give up so easily.

"Sorry. Keep it entry-level. I get it. Let's start with that, then," he said. "What classes are you in?"

"US Government, Environmental Science, Statistics, PE, Journalism II, Band. And AP Lit."

"Cool. I've taken US Government and Environmental Science. I've got notes if you need them."

"Oh. Thanks." I looked down at my lap. "That might be nice."

I had two assignments in each I'd have to complete while we were gone. One of them being the group project I had to coordinate with Morgan on. I had already cratered my grades last semester. I couldn't afford to do poorly this semester with easier classes.

"You must be in one of the other AP Lit classes. We can cross-check to see if we're reading the same stuff. Probably yes, I'm guessing. I'm supposed to be reading *A Streetcar Named Desire* this week," he said.

"*Heart of Darkness*."

"I read that the first week. Maybe we can swap notes as we go through the semester. Start a study group together."

"Hm," I said noncommittally.

"Sorry," he replied. "Not entry-level, huh? I'm scaling it back."

That triggered a smile—a begrudging one, but real.

"What are you taking, then?"

"AP Lit. AP Chem, AP Calc, AP Euro, PE, Orchestra, AP Macroeconomics."

"I see." A full suite. No wonder my parents talked about him like he was a deity. "I was in AP classes too back home," I supplemented.

Once it left my mouth, I felt hot with embarrassment. It came off so defensive, like I was insecure about myself or something. And I really didn't want to seem insecure to him. Was I jealous? Not really—the high-pressure path Sam and, presumably, Alan were on filled me with anxiety. But I still felt a twinge of something. I knew my parents would worry less about me if I were like that.

"Oh?"

"The counselor wouldn't transfer me into the equivalent," I mumbled.

"What? That can't be right." He was indignant. "You should talk to them."

"It's not a big deal. It's my last semester anyway."

"Some of the colleges might care that you dropped down into easier classes second semester."

I shrugged. I wanted to move on from the subject. "Depends on the college, I'm sure."

"Where did you apply?"

"Haven't submitted my applications yet. That's the point of this trip, isn't it? To see if I like the ones on my list?" I thought about my parents' nerve-pinched faces as we had talked about my applications. All the pressure Alan couldn't see, underneath my tidy explanation. "What about you?" I asked.

"Mine are all in. I applied to everywhere on our list that we're visiting. Plus, early acceptance for Stanford."

So he was organized and focused enough to have committed already to a college at the time of application. We truly were at opposite ends of the spectrum. It was almost hilarious. Perhaps my parents had planned this all on purpose. "Don't you find out about early acceptance soon?"

"Yeah. Very soon. Could be before the end of this trip."

"High stakes," I said. "Although maybe not, for you."

"I'm mentally preparing for it to go either way. Although I did a summer program at Stanford between junior and senior year that's application only. Usually people who are picked for that program do get in." He was trying to sound casual and modest. But I could sense the anticipation in his voice.

I turned away, suddenly irritated by this conversation. This was why I couldn't talk to anyone my age about college applications. The things they were worried about seemed so banal. So ridiculously unimportant. I couldn't really care about the aesthetics of different quads or whether one school had better Greek life than another. Other people didn't know the worst that could happen. I did.

"Let's get back on the road," I said, gathering my napkins and trash onto my tray to take up to the garbage can.

"Good idea," he said easily, oblivious to my clouded mood. "Don't want to hit that LA traffic at rush hour."

seven

We arrived at our destination in the midafternoon, after another stop for coffee when Alan needed a pick-me-up. I was happy not to be driving at least. I never liked driving in unfamiliar places, even back home, and the highway was definitely a big no for me.

Our first hosts were Uncle Wang and Auntie Chao. My parents had known them from when they first came to America, and I had seen them only intermittently throughout the years, since we lived so far away.

They lived in Alhambra, a suburb of Los Angeles that was primarily Chinese. The street signs we passed were all in two languages.

We drove down a winding street uphill into the neighborhood. The house the GPS took us to was at the top. And it was big. It had two floors but sprawled wide lengthwise. It was clad in white stucco with a red door. The entrance was on the second floor, with a staircase up from the driveway in front of the garage. There was a broad, floor-to-ceiling window that surveyed the front of the property from the main level. The front yard was perfectly manicured with a tasteful assortment of in-season flowers. It was the kind of front yard that could have been done only with either somebody who was a full-time gardening enthusiast or professional hired help.

It made sense. Uncle Wang was a neurosurgeon.

We disembarked from the car. I pulled my giant suitcase out of the car and looked up at the concrete stairs to the front door.

"I got it," Alan said. He took his suitcase in one hand and mine in his other, and I followed him up the stairs. We rang the doorbell.

"Lai le, lai le," we heard from behind the door.

The squeals of children filtered out.

A minute later, it swung open.

"Ah, you're here! You hungry? I have snacks," Auntie Chao said by way of greeting.

We went inside into an open-concept living area with high-shine wood floors, an expensive-looking beige sectional, and a beautiful white kitchen with marble countertops. The light scattered into the room through a soft white curtain. There was a basket of lemons on the counter and an orchid as the centerpiece of the dining table. It was all so beautiful; I felt as though we had stepped into an HGTV staged house for sale.

"Jia Jia, Fei Fei, come here," Auntie Chao said.

Two nine-year-old girls came bounding into the room with matching braids and Camp Firefly T-shirts. They looked similar enough to be mistaken as identical twins, although I knew they were fraternal.

"Say hello."

They waved. "Hi, Alan," they sang out in unison.

He waved back at them. Of course he must have met them before. San Diego and LA weren't so far apart, after all. Our fathers had all been friends in the past.

"And this is Stella," Auntie Chao said. "You haven't met her before." She turned to us. "You're going to stay in their rooms. I'm driving them off to summer camp later."

Uncle Wang popped in from the sliding door to the back deck. "Hello," he said cheerily. Of Baba's old friends, I knew him as the life of the party. I had heard the story of how he and Baba became friends. Baba and Uncle Zhao met Uncle Wang at a bar with a different group of students, rather than from class. Somehow, Uncle Wang joined up with Baba and Uncle Zhao, and by the end of the night, Uncle Wang had fallen asleep in Baba's bathtub. He was a red-cheeked, jovial prankster. His wife balanced him out as the sensible one, keeping his antics in check.

I gave them a gift from my parents for hosting us: an expensive pack of tea leaves from China wrapped in heavy foil, and they exclaimed gratefully.

Our hosts had put out a whole spread of nuts, sweets, and various other goodies. It would've been rude not to sample at least one of everything, even though I hadn't begun to feel hungry. We sat around the table as Auntie Chao poured us each a cup of tea.

Jia Jia and Fei Fei jostled next to us, poking each other endlessly until Auntie Chao gave them a death glare.

The girls stared at us the way only young children could—with naked curiosity and a lack of awareness about when it was too long to be considered rude. Having not spent that much time with the family, I couldn't really tell them apart.

"What happened to Victoria?" one of them asked Alan.

"Nothing happened to her," he said. "She's in San Diego."

The other one pointed at me. "Is Stella your new girlfriend?"

Alan laughed, catching me out of the corner of my eye. "No, we're old friends. I've known her since I was your age."

I looked away, deeply embarrassed for some reason. I wasn't sure if it was the realization that Alan possibly had a girlfriend who these children had met before but I knew nothing about or the designation of being *old friends*. I couldn't tell if he was trying to be generous with his description. It was both more and less accurate than the truth.

"Girls," Auntie Chao said sharply. "Knock it off."

"Heaven help us when these kids become teenagers," Uncle Wang whispered conspiratorially to us. "That's why we stopped after the twins. I can't handle any more of these little monsters."

"*You* let them stay up to watch K-dramas with us instead of enforcing bedtime," Auntie Chao pointed out. "Now this is all they talk about. Whose fault is that?"

Uncle Wang shook his head sheepishly. "Look at you girls, getting me in trouble, always," he said to them as they giggled.

I wanted to find out more about this Victoria person but couldn't find a way to steer the conversation back without seeming nosy. I didn't want to make it seem like I was interested. I was mostly curious about the kind of girl Alan had ended up with after all this time. I couldn't imagine her, what she might be like.

"Let's change the subject," Uncle Wang said hastily, eyeing his wife nervously. "What colleges are you all visiting while here?

"Caltech, UCLA, and USC," said Alan.

"You must have applied to all those places," said Uncle Wang. "And you, Stella?"

"I'm still deciding."

"Very good. Very good. I know Alan is interested in majoring in economics and going to law school. What about you? We know so little about you since you've been so far away."

My parents and I had never discussed it. There were many things we hadn't discussed. Since Sam passed away, it seemed they weren't much interested in talking to me at all, except when they had to. I was their only remaining life preserver in a vast dark sea, and they didn't want to know that I was full of holes.

Suddenly put on the spot without a rehearsed answer, I found myself blurting out the first random subject that came to mind. "Astronomy."

Perhaps I was mentally listing out options alphabetically and unfortunately only got as far as *A*. I regretted it immediately. I knew nothing about astronomy. Science in general had never been my domain.

Alan swiveled like an owl to stare. I willed myself not to look at him.

"How interesting," Auntie Chao said after a pause. "You mean like studying the stars?"

"Um, yes." I knew I couldn't take it back now. It was too bizarre a lie. The explanation would be too humiliating.

"I had no idea," Uncle Wang said, genuinely impressed. "Your parents never mentioned it."

"Well, it's just something, I'm, you know, exploring." I wondered how my parents were going to receive this information, as it seemed inevitable Uncle Wang or Auntie Chao would mention it to them.

"Astronomy involves a lot of math and physics. Not a major for the fainthearted. I think that's great." His enthusiastic support was painful.

"Yeah, great," Alan said, his eyebrow raised.

"I know it must be difficult for you with Sam gone. But you're still working hard. He would be proud," Uncle Wang said.

There it was again. Those unexpected emotions. I thought by now I would be able to control them, but I was still struggling. I wouldn't cry in front of these people, though. Least of all Alan. I refused to ever let him feel as though he knew anything real about me.

I blinked and blinked until any extra moisture was gone. "Thank you," I told Uncle Wang. I was grateful for my composure. Gracious and crisp. No sign of weakness at all.

He nodded, accepting it at face value and moving on.

Of course it was empty. I didn't know what I was thanking him for. Sam wouldn't be proud of me. How could he, after everything that happened? And anyway, it wasn't true. My grades had plummeted. My college applications sat unfinished in my hard drive, a mere week before deadline. The last thing anyone could say about me was that I was working hard.

But that didn't matter to anyone on the outside. Sam was only an idea to them. His loss, a promise unmet. And me, I was just collateral damage left in the wake of his destruction. I couldn't feel resentful that others would say hollow things like this. It was the best they could do. I reminded myself of that all the time.

Later that night, I couldn't sleep, per usual. I had Fei Fei's room, and Alan was on the other side of the adjoined bathroom, in Jia Jia's room. The twin-size bed with floral sheets was itchy and felt too small for me to do my customary tossing and turning in.

I had long since given up on trying to fall asleep when I knew it wasn't happening. It was late enough that I figured I might sneak into the basement den and watch some brainless TV without disturbing anyone.

I crept out of my room, down the hallway, opened the door to the stairs, and followed them all the way down. I had been flipping through Netflix for five minutes when I heard footsteps behind me.

"Mind if I join you?"

Alan lingered at the foot of the stairs in a T-shirt and gym shorts. Sleeping attire, for someone who should have been asleep.

"What are you doing here?" I asked, surprised and also annoyed.

This boy couldn't be shaken off the trail, not even in the middle of the night. He was like stink on a warthog.

He pointed his thumb upstairs. "Jack-and-Jill bathroom. I can hear everything in your room."

I was abashed, even though it wasn't like I had been doing anything particularly scandalous or noisy in my room. "I feel like that's something you maybe should have disclosed earlier."

"Well, I assumed it wouldn't be a very eventful night. I thought you would be sleeping. You woke me up when you opened the door to your room."

"Sorry," I said not very sorrily.

"It's okay. I'm a light sleeper. Not your fault." He came off the stairs and plopped down next to me on the couch, despite me not having actually extended an invite. "What's wrong, can't sleep?"

"Something like that."

"I have trouble sleeping in new places, too," he said.

I grunted in reply.

He sat beside me quietly for a moment, and I thought he might just fade into the background if I ignored him hard enough. "So, astronomy, huh?" he asked.

"Yeah," I said, my eyes fixed on the screen with determination. I was committed to this lie now. I wasn't about to backtrack for him.

"Really? That's not what I thought you were into."

"A lot can happen in a few years." I glanced over at him at last. "You seem pretty different too."

He smiled then. It was the private smile that I remembered, the one he reserved only for when he was truly sincere. I felt some kind of lurch inside. It still meant something to me.

"That's true." He closed his eyes briefly. A sly look slid across his features. "Still, it's quite a big swerve. You know, I took an astronomy elective last year."

"Fun."

"It was. We got to go out into the field at night a couple of times and use the San Diego observatory telescope. We had this project to find all the different moons in the solar system." He snapped his fingers. "What's the biggest one? I can't remember."

Obviously, I hadn't the faintest clue what the answer was. He was testing me, trying to get me to admit I was lying. I wouldn't cave.

"Galaxia," I said firmly, naming a Sailor Moon villain.

"Close!" He leaned back in satisfaction. "It's actually Ganymede."

I scowled at him. "You made your point."

"Did I? Why did you lie, then? You hate science."

"Why is it any of your business? We don't know each other anymore. You're doing my family a favor. Can't we just go through with this trip in a civil manner and move on at the end? You can continue ignoring me at school and pretending I don't exist. I won't bother you or drag down your reputation as untouchable cool guy."

He winced. "Is that really what you think?"

"Is there any reason I'm supposed to think differently?" I said, my words crowding together in anger. I pinched my nose out of frustration. I was annoyed he had elicited this outburst from me. I hadn't intended on getting into it with him tonight, but he knew how to push all my buttons.

"You're still mad about what happened in Mount Pierce."

I gave him nothing but stony silence.

"Okay, that's fair. I'm sorry. I should've apologized when I first saw you, but I didn't know whether you'd want to hear it. I really am sorry about it."

He sounded so genuine, so earnest. If someone else were listening, it would've broken their heart. But I couldn't shake that seed he'd planted from way back when: I was still a nothing to him, a nobody he could buddy up with when he needed it and drop when he didn't.

I wasn't going to fall for that act again.

"Great, thanks," I said. "Couple years too late, but I appreciate the effort. If you're not going to let me watch TV in peace, then I'm going to go to bed."

I stalked out of the den so he couldn't have the last word and left him behind.

eight

CHUN JIE

Lunar New Year is all wrong. Instead of spending it with Nai Nai, bundled in sweaters, and throwing firecrackers in the street, we are in Illinois.

It's a meaningless day here. Nobody goes home to their families. All the stores are still open. School is in session during the week. My parents are working.

This is the first year we have spent Lunar New Year in America. I wanted to go back to China, but our parents insisted we do it here as a real family. That was one reason; the other was that we didn't have funds or vacation days to travel back.

We sit in the living room with the television on. *Miracle on 34th Street* is playing. It's hard for me to understand sometimes, so I'm not really watching. Mama and Baba are making dumplings in the kitchen.

You sit next to me, reading a chapter book in English.

"I'm bored," I say, poking you in the shoulder. "Let's play a game."

It's hard to do anything fun with just two people; it's not like back in China, when all the kids were around. Since moving here, we've gotten wolfish around each other, as you outgrow me. There is no cultural pressure here for the oldest to let the youngest always have their way, like back home. And you've gotten bossy, which I hate.

But today, you acquiesce to my demands. Maybe because we can't help but miss home on this holiday. To us, it's a day for family.

You lead me to the doorway to the kitchen. Mama and Baba are standing around the counter, filling dumplings in wrappers and lining them up neatly on sheet pans. They are on speaker with our aunt, Mama's sister, who lives in Canada. They chatter away. We are close to the ground. They are not looking at us.

"Here are the rules," you say. "Try to get to the other end of the room without Mama or Baba seeing you. Pretend we're on a secret mission and they're the enemies."

I survey the space between where we are and the other side of the kitchen counter. We have a rectangular dining table in between. I take note of the gap between two chairs where you can crawl underneath. Then there is about four feet of space between the table and the countertop: the danger zone. Once you could get to the counter, you could hide under the ledge on one side and sidle by behind their legs without either of them seeing.

"Me first or you first?" you ask.

"I'll go first." I crouch down as far as I can and peer ahead. I imagine that I really am a rabbit. Stealthy, small. I crawl on my hands and knees. In the shadow of the table so I won't be so obvious. Slowly, so the movement won't catch the corners of their eyes.

It is easy to pretend like they're the enemy. We only knew Mama and Baba through pictures for years. When we saw them in person at the airport in San Francisco, they were different from what I thought they would be. Shorter, I guess, and less attractive. Maybe just because in my mind, they were ideas, and then when I saw them, they became real. And ideas are always better than the real thing.

In real life, Baba is more impatient than I imagined. Mama is less interested in playing with us. Sometimes, when I lie awake in my new bedroom on my new soft mattress and wool blankets, I wonder if there has been a mistake—if our real parents are somewhere else and if they are looking for us.

I make it to the safety of the dining table and huddle underneath. From the doorway, where you peek out just beyond our parents' view, you give me a thumbs-up.

Ahead, I scan the no-man's-land of kitchen tile. The danger zone. I look up. Mama and Baba are still talking. Their heads turn away from my direction whenever they go to spoon the pork and chive filling into a wrapper in their hands. I watch them, waiting to time my escapade to when they are both occupied.

I pick the right moment and burst out from under the table. I dart to the safety of the counter, low to the ground. I press myself against the base. Baba's legs are on one side of me; Mama's on the other. With soft hands and feet, I creep behind Mama so she can't hear me and make it to the cabinets on the other side of the kitchen.

Behind me, you start your journey as well. But you're bigger and louder than I am. Before you even make it to the counter, I hear Baba say in confusion, "Son, why are you crawling on the floor like an animal?"

I giggle. Mama whips her head in my direction. "Aiya!" she exclaims. "How did you get over here?" Her hands are covered in flour, but she reaches down and scoops me up to smack a kiss on my cheek. She smells sweet from her lemon-honey face lotion as her hair brushes against my face. She looks at me like she has been waiting her whole life for me, luminous.

We sit at the counter and watch our parents make more dumplings. Baba pulls out a shiny new penny. He washes it in soap and water and presses it carefully into the center of one dumpling. It disappears as he pinches the edges closed.

"Whoever gets the penny has a lucky year," Baba says. "Eat carefully."

Mama and Baba finish three full baking sheets of dumplings—way too many for four people. They let us stand on the counter stools so we can watch the raw dumplings go into the big pasta pot of boiling water.

"San kai," Mama explains, meaning the water has to come to

a boil three times before the dumplings are cooked. Each time it boils, she adds a cup of cold water and the water settles down again. We wait for the dumplings to bobble up to the surface three times. It feels like an eternity. The scent wafts up from the pot. Baba holds my waist so I don't lean too far over and fall in.

We sit around our dining table, the four of us, like one of those families in American commercials. We fill our bowls with dipping sauces. The dumplings come out onto the platter steaming. I poke them with my chopsticks, as though I can discern where the lucky penny is from the outside.

You start adding five, six, seven dumplings to your bowl.

"You're cheating," I say, annoyed.

"I'm bigger," you say imperiously. "I can eat more."

"All right," Baba says to you. "You eat all of those first. One at a time. That's how the game works."

We start eating. I take small bites so I don't accidentally swallow the penny whole but eat as fast as I can so I can sample more dumplings. I'm eyeing everyone around the table, alert to someone else getting the penny first. We go through one platter without anybody finding it. We're halfway through the second platter. I'm full to bursting. I've eaten fifteen dumplings—more than I've ever had before, and still no penny.

"Maybe it's disappeared," you say.

I scan the plate for the remaining dumplings and push myself to take one more. I pick the plumpest, roundest one. I bite off the corner. Nothing. My heart sinks. But just as I've given up hope, I take a second bite, and I see a gleam. There it is. I grab it with my thumb and forefinger and pull it out. "I got it! I got it!" I shout, waving it above my head.

"Let me see!" you say, even though you can surely see it in my hand. I drop it triumphantly in the palm of yours. In the yellowed light of the shabby chandelier overhead, it shines like gold.

Mama and Baba clap.

"Lucky girl," Baba says. He squeezes my shoulder.

You're sullen, but I don't care, too pleased with my penny.

Later, we settle on the couch to watch the Chinese state-sponsored Lunar New Year program on the one Chinese channel we receive. It airs every year, silly skits with heavy-handed moral messaging and patriotic songs, hosted by blandly smiling celebrities. It's easy to understand and feels familiar. We would watch each year with Nai Nai in China, after all the dishes had been put away, waiting for midnight. We would fall asleep together with the TV on.

Our Christmas tree—something we didn't have at Nai Nai's house—still lingers in the corner of the living room. It's plastic with sparse, fake-looking branches. The ornaments we decorated it with are ugly and unmatching, not like the sophisticated glass orbs I see at department stores. But when Baba turns off the lights and plugs in the tree, the twinkle lights make the whole thing look beautiful anyway.

You and I sit squashed in the middle of our threadbare love seat, and our parents squeeze in on either side. I clutch my lucky coin in my hand. Before I go to bed, I will put it in a special box in my nightstand with all my treasures: my jade rabbit necklace from Nai Nai, my eighteen-karat gold bracelet that was a gift from my aunt when I was born.

Mama caresses my hair. Baba hums along with the music from the show. I lean against your shoulder, full and sleepy. I feel the beginning of a truth: the four of us coming together, maybe, forming a unit.

A chorus of children on TV begin singing the classic new year's song, "Nan Wang Jin Xiao," about how tonight is unforgettable. And indeed, as my eyes close, I wish that every day could be like this: the softest part of a rabbit's den, a golden penny.

nine

The next morning, we had an uneventful breakfast, bid goodbye for the day to Auntie Chao (Uncle Wang had left hours earlier for a scheduled surgery), and headed off to tour Caltech.

I stifled a yawn as we exited the Division of the Humanities and Social Sciences into the hazy midmorning sun. The tour guide was an enthusiastic junior in engineering, who had introduced himself as Kai. He was wearing jeans rolled up to the ankle and a Caltech-branded T-shirt.

He was prepped with facts about the school like a museum curator, and he could deliver them at twenty times a minute. It was a miracle he could breathe. I kept waiting for him to run out of verbal ammunition, but we were two hours in, and he was still going. Alan listened attentively, nodding and asking enough questions for two.

I learned that Albert Einstein had once been a visiting scholar, that Caltech had an annual olive festival that harvested a hundred gallons of oil, and that its admittance rate generally hovers around 3 percent.

I tried to imagine myself going here a year from now. Would I walk around campus in my branded clothes? Would I be happy?

I had hoped I would arrive at one of these places and it would click. It wasn't working. The colleges in California happened to have more tropical plants, but they all seemed the same to me at the end of the day. Places where people could lose themselves and never be found.

Sometimes it still surprised me how much my life had changed in the past nine months. How I could have ended up thousands of miles away from home, because of one singular event.

"So what do you think?" Alan asked. He hadn't attempted to engage seriously with me since I told him off last night.

"About what?"

"This tour? Caltech?"

I shrugged. "Seems fine. I don't think I'll get in. I should focus on more attainable places."

"It's probably my second choice."

"Okay," I said.

There was a long pause, through which Kai droned on up ahead.

Alan sighed. "What can I do to make it up to you after all this time?"

"I'm not a child. I'm not looking for a bribe."

"You know that's not what I meant. I'm just trying to ensure that we get along on this trip. Make it a pleasant experience. Or at least a tolerable one."

I had a thousand retorts loaded up, but instead, something else came out. "Why did you tell the twins that we were old friends?"

He cocked his head curiously. "What should I have called us?"

"I don't know. It just felt mean for you to say it." The memories seemed sharper in relief than they had ever been before. I was a little embarrassed and surprised at how much they hurt. I had thought I'd put it behind me. I wanted to seem unbothered. But I was failing at it.

He paused. "I hadn't thought about it that way. I'm sorry for that too."

I mumbled some form of acceptance, so I wouldn't come off as unbearably petty.

We did the rest of the tour in silence.

Kai dropped us back off at the student center. We stood there, facing each other at last with no buffer in between.

His hair was longer than the short close-cropped cut he had when we were children. I had short hair then too. In China, we were required to have neat, easily manageable hair. Not distracting for class. We had both grown it out in the years since.

The breeze rustled a stray lock of hair in front of his eyes.

I had always thought his eyes were really nice behind his glasses. Big and expressive, impish when he was making a joke, and so easy to reveal his hurt. They were the one part of him that could never sell a lie.

He spoke up finally. "It's funny. I used to be able to tell you everything, and now I can't seem to find anything to say." The corner of his mouth lifted slightly, but the expression didn't reach the top half of his face. His eyes were sad.

I did remember that. He had told me all his secrets, the ones that he was too afraid to tell another soul. The truth was, I knew Alan Zhao better than anyone. At least, I did once. It was strange, in some ways, to be before him now. To not know what other secrets he might have accumulated since then.

"Maybe there isn't anything left to say between us. Maybe there's nothing good here," I said. It could be easier this way, I thought. To walk away and not reopen any more wounds.

"I wonder if that's true. If you really believe that, I mean. I would be surprised. Wo yuan lai ren shi de nu hai zong neng zhao dao yang guang."

I blinked, so startled that I forgot to be angry. It was as though he had opened a portal into the past. For a moment, we were the younger versions of ourselves, before everything between us had burned to ash. I looked away.

Summer afternoons in Mount Pierce had been hot. Hot enough to rival the ones back home, except at least here, we had air-conditioning. It was a marvel that I didn't take for granted. Sam was not much interested in spending time with me that summer, so it was mostly Alan and me left to our own devices.

When we couldn't bear to be outside, we had taken to spending time in the basement of his house, which was fully underground and mostly unfinished. It was cool down there. The cement floor pressed against the underside of our legs like a blessing.

We played tiao qi, Chinese checkers. Alan had a set with beautiful glass marbles with different-colored swirls inside that looked like flower petals. I was obsessed with them. They were the prettiest version I'd seen. Sam and I had a cheap one at home with plain, solid-colored marbles. Three of the colors had at least one missing marble, making those colors unplayable.

He would let me pick my color first. I picked a different one each time, except I left the orange one for him, because it was his favorite. He always played orange.

It was an easy game that didn't require too much attention. We could mindlessly play match after match, exchanging wins and losses while chattering about other things.

There seemed to be so much to talk about. By then I had been in the United States for a year, and I hadn't encountered another soul who shared any commonality with my childhood. None of the kids at Mount Pierce Elementary had watched the same shows or had the same favorite food or knew the right words for what I wanted to say. In school, I was quiet, preferring to keep to myself than sound a fool by letting people hear my broken English. As a result, no one ever wanted to talk to me.

With Alan, it was easy. He talked enough for three people and made it easy for me to chime in every once in a while.

He would tell me about his life in Shanghai, which I could hardly imagine. The glittering buildings and neon lights. The way the night market smelled. How it always hummed and roared with life, no matter the hour. My village in China was nothing like it. Some of the houses didn't even have running water. Sam and I had gone to Xi'An on sporadic trips with Nai Nai. I marveled then at the size and scale of it, but even Xi'An was different from Shanghai. It retained an air of gu dai, antiquity, about it, whereas Shanghai was sleek and Western.

It occurred to me that the two of us would never have become friends in China. We came from such different worlds. But here in the nowhere space between I-55 and I-70, our backgrounds were practically indistinguishable. We were both from a place that people here couldn't begin to conjure up in their wildest dreams.

"I miss the way the air would smell," I told him. I could never describe it right. A little sweet, a little burnt. It was the air pollution, I realized only later, when the scent of it wafted across Mount Pierce from the wildfires in Canada the following year. But to me, it smelled like home.

"I miss the breakfast food," he said. "The yogurt was better."

"I miss the way people would look at you with honest faces. People here smile too much without it being real. It freaks me out."

"I kind of like it."

I sat up, confused. "Why?"

"My dad used to tell me that I shared too much of myself for a boy. I cried a lot as a kid. The first day of school, whenever I would take a fall. I was quick to anger. I was fussy. I warmed up too fast to strangers. He thought I should've been more stoic.

More of a nan zi han." He shrugged, flushing slightly. "Maybe it feels better that other people here have to hide themselves too, you know?"

I didn't know how to comfort him. That sounded horrible, yet it was unsurprising. I had heard Baba say similar things to Sam. But Sam wasn't like Alan. He was always more introspective and reserved. A little old man as a child. The way that Alan would light up when he was excited about something—it made me sad that his father would want to change that.

"I like you the way you are. I like that you're friendly."

He smiled at me. "I like you too." He glanced out the egress window at the sliver of deepening blue sky. "It's probably cooler now. Do you want to go outside and check out the pond?"

We put away the tiao qi set and scrambled out the door with only Alan's mother's voice echoing in our ears to be back for dinner. A small man-made lake in our neighborhood was stocked with fish and ringed with trees. It was much more manicured than the pond I remembered in front of Nai Nai's house. A paved path surrounded it where people could take walks. Still, there was more wildlife there than anywhere else.

We treaded carefully along the banks, combing through the long grass for bird feathers, for which we each had a collection. Although he undoubtedly missed home, he delighted in the rural setting Mount Pierce provided. He was endlessly fascinated by the range of bird species that proliferated the area. He had never seen anything much beyond a pigeon before moving here.

On the shore, we displayed the treasures we had gathered.

He and I had opposite approaches. He was selective, wanting to save the most striking of finds, often emerging from our hunting sessions with only one or two feathers.

He showed me a long feather from the tail of a blue jay. Verdant turquoise with stripes of black. He had the fiery red feather of a cardinal as well.

"Good day," he pronounced.

I had many more feathers than him, but all of them were common brown duck feathers, some with a light spray of white spots, some with irregular dark blotches on them.

"Nice," he said, peering over at them.

For some reason, with his rare finds that day, I felt humbled by my modest batch.

Sensing my discomfort, he nudged my shoulder. "This is what I like about you."

"What do you mean?"

"You find the smallest things beautiful. Bu guan shen me dan diao de dong xi, ni zong neng zhao dao yang guang. If only everyone could be like that."

He made me seem as rare as a jewel-colored feather in the wild. Even years later, I couldn't forget his words. I tucked them somewhere deep, where they could keep me warm.

No one had ever told me anything so kind.

The girl I once knew could always find sunlight, he had said.

The sensation of tears was too fierce. I was so lightheaded, I thought I might float away.

I breathed slowly, each drag of air bringing me closer to the ground again. I couldn't trust him. Not for a child's sentiment. But neither could I shake off my desire to forgive him and start over.

"Look," he said, "I know you want to write me off. Maybe I would too if I were you. But I'm going to leave the door open." He paused, as though considering whether he wanted to share what he was about to say next. "I have a friend from high school who's in college at UCLA. He's invited me out to a party at his frat tonight. I'm going to go. You should come. If you want to get a real sense of the college experience, you're not going to get it on one of these bland tours that say nothing."

"Tonight," I repeated, not entirely sure I understood. "When?"

He scratched the back of his neck. "We'd probably show up just before midnight?"

"I don't think Uncle Wang and Auntie Chao would be down with that?" I was confused at this plan. "Did you ask them already?"

"No, obviously not. The plan would be that we'd sneak out."

I stared at him. "That seems like a bad idea."

"We'll get back at two, three in the morning? Everyone will be asleep. We'll take a house key. Nobody will notice. We can let loose a little."

He was supremely confident, as per usual. He couldn't contemplate getting in trouble. He lived a charmed life.

I had a responsibility on this trip. It was to visit colleges, not tank my grades while I was out and not cause my parents to worry about me while they were gone. "I think I'm going to stay in," I said. "I have homework to keep up with this week. And I didn't sleep well last night. I shouldn't stay up again."

"Okay, sure. No pressure," he said easily, as though it didn't matter to him either way, betrayed only by a small slump in his shoulders. "Just let me know before you go to bed."

My parents had landed in China. They messaged me on WeChat to let me know that they were boarding their connecting flight to Xi'An and would call me once they were settled at Nai Nai's apartment. It would be evening California local time.

After dinner with Uncle Wang and Auntie Chao, I bid everyone an early good night and retreated to my room. I booted up my applications and read them again. I wrote two paragraphs of a personal essay, then deleted one. I tried to read *Heart of Darkness*, but I couldn't concentrate. The language was dense and required unflagging focus, which I did not have.

I was jittery for some reason, as though I had drunk too much coffee earlier. It had been only thirty-six hours or so since I'd last seen my parents, but I felt apprehensive talking to them, especially with Nai Nai there.

At exactly 11:00 p.m., my phone lit up with a video call on WeChat, and I answered.

My mother's face swam into view, slightly blurry, and an arm's length away from the camera. "Hi," she said.

As the resolution cleared, I could see Baba sitting slightly behind her. Baba's sisters, my aunts, were there as well. And Nai Nai, at the head of the table.

My fingers curled in a tiny wave. "Hi, Mama. Hi, Gu Gu, Gu Ma."

"My granddaughter is on camera!" Nai Nai demanded. "Let me see!"

Baba steadied her under her elbow. I swallowed hard, the guilt chewing away at me. It had been months and months since I'd last called her. Her frailty pierced me.

Mama tilted the camera as Nai Nai approached. "Say hello," she said to me. Her voice had a false brightness to it. Her smile was strained.

Nai Nai's hair had thinned and faded to a moon white. Her high, round cheeks had slackened, giving her a gaunt air. But she was still my Nai Nai.

"Mei mei, ah," she said. "You look beautiful. Prettier by the day. But thin. They're not feeding you right in America. Come home next week and I'll make you all your favorites."

"Ma," Baba protested behind her. "You know you can't exert yourself like that."

She waved him off, clucking. "I can cook for one week. I'm stronger than you think. I know my body." She winked at me.

I smiled back weakly. I thought I might burst. "I miss you," I said.

"I miss you too, my sweet girl. And I miss your brother. He must be so busy at Harvard, and now you are all so far away from him. I hope he is not too lonely. I wish for you all to return to me soon. When your schooling is settled and you have time to see an old lady."

I could hardly stand to look at the screen. I didn't see my parents' expressions. They were probably impassive, revealing nothing. It was strength in some ways, hardness in others. One could admire it and hate it at the same time.

Baba was the one who took the lead on shielding her from my brother's death. To him, it was a simple calculation. Nai Nai was an old woman. She had given her years to caring for her grandchildren while her son toiled away in America to make a suitable new life for his family. She could not know that her sacrifice had borne the bitterness of my brother's death. The mantle of sadness should be our burden to bear on her behalf. Many Chinese families would have done the same. We lived far away, and as Sam and I had gotten older, we'd long since stopped regularly calling home, so it wasn't too difficult a ruse to pull.

It was always me who was the problem. I had gotten used to hiding from my parents and showing them my false face. But I couldn't lie to Nai Nai. Unlike all the others in my life, she was the only person who never asked anything of me. It was enough that I existed. She had known me as a guileless baby. She had sung me to sleep under the stars. She knew my truest heart.

The whole family thought of me as the weak link. I was sure this had something to do with why my parents wanted to supervise our interactions as much as possible and keep me away as much as they could.

Little did they know, I could keep a secret better than anyone.

"Soon," I said, my voice shaking.

"Of course, education comes first. You must focus on that and not on my ramblings. I know you are visiting colleges now and finishing your applications. I will look forward to the good news." She leaned back in her chair. "I am so fortunate. To have all these successes through my grandchildren. Chen Wei going to the best university in the world. Xiao Xiao getting married. And my Liang Liang growing up. To live to this age is a blessing. To experience hardship while young but rest easy while old."

"You have so much fu qi, Ma," Mama echoed Nai Nai's sentiments. The pinched corners of her mouth—the only telltale sign of her troubled inner thoughts. Perhaps she was thinking that about Nai Nai's fortune, which had bypassed my own mother. Nai Nai lost her husband young, but all three of her children surrounded her now. A luxury Mama would never have. "We wanted Liang Liang to say hello, but it is late for her. She should go to bed to prepare for tomorrow."

Although I wanted to stay on with Nai Nai, she bid me good night. Mama asked me to stay on for a moment and took me into another room, where she closed the door before sinking onto the bed.

It was probably the jet lag, but I hadn't seen her looking so exhausted since the month after Sam died. I expected her to tell me about updates from the family or share about how she and Baba were feeling. Rather, she dove right into business. "How was Caltech today?"

"Fine," I said, disappointed in how tactical she was.

"Did you like it?"

"It was okay."

"Only okay? It's a very good school. You should take this seriously."

"I *am* taking it seriously." I was irritated at her line of questioning, but uncharacteristically, it was leaking out in my tone.

There was a considerable pause. "Good," she said, softening.

The whole situation sat wrong on my shoulders. My mother's focus on applications, feeling like a ridiculous overlay to the secrets between me and my parents, us and Nai Nai. What kind of family was this, anyway?

I couldn't begin to shape any of these thoughts into the right words to say out loud. They seemed to melt into nothing on my tongue, like snow. I left all these things alone, churning in the darkness where they belonged.

"I don't like that Nai Nai doesn't know. It doesn't seem right. She raised us," I said quietly, the closest I'd ever gotten to challenging her in all these months.

Mama's lips pressed together tightly. I could tell I had annoyed her. She hated being reminded of the years we spent with Nai Nai. "These are decisions for adults. Please do not concern yourself with them."

"But, Mama—"

"It's enough," she snapped. Her face slackened. "You do not need to worry about this. We have it under control." But it was apparent that the reality was the opposite. She was busting at the seams. Something was rocking her composure.

"Forgive me," she said. "We are tired from traveling, and you have had a long day too. We'll schedule another time to talk more." She gave me a long look. "Be well, my daughter."

Before I could respond, she hung up.

My cheeks were hot. Our conversation left me sour and dissatisfied. I was startled at how angry I felt. I was accustomed to my parents excluding me from decision-making, and I had never protested. Yet my insides coiled up as tight as a wire spring.

Inside, the house was quiet. On the other side of the bathroom, I heard light rustling. Alan was right. You could hear everything through the doors. Sleep seemed further than a pilgrimage.

Outside, it was nighttime, the dark gray sky peeping through Jia Jia's pale linen curtains. There was an entire world out there, shaking itself awake and preparing for the stars. With chances to be taken and mistakes to be made.

I knew where I wanted to be.

ten

The Uber drove down a series of boulevards. The streetlamps cast circles of light down on the pavement, flickering across my lap as we passed beneath. Outside my window, the city glowed and the sky overhead was tinged a faint orange.

Alan sat beside me with a seat in between. I looked over at him briefly. The clock on the console read 11:35.

"You have the key?" I asked.

He patted his pocket. "Relax. It's going to be fine. We'll be back before they know it."

I was not reassured. My reckless streak had passed. The cooler part of my head was beginning to take back over. I had second thoughts, but now it was too late. We were already on the way to this fraternity, where I didn't know anybody except Alan. I had somehow deliberately put myself in a position of having to place my trust in the one person I had no reason to trust. Foolish, impulsive, I cursed myself. I could hear Mama's voice in my head. She would be aghast.

"It'll be fun. You'll see," he said, observing, maybe, some of my inner turmoil.

We pulled up to a two-story house with white vinyl siding, an A-line roof with black shingles, and two slim columns on either side of the front door. Above the door, the letters for Omega Phi Epsilon were nailed in. The house was lit up with lamps pointed at the facade. Music wafted out from the windows. It was just nearing midnight.

I felt a nervous lurch in my stomach. "If we get in trouble, just know that I will throw you under the bus so fast that you won't see the wheels coming."

He grinned. "Noted. Come on."

We got out of the car. I watched the driver leave us at the curb. The front door was cracked open. I could see the light from inside, across the smooth green lawn.

I stood there for a moment, until Alan nudged me.

"Let's go."

I followed behind him, trying not to seem intimidated.

Before we got to the door, a guy walked out. He was medium height, very built, and stocky, and he had a full sleeve tattoo on his left arm. His hair was buzzed short on the sides with a long swoop on top, and he had stud earrings. He was wearing a fitted white tee and black jeans. "Alan!" he shouted, and opened his arms. "What up, man?"

They hugged.

He turned to me and grinned. He had a nice smile, full of perfect white teeth. "Hey. Danny Kim," he said, extending his hand, which I shook. "And you are? Alan left out your name."

"Stella Chen," I said.

"Nice. Nice to meet you. Glad you could come around!" He gave Alan a raised eyebrow.

Alan frowned slightly and shook his head.

"Danny and I used to do debate together," Alan said. "He was the team captain before me." He turned to Danny, sizing him up. "You look different, dude."

"It's the hair. And tattoos."

"And the bodybuilding," Alan said. "He used to be scrawny like me."

"Naw, dude, I was always stronger than you." Danny chuckled. "Anyway, let's not keep standing out here. Want to come in?"

The front door opened to a staircase to the second floor. The hallway to the right of the stairs took us to the back, where the kitchen was. It was older, with speckled stone counters and warm-stained wood cabinets that were looking pretty chipped. The entire thing could've used a renovation, but I had to think a kitchen reno was not high on the list of budgetary priorities for a college fraternity. The entire place smelled vaguely of warm beer and Lysol.

There were five guys milling around the living room, and I

could see more in the backyard out the window. A few girls were in the back too.

"You hungry?" Danny asked. "There are snacks in the living room."

I shook my head. "No, thanks."

"Just got up to LA today," Alan said. "Did Caltech. Officially, UCLA is tomorrow. But we thought we'd get a preview tonight."

"That's Gucci, that's Gucci. Well, if you're looking for endorsements, I think you should come here for sure." Danny turned up his bro voice. "Come to play at UCLA."

I suppressed an outburst of uncomfortable laughter.

"Drinks?" Danny opened the giant stainless steel fridge, probably the nicest appliance in the entire place. "Beers in the cooler by the back door. There's jungle juice on the counter."

Back at home, while there had been weekend parties, I was not an attendee. I had never been around such a prodigious amount of alcohol. I hung back to see what Alan would do. He crossed the kitchen and picked out a beer from the cooler. I hesitated, feeling unsure of what beverage I should pick. In my slight pause, Danny ladled a cup of whatever jungle juice was supposed to be and handed it to me.

"Try it," he said.

It occurred to me that you shouldn't take open drinks from people you don't know, but I had watched him pour it. I figured he couldn't have drugged the entire bowl that was out for general consumption, right? It felt rude to refuse.

I took a meager sip. It was sweet, with a slight edge of alcoholic bitter burn. It tasted innocent. I would only have a little anyway. "Thanks," I said.

Alan rejoined us.

"So," Danny said, "how've you been, dude? It's been such a long time. How did the team hold up this year without my presence? I can't believe you applied early acceptance to Stanford. I thought the whole plan was for you to come here so you could join me and the brotherhood. Hold on, I have someone I want you to meet." He put his arm around Alan, the two of them heading toward the sliding door, and disappeared out to the backyard.

Although I could've followed them, no one expressly included me, so I felt awkward trailing behind them. I had never been good at inserting myself into conversations.

Another guy and girl came into the kitchen. The guy looked like he was probably one of the brothers who lived here. The girl had her arm looped around his and a vape pen dangling from her fingers. She was Asian, but she had long dyed-blond hair and a heavy smoky eye.

I moved aside so he could get to the fridge.

"Hey, who are you?" the guy asked, catching me off guard.

I thought he would simply grab a drink and ignore me.

"I'm Stella."

"Never seen you around here before. Are you new?"

"Oh, um, I'm in high school. I'm on a college visit with Alan." I could hear my explanation coming out in the most convoluted way possible. "I mean, my friend Alan is also in high school and I'm doing a college tour with him, but he's friends with Danny Kim, who lives here. They're in the backyard. I think."

The girl stared at me, and I knew I sounded like a babbling idiot. She was impossibly beautiful and so dressed up it made me feel like a little girl.

"Gotcha," he said after a long pause. "I'm Kevin. And this is my girlfriend, Michelle."

"Cool." I took a deep gulp of my drink.

"I'm the president here. So, uh, hope you have a good time."

"Yeah, will do."

He gave me a mini salute. He and Michelle disappeared around the corner. I heard her laughing. She probably wasn't laughing at me, but I had this problem where whenever I saw people talking or giggling and I couldn't hear what it was about, there was no way to convince my brain that it wasn't about me.

I couldn't believe Alan had brought me to this party just to abandon me immediately. I was a fool for going along with it. I thought about calling a car home, but I didn't have the key. A more socially adept person would've been able to strike up chats with new people or go tell Alan that she didn't want to stay. But I wasn't that person. Humiliation settled in like a wool blanket, too itchy and warm.

I wandered around the living room for a while, on the periphery of conversations, too nervous to be noticed and too nervous to join in.

There were other people beginning to filter in and heading

over. Someone made eye contact with me and smiled as if he were going to come over and say hello.

Instead of waiting for him to get to me, I slipped away and found the first-floor bathroom tucked into the hallway behind the pantry. It was small and cramped inside, barely enough room for a single sink and a toilet squished into the corner. I slid to the ground, my back against the locked door. My tips of my shoes pushed against the base of the toilet.

I imagined the messages I might've texted a friend to keep me company in this dismal place if I still had any from before. It could've been an amusing story to tell—how I had snuck out of my hosts' house boldly, only to end up hiding from everyone in a tiny bathroom, drenched in self-loathing and insecurity.

It would've been funny if it weren't so pathetic.

I checked my phone and saw that my cell reception was nonexistent.

I sat there, while the minutes ticked away, wondering how long I could stay before Alan would notice I was gone. Maybe he had already forgotten all about me. I drank heavily out of my cup.

Eventually, somebody twisted at the doorknob.

"Hello?" a woman's voice said impatiently. She knocked.

"I'm almost done," I said through the door. I rose to my feet. I inhaled deeply to prepare myself, unlocked the door, and stepped out.

A girl pushed past me hard without any comment and slammed the door shut.

Back outside, the house had gotten dimmer, and the music was turned up. I blinked in the low light after the brightness of the bathroom. The air was humid. The hallway felt claustrophobic. I thought maybe I should head toward the backyard to get some air and avoid the pulse of bodies pressing everywhere.

As I turned, a shoulder bumped into me, and I stumbled forward.

"Stella?" It was Danny. He grabbed my arm to keep me from falling over. He looked surprised.

"Oh, hi," I said, mildly relieved to have run into at least one person I knew. I peered around him. "Where's Alan?"

"He's around somewhere. Don't worry. He hasn't left. Where'd you disappear to?"

"Nowhere. I was just, um, exploring. Talking to some people."

"Meet anybody interesting?"

"Uh, Kevin," I said. "I think he said he was president."

"Right on. He's a cool dude." We were standing in a somewhat inconvenient position, bottlenecking people who were trying to get into the kitchen with people who were trying to get to the bathroom. Danny gently steered me out of the path of traffic. "Why don't we go somewhere with a little more breathing room?"

I nodded.

"Great. Follow me."

I trailed behind him, expecting him to take me to the backyard or the living room, but we took an unexpected turn to a set of stairs leading down. "Where are we going?" I asked, but it didn't seem like he heard me over the din in the kitchen. The stairs took us to the basement. It was partly finished, and only slightly less crowded than upstairs. We went into the corner, where there was a wet bar overlooking a table where people were playing beer pong.

"You want anything else?" Danny asked, gesturing at my drink.

"I'm good." I took another sip.

"So what do you think?"

"About what?"

"UCLA. You thinking about coming here?"

I smiled and shrugged. "I don't know. I'm not really sure where I want to go to college," I said evasively.

"Aw, well, it's pretty great here. My parents wanted me to go to Stanford or Berkeley, but I didn't get in, so I ended up at my safety." He spread his arms out wide. "But I'm so happy here. I found my brothers. I wouldn't have it any other way. I can tell you, no matter where you go, you'll figure it out. It always ends up fine. You don't have to overthink it."

His words were sliding in one ear and out the other. I was mostly trying to decide what to do next. Like whether I should've been giving the house another loop to look for Alan and demanding that he take me back.

"I do remember what it was like, senior year. Super stressful. Saying goodbye to everyone. The whole thing."

"Yeah."

"And if you came here, I could show you the ropes, you

know. Make sure you knew all the good stuff." He confidently cocked his eyebrow and leaned closer.

"That would be nice." What time was it exactly? "Do you know where Alan might be?"

"Babe, what's the rush? You just got here. Party's just getting started. He's probably chatting up some girls upstairs, you know. Don't worry. I'm not going to let anything happen to you." His hand touched my upper arm.

I had been so preoccupied with other thoughts that I had not noticed what was happening right in front of me. I felt skewered by his undivided attention. He was closing the distance between us. His body was far too close to mine. I had nowhere to go.

My fingers scrabbled for my phone in my bag. "I think I should check to see if he's looking for me." Was this Alan's attempt at a setup? At this point, he probably should've hoped that I would never find him, because if I did, I was going to kill him.

"Stella," Danny said, waving his hand in front of my face. "You there?"

"I don't think—" I said, but before I could finish, he started to lean in. I was against the wall, and the only way I was going to be able to dodge him was if I ducked. It felt like his face was coming at me in slow motion, but I was frozen. Panic clustered in my throat. I could smell the alcohol on his breath mixed with the scent of aggressive cologne. My fingers curled at my chest ready to stop him before—

"HEY!"

Someone's hand was on Danny's shoulder, and he jerked back.

It was Alan. Our eyes connected. "There you are," he said to me, the relief on his face evident. "I've been looking all over for you. I can't get any signal in this house."

No matter the fury I'd been nursing toward him before, seeing him now was like finding a shaft of daylight in a collapsed coal mine. I started to breathe again.

He extended a hand toward me. I grabbed it without hesitation. He tugged me toward him and past Danny's reach.

"You ready to go?" he asked.

I nodded.

"Hold on," Danny said loudly. "We were talking. Why are you out here blocking, man?"

Alan twisted toward him, keeping me to his other side. "What exactly were you doing?" He sounded furious. "This is so not okay. She doesn't know you at all. You didn't used to be like this."

Danny's ears reddened. "It's none of your business. She doesn't belong to you." He took a step in our direction.

My danger senses tingled sharply. Alan was taller than Danny, but Danny was bigger. I didn't want trouble. There was no way I would be able to explain bringing Alan back with a black eye.

I felt a tug on my hand.

I looked down. Our fingers were still intertwined. It caught me by surprise.

"Let's go," Alan said.

Time seemed to pause for a moment as I searched his face, an open question mark. I didn't know where he was going to take me, but it didn't matter. I was going to follow.

We ran toward the staircase, scrambling up the steps and bursting onto the first floor.

I could hear Danny shouting behind us, but the pounding of our feet plus the music playing full blast in the house made it impossible to hear what he was saying. We rushed through a blur of colors and limbs, and then, somehow, we were out the front door, into the warm night air. We narrowly dodged past a group of people who just arrived. The tickle of an uncontrollable giggle crept into my throat.

We could've stopped, since nobody was chasing us, but whether it was the adrenaline or something else, we kept going. Beyond the lawn, down the street, past the line of Greek-lettered houses on the block. Energy sang in my veins as the wind blew fresh on my face. I felt as though I were suspended in a dream, like maybe, if we kept going, we could strip the years away and go back in time. We ran and didn't get tired. We ran into the endless night. And as we flew through campus, he never once let go.

eleven

FAKING

WHEN DO YOU and I become strangers? It is hard to know, except that it seems to begin after we come to America. Things happen slowly, until one day, I realize that I do not remember the last time we played together or when you wanted anything to do with me.

You get older, your face elongating into a man's. With age, our differences become clear, the way the ocean polishes away at the shoreline.

We are so unalike. You are a smaller version of Baba. Your analytical mind grasps concepts after a single lesson. You excel academically. You shrug off social difficulties in a way that I cannot, perhaps because they do not matter to you. You move through the world like a scholar, waiting for a higher plane of learning, waiting to leave this insular world behind. I feel earthbound, wishing to be more American, wanting to share jokes with friends.

Baba treats us both the same, diligently teaching us math beyond the school lesson plans. He scoffs at how slowly the curriculum moves. With you, it is easy, and you fly beyond the schedule until you're doing problems at a college level in eighth grade.

With me, it's another story.

"Why don't you understand?" Baba says one afternoon, a regular replay of our tutoring sessions. "It's very simple. Your brother picked it up instantly."

That's all I hear, how proficient you are, how smart. Baba's tone glows with delight at your name. I shake my head. I don't know why it is hard for me. If I could learn it, I would. Instead, I feel as though I am trying to break into an impenetrable fortress.

"You're supposed to be getting better, not worse." He sighs. He turns toward the living room, where piano melodies drift through the doorway. "Chen Wei!"

The music abruptly stops. Your head emerges. "What?"

"You try." The resignation in his voice slaps me hard. I twist in my seat, embarrassed.

"But, Baba, I have too much of my own work," you protest.

"She is your sister," he says. "You are responsible for each other. She needs your help. And maybe you'll be able to reach her better than I can."

We exchange a look of equal outrage. I don't want to learn from you, any more than you want to teach me. But Baba puts up a hand. His irritation is clear. He has shed his problem off onto the two of us and extricated himself.

You let out a half grunt, half sigh. "Go to your room," you say. "I'll be there in a minute."

I retreat, biting back a retort. I hear you and Baba arguing quietly as I shut the door. I collapse onto my bed. My cheek rests on the cool pillow, beginning to dampen lightly from bitter tears.

There's a knock at the door. "Hello? Can I come in?" You let yourself in and shut it behind you.

Surreptitiously, I wipe my face against the sheets as I sit up.

You carry a red pen and my notebook of problems Baba had begun marking up. "What part of it is causing you problems?" you ask.

"All of it."

Your lip curls. "Can you get more specific?"

"No." I stare sullenly.

"Okay. Great talk."

I turn the other way to face the wall, willing for you to leave me alone. I don't hear anything but paper rustling for several minutes. Finally, you clear your throat. "I'm looking at your answers. You're making the same type of error. I think you're probably just missing a simple thing. What if you—"

"I don't want your help. You can't teach me anything."

Baba's pity and frustration make me feel worthless.

"Everything is so easy for you. You never need help. You don't know what it's like to be me, and I'm tired of trying to be like you."

My resentment leaks out in ugly spurts; directed at you,

directed at the world. I can't begin to articulate it the right way, so it comes out in all the wrong ways. None of this is your fault. All I know is that nothing will be simple between us again. We will always be compared against one another, and one of us will never measure up.

You say nothing, only turn on your heel to leave. I have gotten what I asked for, only I am left with hollow disappointment anyway.

I sit there, trying to decide if this means I'm excused or not. To my surprise, you return shortly. You drop the notebook on my bed. It's flipped open to Baba's prompts for next week. They are all filled out.

"What is this?" I ask.

"Next week's answers. I filled them out for you."

"What? You can't do that."

He shrugs. "Why not? I know them, and you don't. I'm good at faking handwriting."

"That's—that's cheating." My eyes dart toward the door, as though Baba might be standing at the crack, listening in.

"This isn't for school. You're not turning this in to anybody except Baba. That's not cheating." You glance at the pages carelessly. "I left a couple of them wrong so it wouldn't be obvious."

For some reason, this makes me want to laugh. That you pretend to be worse at math so your imitation of me would be more convincing.

"I'll do these for you every week so we can stop getting lectures from Baba," you say.

"I don't want this." But my fingers are curling around the notebook even as I protest. The temptation is too great. We both know that I will go along with it.

You give me a long look that's partly sympathetic and partly exasperated. "Do me a favor, though."

"What?"

"Use your new free time to figure out who it is you want to be. Don't just be me."

I stare at you.

You give me a ghost of a smile, a hint of humor coming out. "There can only be one of me anyway."

twelve

Nine blocks later, we stumbled to a halt at a cluster of trees. I doubled over panting and out of breath from laughter, one hand pressed against a trunk to steady myself.

"Really out of shape," Alan said, breathing hard and cracking up.

"Why did we just run halfway across campus?"

"I—just—really wanted—to get away."

"I don't think Danny is going to find us," I said.

We looked at each other and lost it again.

I was giggling so hard that my stomach was cramping. "I can't. Stop. Don't talk to me."

We stood there, wheezing, until we could catch our breaths again.

"Sorry about all that," he said after we gathered ourselves. "Back there, I mean."

"It wasn't your plan to leave me with him?"

He looked appalled. I felt something inside me unclench with relief.

"I didn't want to leave you at all. I stepped outside, and when I came back, I couldn't find you."

We got quiet.

"He used to be different. Hell of a debater. But he was super sweet and shy," he said. "I don't know what happened."

"People change in college. It's just part of the process," I replied darkly; always, always thinking of Sam.

He didn't seem to get the reference. "You wouldn't have known him from before. You would barely have guessed it was the same guy."

"Hmm. That seems familiar."

His mouth opened and closed again. "Okay. I deserved that."

I felt mildly appeased at my jab. But truthfully, I wasn't angry at him anymore. I had left it behind somewhere between the house and four blocks ago. The moon was high in the sky now, big and glowing, and it was nice to be outside. The air tasted fresh. I felt brand-new. For the first time, I didn't mind being in Alan's presence.

"It's all right," I relented, letting him off the hook. "A lot has happened since then. We are all different people now."

"You're still the same. You're still exactly as I remember."

"And what's that?" I deadpanned. "Awkward, anxious, and uninteresting?"

"Insightful. Funny. Forgiving. And pretty."

I flushed, grateful that we were shrouded in shadow so he couldn't see. "Now you've gone too far."

"What? Danny thought so," he said innocently. "And I never thought you were uninteresting. No matter what you may have believed."

"Well, you're different anyway. To be expected, since you moved to California ages ago and started over."

"What do you mean?"

"I mean I only know the Mount Pierce version of you from back then. And that version of you apparently doesn't figure into your new persona."

He rubbed his chin in bemusement. "I don't quite follow."

"Only that I heard through the grapevine that nobody even knows you ever lived in Illinois. People think you came straight from Shanghai. More worldly and interesting that way, I guess. You are good at curating a compelling backstory."

"I see," he said, raising his eyebrows. "What else have you heard? I want to know what's being said about me in the halls of Weston High."

"That you're popular. I know everyone knows about you, which is not nothing in such a big school."

He grimaced. "I don't know what it means to be 'popular,'" he said, putting his fingers up in air quotes.

"Oh, please, Alan. I think you know exactly what it means to be popular. You've always known how to be popular, no matter where you've lived. Somehow you've found a way, whether you're surrounded by white Midwesterners or West Coast Asians. I shouldn't at all be surprised."

He shook his head, trying to dismiss it. "You have me all figured out, I guess."

"Of course I do. I was your secret keeper, remember?" I said lightly.

"As if I could forget," he replied.

Alan's father had been stern and slow to warm up. He was very smart, very respected. I remembered that Baba always seemed to defer to him in the room, even though they were friends. He spoke deliberately. He did not talk to Sam or me very much, and when he did, he seemed uncomfortable, whereas Alan's mother was chatty and loved engaging with children. I didn't like being around him much.

I could tell that Alan would behave differently around his father. He'd stand straighter, not laugh as much, lift his chin. Once, when his family was at our house and we were having a loose potluck, his father asked him to recite some classical Chinese poems.

"Speak louder," he commanded, two lines in. "You sound like a mouse."

Sam and I glanced at each other, sensing Alan's humiliation rising as though a layer of steam. Our parents were less showy. They never asked us to perform for others.

I tried to catch Alan's eye, but he seemed determined not to look at me.

After that, he always seemed to talk in a loud voice around his father.

"Why do you do that?" I asked him, days later. "Shape yourself around him?"

He shrugged. "It's always been like this. It's just easier. Don't you do the same thing for your parents?"

He wasn't wrong. I worked hard at school, even though it wasn't easy for me like Sam. I wanted to be good at what Baba valued. Still, Alan's outward conformance rubbed me the wrong way. "I think your dad's messed up. What else does he not like about you? Are you just going to stop doing everything he doesn't like?"

"That's why I like hanging out around you. You don't think that I talk too fast or birds are for girls or card games rot your brain. I can just be myself."

"I'm like your secret keeper."

"Yes!" he exclaimed, thrilled at the idea that he had someone on whom he could unload everything he couldn't be at home.

I didn't like it so much. It felt like a big, weird responsibility to put on a person and made our relationship seem too transactional. But I said nothing because Alan was my friend, and it seemed to make him happy.

"Anyway, that was ages ago," I told him. "Maybe it wasn't even real. Maybe it was just another game."

"I was always real around you. You made it easy." He looked at me with the kind of open, disarming expression that made my heart pull sideways. It was then that I had to admit an uncomfortable truth.

Maybe it was the buzz from the jungle juice or the moonlight or the fact that he had rescued me like some kind of knight in shining armor I'd never believed in, but it was impossible right now *not* to think about how much I'd once liked him. Maybe those feelings hadn't been entirely platonic; back then, it would've been hard to pick it all apart. But now it was coming back to me.

Still, we hadn't talked about the big thing between us. The thing that allowed me to guard myself, just enough.

Alan seemed to want to say something important.

I stopped him. I wasn't ready just yet. I had to trust him, really believe that he could no longer hurt me, because I couldn't survive another betrayal like the last one. I wouldn't let him do that to me again. Soon, I thought. Not tonight. Tonight was for starting over fresh.

"I'm glad you made the transition and people like you," I said, softer. "It's a lot to move so much."

"Yes, well. It was hard at first. But it's been good. And now you've moved too."

It went unspoken, but I was never as good at adjusting as he was. No matter where I went, I felt like I was on the outside looking in.

"It's like we switched places from before," he said. "I'm the one who's been here longer, and you're the one who's new." He paused momentarily. "Does that mean I get all your secrets now?"

"Sure. But I'm an open book, don't you know?"

A small smile played on his lips. "You were always very hard to read."

He searched me, and it seemed as though he were trying to find something hidden from view. I felt exposed and looked away, somehow paranoid that he would see my vulnerability toward him, afraid to give him that power.

"I think that we do have one secret in common now," I said, changing the subject.

"And what's that?"

I gestured around us. "We're both on lockdown about where we were tonight. Woke up in the morning with a full night's sleep and no recollection of any disturbances, right?"

He grinned. "Right. Of course." He stuck out his hand. "Should we shake on it?"

I took it. The light thrill as our skin touched again startled me. I let go as quickly as I could and threaded my own fingers together, letting the hum fade away.

We crept back into the dark house, a little before two. "What if they have a Ring camera or something that catches us? How are we going to explain that?" I whispered as we tiptoed down the hallway.

"They don't. Uncle Wang said that they're installing one later this year. He mentioned that insurance is making them get one to maintain coverage next year. He said it was a scam."

I couldn't help but laugh slightly under my breath. Sounded like something Baba would say too.

He locked the door quietly behind us in the kitchen.

"Don't worry," Alan said, speaking through a crack in the bathroom, just before we retired for the night. "We totally got this. Mission accomplished." His impishness was so familiar. He had been the one in the past to come up with our schemes and games. His satisfaction at completing our secret escapade made me smile.

"Good night."

"Good night," he echoed. "Thanks for coming out with me, Stella."

As I slid into bed, my blood still buzzing from our adventure, I thought to myself that next morning was going to be much better. I felt a measure of peace that I didn't have before. I imagined that maybe, even, I'd slide quickly into dreamland.

Then, the doorbell rang.

The neighbors had spotted us creeping around to the back of the house. Not recognizing us, they called the cops.

Uncle Wang and Auntie Chao answered the door with a great deal of confusion before we came out of our rooms sheepishly and explained to the police that it was us the neighbors had seen. Our hosts were sleepy but both looked moderately annoyed. It was two thirty by the time we had settled everything and went to bed. Neither of them asked what exactly we were doing sneaking into the house at the hour.

I had slipped into an uneasy sleep around five in the morning.

I woke up to my alarm only a few hours later and the cold

gnawing sensation in my stomach at the conversation we had to have. My mind a whirl of steady apprehension, I forgot to lock the other door in the Jack-and-Jill bathroom. Alan opened it while I was inside brushing my teeth.

"Oh shit," he said, freezing in spot. His hair was messy, and he wasn't wearing a shirt.

"Sorry! I forgot to lock it," I said through a mouthful of toothpaste. I caught a glimpse of his tanned lean torso before he backed out rapidly and clicked the door shut.

I sat down on the toilet seat and realized that we needed to get our story straight. "Come back," I hissed through the door. "What are we going to say?"

But he didn't respond.

It was too late, I figured. We needed to face the music. Except once again, he was abandoning me. I wondered if he was trying to concoct a story to get himself off scot-free.

I got dressed slowly and emerged for breakfast after I couldn't reasonably delay any further. As I went down the hallway, I heard Alan coming out of his bedroom as well, not far behind me.

Uncle Wang was sitting at the breakfast table, reading his phone. Auntie Chao was turned away from us, stirring something on the stove. Bamboo steamers sat on the table, smelling of shrimp buns. The only sounds were the sizzling from the pan and the coffeemaker on the counter churning out a pot of hot coffee.

My stomach rumbled.

"Good morning, Uncle, Auntie," I ventured timidly.

"Good morning," Auntie Chao said. "I hope you slept well."

Uncle Wang glanced up from his phone and grunted. His face was stormy.

Alan and I grabbed plates like two inmates and returned to the table. I sank into my seat. Auntie Chao poured us cups of coffee, and I whispered a thank-you. Alan was quiet and pale but looked resolute.

Normally, in this situation, he would've been able to generate a conversation to minimize the awkwardness, but he said nothing. Try as I might, I, too, could not muster up a distraction to save us. We all ate in silence. The sounds of chewing felt deafening. At a certain point, the tension was so unbearable, I was practically praying for someone to bring up last night so we could all be put out of our misery.

Finally, Uncle Wang sat back in his chair and folded his hands together on the table.

"We should talk about yesterday," Uncle Wang said formally.

Auntie Chao shot him a look that I couldn't read.

"What exactly were the two of you doing with our house keys, out in the middle of the night?"

Alan and I exchanged a look. This was it, I thought. He was about to flip on me. His father's rage would be incandescent if he had anything to do with this.

I imagined my parents' reactions if they found out I had snuck out in the middle of the night to go to a frat party and drank alcohol. That was not the kind of girl they thought they had raised. They'd lose it. Maybe they'd even hop on the next plane back to America. And then I'd really be in for it.

It was all a matter of who would go first.

I opened my mouth, not even sure what I was going to say, but Alan beat me to the punch. "It was my idea, sir," he said without a hint of hesitation.

I gaped at him.

"I wanted to see my friend, and I dragged her along with me. She didn't want to go, but she didn't want me to go out alone."

Except, of course, that I had gone entirely of my own free will. He was taking the fall for both of us, or at least trying to. It caught me so off guard that I couldn't protest.

"Well, that is very disappointing," Uncle Wang said. "You are supposed to be responsible for Stella's well-being on this trip. Asking her to sneak out with you in the middle of the night to get drunk is not protecting her well-being."

Alan winced.

"But, Stella, you too should have known better. You could have told us."

"Yes," I said, knowing I never would have tattled even if this story we were going with were actually true.

Uncle Wang cleared his throat. "Since we're your guardians and the police were called, I'm afraid we had to let your parents know."

"Do you?" I asked timidly. "Nothing happened. Nobody got hurt."

His gaze pierced me. "Yes, we do. I have already called them. I had no choice."

I swallowed. I hadn't checked my cell phone but wondered if my WeChat app was getting blown up with messages. I was going to be ill. Alan looked pale.

Uncle Wang's mouth twitched. Then he slapped the table so hard, we all jumped. "Just kidding!" he shouted. He started howling with laughter.

Alan and I exchanged looks, stunned.

"You should see your faces," Uncle Wang hooted in glee. "I got you so good."

Auntie Chao rolled her eyes while bringing over a pot of tea. "I'm sorry," she said. "I tried to talk him out of it."

"So—worth—it," he wheezed.

We sat there for a moment, trying to figure out how to respond to a grown man acting as though he had just pulled off the greatest prank of all time, laughing hysterically by himself. "You're . . . not going to call our parents?" I ventured.

"No, of course not. You're almost eighteen. No harm done, right?"

"To be clear," Auntie Chao said, ever the levelheaded one, "we would not have signed off on this had we known about it."

"But that's what you get for waking us up to talk to the police in the middle of the night," Uncle Wang said, jabbing his index finger at us. He took a sip of his coffee and let out a long, satisfied sigh. "I do think you both are a little too serious about this. I'm sure your parents would've been mostly concerned with you being safe and happy that you had come back unharmed."

I knew he was wrong about that, but I didn't need to correct him. The feeling was coming back into my limbs. I managed a weak smile. While I was glad he could find the humor in the situation, I was sure Baba would not have, if he had really gotten that phone call. And if Baba wouldn't have been cool with it, Alan's dad would have been on a different stratosphere.

As though Uncle Wang knew what I was thinking, he piped up. "Your ba doesn't have any room to be judgmental. The things he got up to when we were in school? We used to play mah-jongg every weekend. Loser had to crawl under the table and take a shot. For the record, your ba was terrible. I think he must have permanent bruises on his knees and still owes me thousands of dollars. You should tell him that. Plus he got arrested once for openly carrying alcohol. Bet he didn't ever tell you that either."

The shock must've been transparent on my face, because Uncle Wang guffawed slyly.

"Really appropriate story for the kids," Auntie Chao said dryly. "That was when you all were in your twenties, not in high school."

"Sorry. Gambling is bad," he added with a cheeky grin. "But when we weren't playing mah-jongg, your ba was the best at karaoke. He had an unbelievable voice. Could win that show—what is it called? *American Idol*?"

I still couldn't imagine the Baba in Uncle Wang's story. Sure, he had his goofier moments, but in general, he was a sober, deliberate man. I'd never seen him play mah-jongg. And I'd never heard him sing. But Uncle Wang was one of Baba's best friends and knew him better than anyone. He winked at me, and even with his penchant for exaggeration, I had to believe him.

I had never asked my parents about their years in America before Sam and I came to join. They didn't like talking about it. In fact, I knew very little about them in general, something that suddenly struck me as a startling hole in our relationship.

"But on a serious note," Uncle Wang said, "please do not leave the house tonight."

thirteen

A FEW HOURS later, I found myself staring down the barrel of what looked to be an ordinary cheeseburger. But as I was learning, appearances could be misleading.

"It's just a burger," Alan said. "Don't psych yourself out. Give it a try."

I was all about extending trust to him these days it seemed, so there was no reason not to keep doing it. I took a bite, carefully running the flavor and texture along my tongue. It was savory and chewy. It tasted like—well—a real beef patty.

"Good, right?" His face was expectant, intensely curious.

"Yes," I said, surprised at how thoroughly convincing imitation meat could be. We were at Monty's Good Burger for lunch, after touring UCLA in the morning. It was, as Alan had told me, a famous vegan burger joint in Los Angeles.

"I've always wanted to try this place."

I chewed my burger, enjoying its juiciness. I didn't need to out my lack of worldliness to him; he had lived in Mount Pierce too, after all. We didn't have any vegan restaurants there. Tofu was a thing I still viewed as a fundamentally Asian ingredient, to be cooked in its own right and not as a replacement for meat. "Why? Why not just eat a normal burger?"

"Because I'm a vegan now. Mostly."

I put the burger down. "You are? What do you mean by *mostly*?"

"I generally eat vegan, except at home." His mouth twisted slightly—so slightly that only someone who knew him as well as I did would have noticed. I didn't say anything because I understood why. But he must've read something into my expression. "It's just not worth the fight." He sounded defensive, as though he feared I was judging him for his cowardice. "Why pick one if you don't have to?"

"I'm not criticizing you," I said. And really, I wasn't. I could predict his father's reaction to him wanting to be vegan.

"Anyway, now you know." He looked out toward the distance.

"I feel like we're in a confessional," I joked. "Is there anything else you want to tell me that you've been keeping close to the vest?"

"Oh yes. Always."

"What else?"

He leaned in. "I've gotten really into writing *Neon Nights* fan fiction."

"Interesting." *Neon Nights* was a popular anime about a former yakuza member and his efforts to escape his past life. I knew it was based on a successful manga and had been adapted into six seasons of television. That was about the extent of my knowledge. I associated it with the nerdier set. The thing that caught my attention was that I had never known Alan to be a writer. That was always me.

"You're one of only a few people I've told."

A few people. So I had been downgraded slightly, to one of a circle of confidants. It was only fair, I supposed. "Why?"

"Why am I telling you, or why have I told only a few people?"

I thought about it. "Both, I guess?"

"Well, you can guess why I'm telling only a few people," he said easily. "It's not exactly the kind of thing people expect out of a two-sport athlete and homecoming king. And I write a lot of romance. I'd never hear the end of it from my teammates. And I'm telling you because you already know everything embarrassing about me and you're still around, so I figure this wouldn't drastically change how you feel about me. We're already in too deep. I like telling you things. I like seeing your reaction."

I paused. "You were homecoming king?"

He grinned happily.

For any other person, this level of clout-chasing would've been off-putting and shameful. But he was too likable for it to matter. It came off as a charming quirk, rather than thirstiness. In any case, I knew it all sprouted from the same source. Alan had a deep-seated need to be loved, and he sought love everywhere to quench this need. He needed this love from strangers as equally as he needed this love from me. It was no wonder he wrote romance. He was an intrinsically romantic person.

"And what about you?"

"What about me?" I asked.

"Tell me something you're keeping close to the vest," he said, parroting my words back at me.

"I don't hide things like you do from the world."

"Just from me."

I looked at him, not fully comprehending.

"Let's step back to the day before. You tried to convince me that you wanted to major in *astronomy*. You."

"I don't know what I want to major in."

"That's not true."

I drew back. "What, you're going to tell me about myself?" I was full of indignant offense.

"I could guess. You want to major in journalism, obviously."

He truly surprised me this time. "Why would you think that?"

"You told me you were taking Journalism II," he said slowly. "What kind of person takes Journalism II without a serious interest in it?"

Ah yes, I thought. We had shared class schedules. But only in passing. It didn't occur to me that he was paying such close attention. I hadn't paid that much attention to what his schedule was.

"And you know, Kit," he added.

I was startled. "You remember Kit?"

"She was your most prized possession. Of course I remember."

Kit was a Kit Kittredge American Girl doll that my parents got secondhand from one of their friends who had a daughter ten years older than me. I got it for my first Christmas in America, wrapped up and regifted in a Payless shoebox along with a hardcover companion book and a set of accessories. I didn't know anything about American Girl dolls, but I knew it was the most expensive gift I'd ever gotten. I didn't have anything like that in Da Ji Cun. She just looked pricey with her finely stitched clothes and smooth artificial skin. "American Girl," Mama had said softly when I opened the box, wrapped in old newspapers because we couldn't afford flashy wrapping paper. "Like you."

Even though Kit had a perky blond bob and blue eyes and looked nothing like me, I immediately felt like she was mine. I took her everywhere. She was the most American thing I owned. Having Kit made me feel a little bit like I had a road map for fitting in with other girls. All I had to do was be more like her. I read Kit books from the library and ran her traits through my fingers like shiny coins. Spunky. Intrepid. All-American. In the Kit Kittredge canon, she was a reporter.

I had completely forgotten.

I shook my head. "I don't want to be a journalist because of a child's doll. That would be ridiculous."

"Who knows why people do anything? Maybe it wasn't a linear A to B. But maybe there was a spark in there, somewhere."

"Not a very good origin story," I said dryly. "Would make for a trite college application essay."

He hummed. "Aren't all college application essays trite? Isn't that the whole point of them?"

"I wouldn't know. I haven't finished mine yet."

"So, what's holding you up? They're almost due."

"I don't know," I said. "I'm not sure you would understand."

"It has to do with Sam, doesn't it?"

I blinked rapidly, struck sharp with a pain that I couldn't describe. I kept underestimating him. He was far more perceptive than I gave him credit for. It made me uncomfortable. Even after only a few days, it seemed impossible to bury anything deep enough that he couldn't find it.

I couldn't figure out what to say or where to begin about Sam, so Alan shaped the words for me. "What happened to him? How did he die?"

It felt so crude, the English language. Short sentences looking for hard truths. They were the questions that people wanted to know and that my parents had invited by keeping it all in the dark. So few had directly asked. And I had never told anybody. I looked up at Alan's face and knew so clearly that he was not probing out of nosiness. He was tender and sad. I wondered if he was remembering Sam as a boy, when we were all children.

I had rebuffed him once before on this question, but now, it seemed different. Before, it felt like trading gossip. This time, I was telling him a story about Sam. But really, I was telling him a story about me, because Sam's story was part of mine, and mine was still going.

"He died of a drug overdose," I said. "Adulterated Xanax,

laced with fentanyl. He didn't have a prescription for it. They never figured out who his dealer was."

His face whitened. "Jesus."

I was strangely calm, my eyes dry. I had imagined before, maybe, if I had said it out loud to someone—anyone—that I might unlock some kind of peace or acceptance. The truth will set you free, or so people said. But mostly, I felt hollow. Which was to say, I felt the same as I had before.

"It was accidental?" he asked, transforming his statement into a question only right at the very end.

"That's the thing, actually. It's impossible to know. I think it's what kills my parents the most."

"Is that what bothers you too?"

It was, and it wasn't. Sam was gone. However it happened—intentional or not—didn't matter, because the end result was the same. At least that was one way to think about it. But I couldn't convince myself of that. Of course it mattered. The whys and hows of it were all that I had left. They were what kept me up at night.

"Yes. All of it bothers me," I told him.

"This is what's stopping you from finishing everything."

He still didn't understand.

"He went to college, and then he never came back," I said. "How am I supposed to get over that in nine months' time? How am I supposed to look forward to the thing that killed him?"

It was a peculiar sensation, the knowing steady onward march of time, toward what felt like an executioner's block. Logically,

I knew I could probably go to college and not die. Most people went to college and came out of it just fine, proceeding to adulthood a little more educated, a little more mature. Most people. But not Sam.

And why? He had been the best of us. He was built for college. It seemed particularly cruel that he didn't survive it. If he couldn't do it, then how could I? We were of the same stock, and I was the lesser one in every way.

"College didn't kill him," Alan said.

"The drugs did. I know." But it was easier said than believed, given what I'd experienced. College had changed him. That much I knew.

I straightened and shook it off, pulling back from the brink. Alan was watching me intently as I carefully tucked the messy and dark parts of myself out of sight again. These were not things I wanted to share with him. And there was still more he didn't know—that no one knew. My grief was the loneliest grief there was. I deserved that.

I loosened a wry smile. "So there you go. You're not the only one hiding things at home. You're vegan. I'm afraid college will kill me," I joked. "Normal things, right?"

He looked at me very seriously. "You should tell your parents that."

"Sure I will. I'll tell them when you tell your parents everything."

"Your parents aren't like my dad," he said gently. "They will care about this. They won't want you to suffer."

Even in the same house, we all wandered around in our own ghostly worlds. It was hard to share my suffering with people who were also suffering. Whose suffering counted for the most? Alan wasn't there for the aftermath. He couldn't comprehend the level of wreckage Sam left in his wake. We were all barely alive anyway, but for what it had been worth, we *were* still alive. There was nothing to do but move forward.

"Don't worry about me," I said. "I'll get over it. That's what this trip is for, isn't it?" I refused to look at him. Instead, I crumpled up the wrapper on my burger and pointed at the clock in the corner. "We have to go. We're going to be late for our tour at USC."

How had I found myself back in this situation, orbiting around Alan's gravitational pull? It was years ago when he had betrayed me, but if I were to be honest, I had never really let it go.

That summer, the long days wound down until school was finally around the corner. Alan was nervous, because it would be his first time going to school in America. I couldn't fully assuage his concerns. Public school in Mount Pierce could be a brutal place. I survived only by keeping my head down and my mouth shut as much as possible.

He did have one advantage over me. His English, although mildly British, was more fluid than my own. Mine was getting a lot better, but first impressions were hard to overcome. He would probably set a better one than I did.

A few nights before school resumed for the fall, he came over to my house with his tiao qi set. We played several games quietly in my room, both consumed by our own thoughts. Perhaps we could sense, even then, that things were about to change. The summer had been a capsule, and there was a gentle waft of melancholy in the air. I had felt, briefly, transported back to the days of Da Ji Cun, where I could be myself. But I was comforted by the notion that at least this time, I wouldn't be going back to school alone.

"Don't bring tea leaf eggs for lunch," I told him. "Or anything that has a strong smell."

"I'll just buy hot lunch. I already asked my mom for money."

I nodded in approval. "It doesn't taste very good, but at least you won't have to explain yourself."

"We don't have the same teachers," he said anxiously. "Do you think we'll have the same lunch period?"

"We will," I assured him. "I double-checked."

We went through other suggestions I had for him, like not sitting too near the front of the classroom, if he had a choice, especially in math classes.

He stayed for dinner, not wanting to go home, maybe. We watched television for a bit, and then at last, he had to go home for bed. Right before he left, he gave me a hug.

"Thanks for being my friend," he whispered.

Over the next few days, I contracted a scratchy throat that turned into a full-blown fever and chills. It was one of those fierce late-summer flus. The unfortunate timing meant that I missed the entire first week of school. I didn't see Alan in that time to keep him from catching what I had. I had no idea what his first week was like.

In time, I would think about that week and wonder, endlessly ruminate, on whether everything would've been different if I hadn't gotten sick. How much a small, serendipitous event could so radically change the course of two people's relationship. Because I refused to believe that when he had left only a few nights ago, he had said thank you with the intention of letting me know it was goodbye forever. What kind of person would do that?

When I returned, I felt disoriented. I had missed only a week, but people had already begun to settle into their routines. I was slotted into the only remaining seats left in each of my classes and asked to play catch-up on assignments.

By the time I got to lunch, I was already feeling weighted down by the heaviness of returning to a life I had managed to break free from over the summer. As I went down the line to collect my food, I caught a glimpse of Alan.

He was sitting at a table with a group of boys I'd never talked to. He seemed relaxed. I was surprised and then a bit envious that he had already found people to surround himself with. I had sat alone for weeks on end before clinging to a group of outcasts.

I wasn't sure whether I should wave to him, or what the right thing to do was in this situation. He hadn't been looking around for me. He seemed perfectly content.

As I passed his table, I must've paused for a moment, just briefly. Maybe our eyes met. For once, I saw nothing in them.

One of the boys piped up, "Do you know her?"

"He has to. They're both Asian, so they're probably related," another one said before bursting into laughter. He nudged Alan. "Lighten up, buddy. It's just a joke. We tell jokes here."

Alan shook his head and laughed in response, like a puppet, jumping for his puppeteer. My heart sank. My skin burned so hot that if it were a flame, it would've been the blue kind.

I looked at him, hoping he would say something but already knowing that it was too late.

"But you came from China too, right?" the first boy asked.

He nodded. "I came from Shanghai." He pronounced it in an exaggerated American way. Shang, like orange Tang. Hai like hi. "I heard she came from some village in the middle of nowhere."

It was funny hearing him say that. Mount Pierce was more like a village in the middle of nowhere than Da Ji Cun, which was at least on the outskirts of Xi'An, a city four times the size of Chicago. Not that any of these boys, who probably had barely left the state, could ever imagine.

The boys turned back to each other to talk about something else, and I was forgotten, just the butt of some guy's joke that day. I went to a table somewhere on the far end of the cafeteria. I couldn't remember who I sat with, or what I ate. Whatever it was, it probably tasted like ash to me.

All I could remember was the numbness. How it felt, to feel nothing at all.

At USC, I learned that there were thirty-nine fountains on campus, and that was the only fact I retained from Lakshmi's tour, mainly because I did feel like we walked past a surprisingly large number of fountains. I had counted nineteen on our route.

The LA schools were starting to blend together in my mind. They were all palm trees and brick paths and cloudless blue skies. I didn't know that I could've distinguished one from the other, if you showed me a picture. Certainly not enough to have a firm opinion about which school I preferred.

Alan suggested we go for boba milk tea after the tour was over, so I followed his lead to a popular chain. I ordered my drink, half sugar, and took a sip. It was creamy, silky, and fresh. The boba had the right amount of bite, coated with a fine layer of sweet syrup. It was, I had to admit, wildly delicious. Even better than anything I'd had when we made trips to Chicago. So far, the food-tour portion of this trip was impressing me more than the main attractions.

We sat on a bench in the shade, resting our feet after walking all day.

Alan had been quieter and more pensive in the afternoon, after our conversation at lunch.

I caught glimpses of him out of my peripheral vision. His fingers tapering around the circumference of his cup. The particular shape of his knees.

"I meant to thank you for this morning," I said.

"For what?"

"For trying to take the fall with Uncle Wang."

His eyebrows did a little jump. "Oh. Well, it didn't really matter. All's well that ends well."

"Right, but you tried." I glanced at him sidelong. "If I had said something first, it would probably have been to implicate you."

"That would've been fair. You didn't owe me anything. And it *was* my idea to go to the party. My friend who I wanted to see." He flinched slightly at the reference to Danny.

"But it was my choice to come with."

He opened his mouth to push back again, but I interrupted him.

"It was nice, okay? That's all I'm saying."

He blushed. "Okay."

"I didn't expect that from you, if I'm being honest. It made me think—" I stopped abruptly.

"What?"

It still tasted bitter to me. The memory of before. My throat was tremulous. My pulse trembling. But I couldn't leave it alone anymore. Not if we were going to try to find our way back to each other again in any manner resembling forgiveness.

"Can we talk about it?" I asked. "I mean, the thing you don't want to talk about. What happened after that summer." Everything around me seemed to flutter, like I was afraid of what would come next. I had waited for so many years to hear what he had to say about it all. I imagined confronting him so many times. In all those scenarios, I was sticking it to him in some way, forcefully getting my revenge, making him feel sorry. None of them were like this. Somehow, no matter what, I would always be the one trying to gain the upper hand on him, while he held the high ground.

At the end of the day, I was still my younger self, hoping that he would choose me.

He heaved a sigh, as though he had been waiting for this moment too. "Ah," he said. "Yes. Yes, we should."

"Why did you do it?"

"You know why. It wasn't anything deep or complex. I was scared. Isn't that why anyone does something horrible like that? I was so riddled with fear that those kids would make me their target. I was willing to do anything for it not to happen to me." He couldn't meet my eyes.

"You chose yourself over me."

"Yes. I was wrong. I think back all the time to that moment and how I wished I could do it over again. I figured I would probably never see you again. But then you ended up moving here. When your parents asked if I'd take you on a college tour trip, it was an unbelievable thing. It felt like fate intervening to give me a second chance to make up with you." He slumped forward slightly. "I'm sorry, Stella. Do you wish I would've said no?"

Unable to speak, I shook my head. At the beginning of the trip, I did wish I had the option of doing the trip with anyone other than him. But I didn't feel that way now. I felt like I was finally being given a chance to let the bad parts of us go. Maybe that was how it was for him too.

There was one more thing I needed to know. "Do you

remember the last time you were at my house before school started?"

"I do."

"Did you know what you were going to do then? Had you already decided?" I could hear my heart beating in the question, like wings pounding against a wire cage. Tell me it wasn't part of your plan, I thought. Tell me you couldn't be so cruel.

He didn't answer for a long pause. "No," he said. "I didn't know that night. I thought I was going to see you at school on the Monday."

I leaned back on the bench, relieved. It seemed that after so many years, I could finally put this persistent worry to bed.

I didn't talk to Alan again after that day in the cafeteria. What was there to say? What could he have done to make up for it? I wasn't interested in being his off-hours friend. To his credit, he didn't try to contact me either. At least he recognized that what he had done was unforgivable.

Of course, our families still saw each other. But I went out of my way to keep from being alone with him when they were over. Gone were the days that we would go to each other's houses to play, even though we lived down the street.

A year later, his family moved again. This time to California. I didn't say goodbye.

The sunshine boy who entered my life so easily, slipped away like a shadow. And that was the end of it. Except for one thing.

A few months after he was gone, I was reorganizing my room

during one of my mother's whole-house frenetic deep cleans, when I found it, tucked away in a back corner of my white bookcase, right next to Kit's foot. An orange marble from Alan's tiao qi game. I picked it up and turned it over in my fingers, admiring the delicate petal design encased in clear glass. The orange set of marbles was unplayable now, with one missing. It was a shame. A beautiful set, ruined by carelessness.

But then, how had it gotten there? It didn't seem like it could've rolled there on accident. Maybe he had left it for me, a single memento of our summer. A reminder of what could have been.

I kept it in my jewelry box with my family gold and Nai Nai's jade rabbit necklace.

fourteen

As WE GOT farther away from Los Angeles, the sea breeze drifted in, pushing away the sallow air. Our drive was lined with blue mountains and ocean on one side, palm trees and red-tiled roofs on the other. The colors were more vivid and sharp here, no sign of the haziness that drifted over the city.

Leaving Los Angeles felt like a brand-new start. Already my limbs were lighter, my mood uplifted. Maybe the beautiful climate was finally beginning to thaw my frostbitten Midwestern exterior. I had even gotten a fairly decent night's sleep by my standards before we departed from Uncle Wang and Auntie Chao's house. They'd sent us off in the morning with tight hugs and full thermoses of coffee for the road. I had a tinge of sentimentality about them as we left. They had been such good hosts. I could see the younger versions of them through their present selves. For some reason, it made me feel closer to my parents in a way I hadn't before.

I rolled down the window and felt deliciously awake from the salt tang of the sea.

"I don't get it," I said after a moment, continuing my conversation with Alan, who was impatiently awaiting my response. "So other people can see the ghosts playing baseball?"

"Yes."

"Why isn't the entire movie about how ghosts are real? That seems like a big deal. Wouldn't there be national news stations reporting about how there are ghosts playing baseball in the middle of Iowa?"

He sighed. "It's not really about the ghosts, Stella. It's a movie about second chances and the relationship between fathers and sons."

"But the main character guy—"

"Ray."

"Whatever. He saves his farm from the debt collectors because he builds a baseball field in the corn and people pay to see the ghost baseball players play? Is that not the main plot of the movie?"

"You're really focused on the mechanics of ghosts in real life. It's about him getting to play catch with his dad one last time."

We were somewhere between Santa Maria and San Luis Obispo, after a long leisurely stop for lunch. I had put on my sunglasses to cut the glare, and Alan had a pair of clip-ons over his glasses.

I frowned. "I thought this movie involved ghosts helping a baseball team win a championship improbably. Against all odds. Like all sports movies."

Alan almost choked. "Are you talking about *Angels in the Outfield*?"

"Is that the one?"

"*Field of Dreams* and *Angels in the Outfield* are completely different movies. Like, how could you possibly confuse them? *Field of Dreams* is an actual classic, with Kevin Costner, that makes grown men cry. *Angels in the Outfield* is a schlocky movie made by Disney that nobody likes," he said heatedly.

I adjusted my seat farther back and lowered my sunglasses. "Oh, sure, no way I could confuse those two movies. Just both old, about baseball, and involving ghosts."

"Ghosts are not angels. They're different things."

"Don't you think it's kind of weird that there are multiple baseball movies involving ghosts and bonding with your family? I mean I feel like one is probably enough, right?"

"Ghosts aren't angels!" he said, pounding the steering wheel.

"Close enough."

He shook his head in despair. "You're hopeless. You don't get the magic. One day, we'll watch *Field of Dreams*, and then you'll understand."

I smiled, amused at the idea of us spending time together in a basement again, like old times. It was a small and delicate hope, like a snowflake on cold glass. It was a thing that could dissolve easily, of course. Still, I let myself imagine it, suspended for a moment in a limitless future.

"One eight eight, Viejo Pass, Montecito, California," I said later, reading the address into the GPS as we got back in the car after a gas refill. "Auntie Yang and Uncle Ma live in Montecito, not Santa Barbara?"

"It's just in the hills. It's fancy."

Santa Barbara was like a city on a postcard.

We drove along its picturesque streets until the GPS took us up a hill to a neighborhood where the houses dotted the incline with generous plots. It was a gated community. We had to punch in a code we had been given to get inside. These houses didn't so much have "yards," as much as they had "land." The houses themselves were modest in size but were very pretty in design.

My mouth must've been agape. Alan grinned.

"Welcome to Montecito. You should check Zillow."

I googled their address on my phone. The house came up. It had sold five years ago for four million dollars. Real estate in California was wild. "Wow, they're rich, huh?"

"Uncle Ma is the head of the MatSci department at UCSB," he answered.

Eventually, we approached the top of the hill and turned onto Viejo Pass. We drove through a large plot landscaped with gorgeous trees and arid shrubs. The house was a one-story hacienda-style home. It had a brick exterior and a red-clay-tiled roof, but the brick was whitewashed in front.

We parked in front on the gravel driveway and stepped outside. I blinked a couple of times, as the landscape all around was surreal. Auntie Yang's place had a stunning view of the mountains, the harbor, and the ocean. I thought it was the most beautiful property I'd ever seen, like the kind of place a Hollywood celebrity would have as a summer home.

I hadn't ever met them before. Both my and Alan's parents all ran in the same circles in graduate school, but I knew that Auntie Yang in particular was a close friend of Mama's at the time. It was only much later that she met Uncle Ma. She had done so through, of all people, Alan's father. Alan's father was a professor as well, and they had both worked at the same university for their postdocs. Because Auntie Yang and Uncle Ma married later, their one child was also much younger than Alan and me.

We brought our suitcases up a neatly maintained gravel walkway to an arched wooden door with iron hinges and rang the bell.

Uncle Ma answered. He had black hair shot through with silver, a crooked nose, and a pronounced Adam's apple in a long neck. He was wearing pale linen pants and a white shirt, very coastal and high end. "Ah, you're here. Alan and Stella, right? Welcome, welcome."

He had better English than my parents. His accent was barely noticeable. Made sense, since he had spent almost two decades as a professor in the United States. He seemed more American than any of my parents' other friends.

He stepped aside and ushered us through the front door.

The inside of the house was like a gorgeous, sunlit little jewelry box.

There was a high-vaulted ceiling of wood planks and exposed

wood beams. A big rounded vertical wood beam held up a loft area with an iron railing. The living area was open-concept, with a grand fireplace, two sitting areas, and a chef's kitchen of polished wood and stainless steel. The decor was themed in warm brown leather and wood and soft white fabrics.

I felt dusty and out of place in this cozy, clean wonderland.

Two women and a child around the age of four emerged from the back patio inside. One of the women was Chinese and my parents' age. She exclaimed, "Yah! Our guests are here and you didn't tell me," and bustled over to give us hugs.

"They just got here," Uncle Ma said.

Auntie Yang held me at arm's length. The corners of her eyes crinkled with pleasure. "You look just like your ma."

I had never had anyone tell me that before. People usually said I looked like Baba. I wasn't sure whether that was the type of comment that merited gratitude—was it more flattering to be told I looked like Mama or Baba? I didn't say anything in response.

"I talked to her just this morning," she said.

"You did?" Mama hadn't even bothered to message me.

"We got carried away with the time, as we usually do. I'm so happy to meet you at last."

I tried to visualize how Mama behaved around this gregarious, stylish woman, who was supposedly her good friend. Before I could ask for more on what they talked about, Auntie Yang had turned to her companion.

The other woman was a young white woman, her pale brown

hair tied up in a high ponytail. She was wearing yoga pants and a white tank top, and she was holding the child's hand.

"This is our nanny, Juliet," Auntie Yang said. "She's a grad assistant in Peter's program." She motioned for the boy to come over too, which he did reluctantly, hiding behind Auntie Yang's leg. "And this is James. James, can you say hi?"

He shook his head.

"He's a little shy right now," Auntie Yang said apologetically.

Alan knelt down and held up his hand. "You wanna give me a high five instead?"

At first, James didn't move, but Alan was patient and stayed in the same position a beat longer than was comfortable. Slowly and deliberately, James reached out and smacked Alan's outstretched hand with his own.

"Yeah!" Alan said. "Great job."

We all clapped, and James looked bashfully pleased.

Alan had a particular knack for talking to children. I was insecure around them, and I swore they could sense it.

Uncle Ma clapped him on the back. "Your father doing well?"

"Yes, sir," he replied solemnly. His spine straightened. He stood the way I remembered when he talked to his own father.

"Good. Glad to hear it."

"Thank you for letting us stay here, Uncle Ma and Auntie Yang," I said.

"Please, call us Peter and Molly," Uncle Ma said. "We're not formal like that."

"Okay," I said, not repeating it back to them. I couldn't

imagine actually calling Chinese people of my parents' generation by their first names. I'd be seventy years old, and I would still call the hundred-year-olds uncles and aunties. On the other hand, my parents' other friends tended to still speak Chinese among themselves and to me. Uncle Ma and Auntie Yang spoke only English to us. Auntie Yang's was mildly more accented, but she spoke without halting or searching for words, the way Mama did.

Should we give you the tour?" Auntie Yang asked. Juliet took James back out to the patio so he could run around.

Uncle Ma and Auntie Yang had a big master suite at the end of the hallway, layered in gauzy blue linen, with a sea view. James's room was next door, tastefully done in forest greens with an animal motif.

"I'm sorry we have only one guest room with a bed," Uncle Ma said. "We have a pullout couch in our exercise-meditation room."

He showed us both. The guest room had a big white queen-size bed with double glass French doors that opened into the garden. The "exercise-meditation" room was next door and smaller. It had a Peloton, a rack of hand weights, a pullout couch, and a yoga mat next to a table full of incense sticks. Alan took the exercise-meditation room, and I took the real guest room.

Auntie Yang clapped her hands together. "Shall we have lunch?"

We all sat around a rectangular reclaimed wood dining table. Juliet was seated next to James and attending to him while he ate.

Auntie Yang had prepared grilled chicken and fajitas rather than Chinese food. My parents' repertoire of non-Chinese food was zero, if you didn't count jarred marinara sauce and boxed pasta.

"We bought this house right when I was pregnant with James," she said. "Total renovation and had to do it all in under a year. We moved in when James was three months? I was on maternity leave."

I couldn't recall what Auntie Yang's job was. "What is your work?" I asked.

"I'm a paralegal at a law firm in town. Horrible," she said.

"I keep telling you that you can quit," Uncle Ma says, pained. "We don't need the money, if you don't like it."

She shrugged. "I have to do something. What would I do around here, now that James is in school? Just hang around here and water the plants?" She forked another chicken breast off the center platter. "Lifesaver that we have Juliet here to help. What will we do when she graduates?"

"Well, she still has two years," Uncle Ma said. He was the quieter of the two of them. Cerebral and reserved, he spoke up sparingly.

There was a long pause. Our silverware clinked loudly against their custom clay plates.

"Pity you will only stay two nights," Auntie Yang said. "It's so beautiful here. You should certainly use tomorrow to enjoy yourselves in Santa Barbara."

"You both applied to UCSB?" asked Uncle Ma.

Alan looked at me quickly.

"Yeah," I said. No reason to explain my situation. "He's doing early acceptance at Stanford, though."

"Well, I can't begrudge him that," Uncle Ma said approvingly.

The two of them began engaging in a separate conversation about the college application process.

On our side of the table, Auntie Yang smiled at me, her eyes unwavering from my face. I started to feel mildly self-conscious, as if perhaps I had something in my teeth. "Don't mind me," she said. "It's just so wonderful to meet you at last. Like seeing a celebrity. Your mother used to talk about you all the time before you came here with your brother."

Strange. Not that a version of me had existed in someone's mind before I had come. It was the fact that Mama talked about me to other people. She was so circumspect about those years in America before we arrived, so openly unemotional. Up until this moment, I realized that I hadn't ever considered whether she had missed us at all.

fifteen

THE HALFWAY POINT

UNLIKE MOST PEOPLE, you could fold our lives in half, with two different existences on either side. One half was China; the other half, the United States.

Your life is frozen in time, and as such, a perfect split. Mine will keep going—if all goes well. One day, the China portion for me will be a smaller and smaller piece, until it'll be only the beginning, the mere introduction of a version of myself I still do not know.

But today, the inflection point is in the middle of everything, and that's what I think about when I try to see when things changed.

We are never the same once we come over the ocean. In the before life, I am your partner, your double, and I follow you everywhere. You teach me everything I need to know. From you, I learn how to skip rocks the farthest across the pond by flicking my wrist just so. I learn how to spread the exact right amount of chili crisp on my mantou. I learn how to leap over the garden walls of our house perfectly without messing up Nai Nai's climbing roses.

We sleep in the same room, whispering in the dark. I know that you share generously but fear being taken advantage of, that you dream of making our family proud by making a big discovery that you can put your name on. You long to come to America and join Mama and Baba, while I dread it. I don't know them, but I know you.

After, you become quieter and more introspective. You seem to make the transition with ease, yet I wonder what toll it takes on you. I want nothing more than to cling tighter, but you push me away. You tell me I'm a baby, that I need to grow up and be on my own, that you are too busy, always so busy. Maybe it would've happened even if we had stayed in China, but I'll never know. To me, it seems as though the move is what changes you. And I cannot let go of that, as hard as I try.

You do not try to teach me anymore. But still, I learn.

I watch you work yourself to the bone late into the night and never ask for help from anybody.

I watch you carefully edit information to Mama and Baba to exclude what might make them uncomfortable or disappointed. I watch you polish away at yourself like a river stone, until you are hard, smooth, and bright, all the imperfections rubbed away.

Once I start middle school, I realize that all the girls have started wearing makeup. Shiny gloss across lips and eyelashes long and inky dark with mascara. My bare face feels like yet another way in which I stand out. I begin to swipe makeup samples from mall counters. I watch videos in the dark, of how to shade colors without a crease on my eyelids, how to make my sparse lashes curl.

Mama asks, "Is school going well? You fit in?"

Her anxious worry fogs up the windows.

I know without hearing it directly that she would not like her eleven-year-old daughter wearing makeup. A frivolous distraction, she would think. The mark of an unserious girl.

I also know other things about her, because once upon a time, you told me. That our mother's family was poor. That they wished for a boy, but in China, they could have only one child, which turned out to be an undesirable girl. That she worked harder than anyone and outscored everyone at her school on the gaokao, the college entrance examination. That you remembered her crying bitterly when she left us behind. I had been only a baby.

I weigh all these things together. What I owe her against what I owe myself.

I tuck my makeup, precious as gems, into the inside pocket of my backpack, where she won't look. I go to the girls' bathroom in the mornings once I get to school and methodically apply my armor before facing the day. Before I go home, I wash it all off so I can return home a barefaced innocent child.

I tell Mama nothing.

This is what I learn from you.

sixteen

Of all the colleges we'd seen so far, none of them had stood out to me, until this one. UCSB was astonishingly beautiful.

We walked along the lagoon on campus, a huge body of water that linked up to the ocean. The water was deep blue, lined with paths where people jogged around the perimeter. Far in the distance, you could see the purple blue of the ocean beyond and the low rise of mountains. It was hard to beat having access to the beach on campus.

UCSB didn't need a tour to sell the experience. Just walking around was enough. It felt like we were on vacation. It was incongruous. Being here should've made the application deadline loom harder rather than seem far away.

I thought about what this trip would've been like had I done it with my parents instead. We had taken a week off to visit colleges with Sam when he had been applying. We marveled at the aged redbrick campus of Harvard and the impressive gothic architecture of Yale, each lending a sense of weight and history. Sam's face was tight with suppressed excitement. He didn't want to seem too eager to leave the nest, but I could tell that he was no longer with us in the present. He was soaring toward his future, already gone.

I could not have felt more different about it.

It made my parents' absence on this trip feel all the more conspicuous. We hadn't talked since Mama and I had the spat about the secret we were keeping from Nai Nai. It seemed that they were hell-bent on avoiding anything difficult with me, from the beginning of this trip to now, where even apparently talking to me was too much.

I wondered what they were doing. And I wondered about Nai Nai, whether she was thinking about me.

"What's turning in that brain of yours?" Alan asked as we circled the lake.

"Oh," I said. "Just thinking about everyone in China. Without me. What's happening, and all that."

"Ah," he said.

"I feel like I was just dumped on this trip as something to be rid of."

"Ouch. And what am I? Chopped liver?"

I smiled. After everything from the past few days, I could let myself feel grateful that he was here. We were tentative but feeling our way toward openness again. And it was nice. I could admit it now. I *had* missed him. "You know that's not what I meant." I folded my hands together. "It's been years since I've gone back. Hard to believe. What about you?"

"Three years," he said. "Three and a half. I don't have any relatives there who I'm close with anymore. They've all passed away. And everything is so unfamiliar. The last time I went back, I felt so out of place. It almost hurt to be there, you know? To be somewhere you used to fit in and no longer fit anymore."

He always seemed to say my innermost thoughts. That was what made us so deeply connected back then. I knew, logically, that there were many children like us, even if in Mount Pierce, we were a special set. Maybe at Weston High, we weren't special at all.

"Sometimes, I try not to talk to my grandmother," I confessed. "It just makes me too sad. So I avoid her."

"Even though avoiding her hurts too," he finished for me. He had been raised temporarily by his grandparents as a child as well, but his parents had rejoined him in Shanghai in the later years, before they all moved to the United States.

I nodded. It was shameful, but he understood, at least. "The more I avoid her, the more I don't know what to say to her when we do talk. I'm just in a constant cycle of guilt. Guilt building on more guilt."

"I get it. You ever heard the term *satellite babies*?"

"No. What's that?"

"I learned it only when I moved to San Diego. They're kids who were raised by extended family, usually grandparents, while their parents worked in a different country. And then they go back to their parents when they're older. Common mostly among Chinese families."

"Huh. Satellite babies," I repeated. It conjured up a lonesome image, floating in space, touching nothing. Was that why I felt so rudderless all the time, so unable to fit in anywhere? But then, Alan had never had this problem. Maybe he was an exceptional satellite baby. One who had overcome our fundamental nature. He had found his way back home.

"It's a very specific experience. It's no wonder it's hard for us, right? Leaving our grandparents, joining our parents. It was so strange when my grandmother died. That was the last time I went back. For her funeral."

"I'm sorry."

"It's okay," he said. "Sometimes I wish I hadn't gone. That's terrible to say, isn't it? But I wanted to remember her the way she was. It didn't feel real until I saw her body."

Although Nai Nai was getting older, her dying still felt like an abstract future thing. The idea of it made me shiver. One day, I wouldn't have the chance to talk to her anymore. Would I regret all the times I'd been too busy to call? Or the summers I hadn't visited? Nai Nai never complained. She never made me feel bad about it.

Even now, she was probably patiently waiting for the day she would see her American grandson again. She was the only one who didn't know that she never would. Not in this life, anyway.

As we meandered through the grounds, he gave me tips about the teachers he was familiar with and what groups of people at school to avoid. We had flipped roles from when we were at Mount Pierce. I found myself enjoying his descriptions of Weston High and how different it was from what I knew. He had been so anxious before, and now he was confident about school and his place in it.

I wondered what it would be like when we returned to class next week. Would it be like how we were now? Walking and laughing side by side in the sun? And how surprising it would be to everyone there, that we went so far back.

I had a tiny nagging question that had been tickling the back of my mind this entire time, but it had never seemed like the right moment to ask.

"There's still one thing we haven't talked about," I said.

"Oh? What's that?"

"Who's Victoria?" I tried not to let any trepidation enter my voice. It was an innocent question. I prepared myself mentally to feel no attachment to the answer either way, and yet for some reason, my body was not getting the message. Beneath my skin, my blood vessels surged, heating the surface, but hopefully not turning me red.

His eyebrows did a tiny jump. He coughed lightly, surprised. I knew then that the answer was not nothing.

"How do you know about her?"

"The twins asked. Remember?"

"Right. She was my girlfriend."

"Was?"

"Yes. Was. Which I guess makes her my ex-girlfriend, for clarity." He laughed. "Are you worried?" he teased.

I definitely flushed then. "No, I don't care." But I knew my face belied my words. I had so many questions. How long? How did they meet? Was he in love? I had to lower the temperature of my interest, though, for self-preservation. I shrugged. "I was just curious at how the twins knew about her."

"Is this the portion of our conversation where we talk about our past love lives?" He grinned easily.

"I think mine would be a very short update, but sure."

"Okay, why not? I'm curious. I dated Victoria for two and a half years. Long enough that I once invited her on a family trip to Los Angeles, so the twins met her then."

"Oh. Serious."

"I guess so."

"Sounds pretty serious to introduce her to your family and go on a family trip together. What was she like?" And why did you break up? I wondered silently.

"Smart. Intense. But very funny when she wanted to be. We were both on student council together. We ran against each other for president. She won. She was Chinese American. Born in the Bay Area. My family really liked her."

I felt intimidated at his description, as though I were being measured up to it, and I wasn't comparing favorably. "Wow," I said, my bones feeling loose and unwieldy. "So what happened?"

"It's odd, right? She was perfect on paper. It was like one of those things where it just seemed inevitable that we would get together." He paused. "I make it sound so mechanical. I did like her. But we seemed to be lesser than the sum of our parts. Over time, it felt like she was more interested in a vision of who I could be rather than who I was. It was small stuff at first, but then it became bigger and more existential. Eventually, we got closer to post–high school life, and, of course, it got complicated. It was her dream to go out east for college, and she wanted us to apply to the same colleges. And I didn't want that. So that ended up being a deal-breaker, because she said she couldn't see a future with me." He went quiet. "It was fair. She was always the one thinking about who we could be, and for some reason, I never thought about us at all."

"So you broke up with her?"

"No. She broke up with me."

It hadn't been his decision in the end. Maybe, then, this was all an ex post facto justification for what had happened. Who knew if it was even true? I tried not to look disappointed.

"The truth is," he confessed, "I knew it wasn't quite right for a long time, but I could never bring myself to do something about it." His eyes went misty and distant at some painful memory I couldn't see, before he gathered himself again. "And, you know, it's shallow, but I really didn't want to go to homecoming alone."

"You're so noble. Did she break up with you before or after?"

"Before," he said promptly. "She was always braver than me."

That must have been early in the fall, only a few months ago. "Did you love her?" I asked.

"Wow. No pulling punches from you, huh?"

I shrugged.

He hesitated. "We dated for over two years. We said 'I love you' to each other after one."

"That didn't really answer my question."

He shot me a sharp look. "I guess it's complicated. I don't know."

I wanted to keep pushing, but I stopped myself. There were things that I wouldn't be able to understand about that period of his life, and it was fine.

"Okay," he said. "Your turn."

I sighed. "There's really nothing to tell."

"Really? Nothing?"

Now I was heating up like a raw sunburn. All I had were flashes of embarrassing escapades that I barely wanted to remember myself, much less share with another human being. Fleeting unrequited crushes, and once, an awkward kiss in a car that didn't lead to anything. Nothing resembling love, or anything close to it. My romantic life was a mostly barren wasteland, but Mount Pierce wasn't exactly a place that offered a lot of promising prospects, if I were being honest. As I approached seventeen, I did worry, every once in a while, that maybe there was something about me that was just fundamentally unlovable. Or maybe that I was broken, because I didn't know what it was like to fall for someone. But unlike Alan, I felt confident that if it happened to me, I would know right away.

These were not thoughts I could say aloud, so I just nodded. "I told you it was a short update."

I was worried he would press, but he didn't. He only smiled in mild disbelief and resignation and backed off. I was relieved.

We passed through a butterfly garden, bursting with orange and purple flowers in alternating clusters.

"Look," he exclaimed.

"What?"

"Cassin's kingbird." He peered up keenly, leaning toward me and guiding my gaze up to the branches of a nearby tree with his finger. "See its yellow belly and gray head? It's rare to see around here. I have to log it. I've never seen one before." He turned toward me. His expression was so open, you could read the palpable delight all over it. His excitement was contagious. He could make you care about some bird species you'd never heard of until right that very moment.

There it was, I thought in surprise. Standing on the edge of a sheer cliff, right before the sensation of falling.

We had dinner with Auntie Yang, Uncle Ma, and James. They made spaghetti and meatballs. They were perfectly fine spaghetti and meatballs, but it was still strange to me that they cooked American food and spoke no Chinese with us. Auntie Yang wore an apron with branches of lemon trees along the edges that she told me she had bought on the Amalfi Coast. They were like a standard upscale white family.

Auntie Yang was a vivacious host. She regaled us with stories of their vacations and the funny passive-aggressive land battles they were having with a neighbor around the perimeter of the property and where it was properly located. "They are putting up a fence," she said. "And the official survey of the property has the boundary four feet closer to their house than they thought it was—meaning the plot is supposed to be smaller. But they want us to honor where they originally thought the line was, which means they would rip out a line of beautiful birches we've had to accommodate their fence, and I just can't accept that."

"Who cares where they put their fence?" Uncle Ma asked. "The property is big enough. It's not like we'd notice the loss."

"It's the principle. They're legally in the wrong about the property line and morally in the wrong for what they're going to do to the birches. And I'm going to fight them over it."

"Seems a bit far to declare them morally wrong over some trees," he said. "They seemed like nice enough neighbors until you started antagonizing them."

"Peter doesn't have any sense of principle outside of the sciences," she told us, her lips twitching.

I laughed.

Later, we all went to our own rooms early for the evening. Alan said he was tired from the drive this morning and was going to collapse in bed. I was going to work on homework and possibly, possibly my college applications—the entire point of this trip.

I opened the French doors to the garden. The sea breeze flowed in. I did a couple of math worksheets because they were mindless and easy. I had three short essay questions to send via our online learning platform about *Heart of Darkness.* I finished everything for school I could as a valiant procrastination attempt before I turned to my applications again.

Alan had been right. Of course I wanted to study journalism. I couldn't realistically imagine myself doing another job. What else would I study in college? Why hadn't I even thought about it before? Why hadn't I ever had a conversation with Mama and Baba about it? Sure, possibly they would object, but I didn't give the option to in the first place. I accepted defeat before an opening move.

That was how I continuously chose to navigate our lives. Follow the path of least resistance where I could. Hide or minimize everything else. I didn't know how to have any difficult conversations. Neither Sam nor I did. Maybe it was a skill we should have learned—maybe it would've saved his life.

I opened the page to the personal essay I had barely started. I wanted to vomit. I wanted to delete everything before it. Name, birth date, high school, everything. I wanted to delete myself from the system.

It was dark now, and still, my parents hadn't called me. I lay in bed, feeling like a kettle, slowly reaching a boiling point. But there was nobody to yell at, nobody to hear the whistle.

I sat up. Opened the WeChat app. Our family chat was silent. Warm and reckless, I dialed Mama directly without asking to see if now was a good time. I would make her worried, calling out of the blue like this. She might've thought something was wrong, but that was a small benefit too. It was mean, but I wanted them to worry for once.

I didn't know exactly what I wanted to talk about. Only that I was tired of being ignored, relied upon to do the right thing all the time.

"Hello?"

It caught me off guard. I'd half expected nobody to answer so I could feel self-righteously neglected.

Baba was there too. They were both sitting in Nai Nai's kitchen, but nobody else seemed to be there.

"Liang Liang? Is everything all right?" she asked urgently, her anxiety manifest.

I swallowed. The pressure I felt to reassure her was already there. "Yes. We're in Santa Barbara now. At Auntie Yang's house."

Her shoulders relaxed. "Good. I meant to call, but things got busy here."

"The wedding?"

"Yes. That."

Her voice was tense and clipped. I wondered what was going on. "What's happening?" I asked. "Is there anything I can do to help?"

"Oh, nothing. Just a bunch of silly things. Weddings are complicated. You don't have to worry."

I felt myself being brushed off like an errant fly.

"Have you turned in your applications yet?" she asked, pivoting quickly.

I thought about lying, maybe, just to get her to leave me alone. "No. Not yet."

"But you're getting closer?" she pressed. Beside her, Baba leaned in too, both of them listening intently for my response.

I stared at the screen at them. These two people who cared deeply for me but knew so little about me. And truth be told, it was the same the other way around. Their lives before Sam and me, a total mystery.

It made me suddenly, deeply sad. We had been lonely for so long, that it had permeated our lives, and we didn't even notice it. We were like fish, oblivious to the water.

"I'm not," I said abruptly.

"Not what?"

"Not getting closer to turning in the applications."

They exchanged looks, twin alarm bells. "Why? Is there too much homework? You have to prioritize this over your homework. This is your future," said Mama.

I tried to figure out how to say it. *You should tell your parents that*, Alan had said. I couldn't tell them exactly the way I had told him. "It feels like this big thing," I said. "Turning in the applications. It means I have to do the next step. Go to college."

"Yes." Mama's brows were furrowed. She did not understand, so I had to say more.

"I'm scared." The words dropped hard. One-two punch. Heavy tomes hitting the ground, one after the other. I felt oddly exposed talking about my feelings, like an oyster pried open on its hinges. We did not talk about feelings in our household. Only American families got into those things. I couldn't ever remember my parents asking me, "How do you feel about that?"

Not even after Sam died.

There was a long, empty pause.

"Why are you scared?" she asked at last, tentative.

"Because of Sam. I'm afraid to go. I just can't do the applications. I can't get over it."

For the first time, I saw my parents' expressions ripple with fear. Okay, I thought with a little measure of relief. Maybe for once, we were on the same page. They had felt it too.

Mama looked fragile. She touched Baba's arm. He had been sitting quietly, but now he cleared his throat and spoke.

"There is nothing to be afraid of," he said firmly.

Mama nodded in parallel, as though seeking to be convinced by his words too.

"You are not like Sam."

But I was. I was literally the same set of DNA, half of Mama and half of Baba. All his latent weaknesses in me too.

When we first came to the United States, everything was so strange, but we used to take solace in the fact that the two of us had always experienced life together. We could always relate to each other. We had the same upbringing, the same background.

I hadn't said anything yet. Across the ocean, Mama wrung her hands in despair.

"This," she said to Baba. "I worried about this. We should have stayed with her. We cannot just put Chen Wei away and think that Liang Liang will not be affected. We cannot let him ruin her life too."

Ruin my life? As though my life were some kind of object whose sole purpose was to be maintained and protected rather than experienced. I flared.

Baba shook Mama off like a shriveled leaf. "You will go to college," he said, declarative. "You are worried because of the unknown. You'll go and see that everything will be fine. What will you do if you don't go to college? There is no job without it, no future without it. This does not have to do with your brother."

"It has everything to do with him!" I snapped. I lowered my voice so as not to alarm anyone in the house. My chest hurt like a bruise.

"Why can't we talk about that? Why can't we ever talk about him?" And then— "You won't even unpack his room," I said, so softly that I wasn't sure they could hear me.

Sam's passing, all the secrecy around it, a rot at the center of our lives.

I was holding back tears. I wanted to tell them the truth. The most important thing that I had kept from them. After Sam died, I thought I would take it with me to the grave, but I knew now that I could not move on with it locked inside me like a growing mold. I was being poisoned from the inside out.

I thought they might yell at me. Maybe cry. But they stayed silent and impassive. Eventually, Baba exhaled slowly. "Talking about it changes nothing. He is already gone." He looked as though his bones were the only thing holding him together. "All I want now," he said, "is to protect my remaining child. Please."

I felt all the air go out of me too. "Okay," I whispered. "Okay."

I couldn't bear to end the call like that, but there was nothing else left to say.

My mouth was desperately dry. I needed a glass of water.

By this time, the house seemed mostly quiet. I couldn't hear anything except the gentle billow of the curtains against the open door to the patio.

I crept out of my room. The hallway opened to the living room, with the kitchen on the other side.

As I emerged into the living room, I saw that a lamp was lit, a figure sitting quietly on the leather couch off to the side. It was Auntie Yang. Her head was tilted back. She had a white sheet mask on, but her eyes were open. She looked like a ghost, lounging in the shadowed corner.

I wanted to slide backward, return to my room to nurse my wounds alone. But she spotted me and sat up. "Stella?"

It must have been midnight by now. Everyone else was probably in bed.

"I'm just getting something to drink," I said.

"There's a bottle of sparkling in the fridge. Or drink out of the filter on the main faucet."

"Thanks."

I tried to pass her as quickly and inconspicuously as possible. I went to the kitchen, poured myself a glass of tap water, and attempted to return to my room without engaging in small talk.

But she had peeled off her mask and leaned forward in her chair. Her face was shiny from the moisture. I nodded to her as I headed toward the hallway.

"Is everything okay?" she asked.

I didn't know what it was, exactly. Whether she had noticed a rim of red around my eyes, or the way I shrunk into myself as I moved. It was one of those things where everything actually was fine until you heard someone ask you the question directly. But through most of my life, nobody had ever really asked.

To my horror, tears started sliding down my face in earnest. "Oh my God," I said, trying to stem the uncontrolled overflow from my eyes. "I don't know what's happening. I'm fine. Really, I'm fine." There was nothing worse than crying in front of a near total stranger and not being able to stop yourself.

"Oh my, come here," she said.

I could do nothing but obey.

She rose up and gave me a hug. "Sit."

I sat on the adjacent sofa, while she handed me a tissue. I wiped my cheeks hastily. She waited without saying anything until I pulled myself more or less together.

"I don't know what came over me," I said.

She nodded. "Sometimes it happens when you hold it in for too long. It all comes out when you least expect it to."

To my surprise, she had switched back to speaking in Chinese now that we were by ourselves.

"Is it a problem?" she asked. "I get tired of English at the end of the day." Her voice sounded different in Chinese, softer and more contemplative.

I told her it was okay.

"What happened?" she asked. "You don't have to tell me, if you don't want to. You can go to bed. But maybe you want to."

"It was nothing. Had a disagreement with my parents," I said before realizing that I didn't want to air our dirty laundry out in front of Mama's friend. It would be my mother's worst horror. "I mean, we don't fight very much," I added, which was true.

"I won't say anything to your mother, if that's what you're worried about. She has enough on her plate. But I understand. You must be missing them. Such a big trip to be taking without their input. I'm sure they are sorry to be away."

I wasn't sure they felt that. It seemed to me that they wanted to escape. "Mm," I said in tepid agreement. "Maybe."

"Oh, certainly. They do. I was there in the years you and Sam were still in China. They were long years, and your mother counted the days like gold coins. She wondered, often, if it was worth it. To keep you there while she and your father worked here. She said to me that once you came here, she could never imagine letting you go again. She would sleep in your rooms until you graduated."

"How can that be true?" I blurted out. "She was not like that when we came over." I hadn't meant to say it out loud, but Auntie Yang's confession astonished me. I believed that my mother didn't have a sentimental bone in her body. She spoke awkwardly around us. She could hardly look us in the eyes for weeks in the beginning.

"I remember that she had this idea to keep a box of all the things that represented every year without you and she was going to give it to you and Sam when you arrived, so you could know that she had kept the time while you were gone. A stuffed tiger from the first American zoo they went to. A pressed flower from the tree outside their first apartment. She showed me. Did she give it to you?"

I shook my head. "I've never seen it."

"Ah."

"I thought she didn't even like us. I imagined that the wrong people picked us up at the airport. That maybe other people out there were our real parents." I had never told anybody that before. I probably should have kept it to myself, but it was too late now. "Why didn't she give me the box, then? Give us the box?"

Auntie Yang didn't say anything for a moment. "I think she feels a lot of guilt for leaving you behind. I think she felt that there was nothing she could do or say to make up for her perceived shortcomings of not being there for you for so many years. Sometimes the hardest thing to do is to be honest with the ones you love."

I didn't know what to say to that. Her words seemed to pierce me. Mama had kept herself hidden from us, but then, who was I to judge? I was keeping myself hidden too. It all felt like a pointless shell game we were playing. To what end? Who were we protecting, after all?

There was still so much I wanted to know, but I needed to get it from my mother, not from Auntie Yang.

"Your Chinese is still very good," she said after a long pause.

"Thank you."

"James doesn't speak it at all. Peter wants us to speak English at home, and the nanny only speaks English too." She looked over me, toward the wall of glass windows on the other side of the house. "It's strange, feeling like there are things you will never be able to tell your child fully. Things they'll never understand. For me, literally. I am afraid he will lose this part of himself. The Chinese part. But I can tell you that no matter what, every choice I make is for him, whether he knows it or not. So I can see where your mother is coming from."

"Why can't you teach him Chinese?" I asked, and then I realized that maybe my question was poking into a part of her life that she didn't want to share with me. From the set of her jaw, it was apparent that she and Uncle Ma had discussed this.

"Oh," she said lightly—so lightly that it was clearly artificial—"that is a story for another day. But now it is late, and you should go to bed. I didn't mean to keep you up with these old memories."

I was being gently but firmly dismissed. I stood up with my glass of water. "Thank you for this," I said. I figured she understood what I was thanking her for. "Good night."

She nodded.

I left her in the living room and went back to my room. I got ready for bed slowly, preparing to face down a long night of wakefulness. The insomnia was an ever-present part of my routine now.

As I tucked under the covers, I mulled over all the things she said—the price of secrets, the importance of honesty. I thought about the bond between my parents and me, amorphous and flexible. Hard to define, yet impossible to sever. I considered calling them again, but I needed time to let it all settle. I still didn't know what to say to them. I never knew how to start.

So instead, as always during these nights, I waded through the endless time before morning by curling into my own head and bringing Sam back to life.

seventeen

REQUISITION

FAMILY IS AN organism. Multicelled but operating in unison. Decisions are made for individuals by the group, opposition be damned.

We learn that life is like a bell curve. Children are powerless, and elders are too, in the end. It's the middle generation that holds up the sky.

This is what happens when the family decides that Nai Nai is too old to be living in Da Ji Cun by herself. The village is too far away from high-end medical care. The winters are too cold for an old woman's bones. Gu Gu and Gu Ma will keep a closer watch on her in a new city apartment. Baba will financially cover the cost of a full-time live-in aide. These are things Baba and his sisters talk about in hushed tones over the phone, until at last, they agree to the plan. Three to one, they will overcome the will of their aging, headstrong mother.

We call her to break the news, the American arm of the

family. Baba sitting closest and Mama at the other end. You and I sandwiched in the middle. We, the grandchildren, are here to soften the blow of the news.

"What's the occasion?" she jokes, seeing us all sitting around the table on a Wednesday.

I shoot a sharp glance at Baba. Surely she can see through this charade. Baba and Mama still call her regularly, but it's been months since you and I have. Six months between calls is nothing unusual for us now.

Nai Nai looks rosy and bright-eyed. She looks spry and alert. Shouldn't she be allowed to decide where she wants to live?

"We just thought it had been a long time since we all talked," you volunteer uncomfortably.

"I thought you'd all forgotten about me."

"Ma," Baba says with a mortified voice.

She laughs. "I'm kidding. You're busy, everyone's busy." She has a big sigh. "Everyone's busy these days with their own lives. Me? I'm the only one who's slowing down. That's getting old. You young people still have to work hard."

Baba nudges me, because I haven't said anything yet.

"We want to see you soon," I say. As part of the sweetener to coax Nai Nai out of her house, Baba told her that we would visit her this summer. "We miss you."

It's strange. We moved late to the United States, late enough that our Chinese was firmly rooted. But once we started going to school, it was startling how quickly our tongues began to get used to different sounds. Sometimes I can even feel my *zh*'s and *z*'s getting mixed up, my vowels getting wide and sloppy.

"Me too," she says. "It will be a good trip. Been so long since you've been here. The people in town won't even recognize how big you've gotten." She shrugs. "The ones who are still here."

Much has changed in Da Ji Cun. Nai Nai recounts those changes whenever we call. Our neighbors on either side have moved away in search of better lives, better jobs. Half of the houses now stand empty.

"Xing Xing gu gu got married this year," Nai Nai says. "The wedding in the village was wonderful."

She is Peng Tao's older sister, and accordingly, we call her auntie, even though she is seven years older than me. That makes her twenty-three. I can't imagine getting married at twenty-three.

"You know she remembers you both and asked after you."

Xing Xing was around less than her brother when we were there. I remember a round face, wavy hair, and crooked teeth, but a sweet smile.

"Who did she marry?" I ask.

"A boy from college," Nai Nai replies. "Grew up in Henan. In older days, the wedding would be in the boy's hometown, but these children have two weddings now." She nods. "Good for Xing Xing. That girl studied hard. She put in her heart's blood. She got out. And she found an educated partner too. She will have a good life."

I am humbled. I know how hard the kids in China have to

work to have the hope of a future. The line between poverty and stability is razor-thin. By a trick of fate, we were destined for America, where the pressure in school is nothing in comparison.

"Now we all worry for Gou Gou," Nai Nai says.

My attention is seized. "Gou Gou?"

"Yes, she is taking the college entrance exam next year. But she's not focused like Xing Xing. She's thinking of the present, not the future. She's too busy chasing the boys." She makes a snorting noise. "Those boys will be nothing. They'll go nowhere. And she'll end up just like her mother."

I think of Gou Gou when we were little. The tiny gap between her front teeth, her pigtails. The last time I saw her, she had grown out her hair and her face was losing its childish chubbiness. She was growing into her looks. It was clear that she was going to be pretty, prettier than me.

"She's too good-looking," Nai Nai says. "Beauty is wasted on these girls. Not serious." She looks right at me. "My granddaughter is different. Pretty and smart. She'll be able to go to any college she wants."

I feel myself getting red at the kind of unabashed praise you can only get from a grandparent.

"And my grandson. Going to the best university in the world next year." The pride vibrates in her voice. "I always believed. I'll die happy now."

Her words are too on the nose to be real, because no matter what Baba says, we all know the reason they are moving Nai

Nai to the city is to prepare for her eventual deterioration. Time catches everything. I meet Baba's eyes, and his jaw tightens. He clears his throat. "Ma, we've been thinking."

She rolls her eyes. "Aiya, here we go. I knew you were calling me because you have some plan for me that you have to unveil."

Baba colors. Even though my aunts are in China, when the family needs to ask Nai Nai to do something, it's always Baba who lands the messenger. It's a combination of him being favored because he's the child who's far away and being the only son. Nai Nai's favorite. "Don't be like this." He sighs. "But you're right. I've been talking with jie mei, and we've decided that it makes sense for you to move to the city. It's too isolated out in the village, and you're getting older."

"You don't have to remind me," she says tartly. "You and your sisters have *decided*, eh? No talking to me first?"

"I'm talking to you now."

She sniffs.

"We can get you an apartment close to jie. Wouldn't that be nice? Don't you want to be closer to your daughter?"

"My daughters, both of them, could visit me more out here." She is stiff.

Baba wrings his hands in his lap. This conversation is not going the way he wants it to, but it's going exactly the way I expected. Nai Nai has always been like this. Of course she wouldn't just roll over and do what they want just because he's asking. "Aren't you always complaining about how the winters are getting too cold for you with the coal heater? In the city, we can buy an apartment with radiant floor heating. Your feet will never be cold again. Your arthritis will be better." He's pleading.

She turns her head as though she doesn't want to hear.

I think about the village in winter, our big puffy coats as we cuddled by the coals. The green skim of ice on the pond in front of our house. The gray branches of the trees reaching for the white winter sky. The smell of cold.

"Did you already get the apartment, or do I get to tour them at least?" she says finally.

Baba is encouraged. "You can pick, certainly. Jie will come get you next week to see a few if you want." He sounds artificially gentle, as though he's afraid if he presses too hard, she'll scamper away like a skittish horse. "There are lots of good places out there, Ma. It'll be nice. No more stairs. You can have a washing machine and a dryer."

"I never needed those things," she says. Her eyes glitter. It seems as though she is going to fight us. Then she deflates and speaks dully. "But I have to move anyway. The government is requisitioning the village for land developers. We have three months to vacate."

Everyone is stunned, except me. I don't understand what's going on. I'm not familiar with the word. I look to you for an explanation.

"Requisition," you say quietly. "It means the government is repossessing the land so they can use it for something else."

Our childhood home. Gone in three months. The entire village cleared out. Where will they go? It doesn't seem real.

"Are they paying you?" Baba asks.

"Some." She doesn't elaborate. Her tone tells us it isn't very much. Not that it matters. There's no appeal. No way to change the wind. "So you see, I have to find something anyway."

"Why didn't you tell us sooner?" Baba says, pained.

"Your sisters would know if they were around more. Three children, none of them to be seen. You don't care about lao jia, our home."

Baba looks like he's been stabbed. I feel bad for him; it's not as though he had the choice of being around more. "Well, if you have to move anyway, then I suppose we are all on the same page at least."

"The family plots are going too," she says abruptly. "So we need to find a new place to bury our dead."

"We'll find something. We'll work on it. You don't worry about anything," Baba says.

She sighs. "Chen Wei, Chen Liang," she says to us. For the first time ever, she sounds old to me. "You come back home soon, okay? You come back one last time to see everything."

My throat is thick. I wish I could reach across the screen, across the years, across the words I don't have. "Yes, Nai Nai," I say. "We are coming."

eighteen

We had one more day in Santa Barbara and one more night before we'd make the drive up to Palo Alto for the last leg of the trip. Once we went to Palo Alto, Alan and I would split up with two different Stanford students hosting us in the dorms. Then up to Berkeley for a visit and we'd make the long drive back home.

Today was a free day. I was planning on trying to catch up on the pit of schoolwork that seemed impossible to dig myself out of and write my personal essays (really this time). Baba's words from the previous night echoed roundly in my skull. I would need to get over this hurdle. I couldn't keep pushing it off forever. Maybe it would be easier if I sat outside in the light of day, rather than working at it in my bed at night, insomnia bearing down on me. Maybe the bright bluish air and sea breeze would brush away my neuroses.

I had mentally committed to this in full, until Alan came into my room midmorning sometime after breakfast and plopped down on the edge of my unmade bed.

"What are you up to?" he asked, which I knew was the prelude to ruining all my plans.

"A lot. I'm so behind."

"I've just been thinking, you've moved to California, and you haven't even done anything fun while you're out here. You haven't gotten any kind of welcome tour."

"I don't think people normally get a welcome tour when they move to another US state."

He waved his hand dismissively. "This isn't just another US state. We used to live in a cornfield, Stella. This is like moving to a different world. Especially Santa Barbara. Isn't it magical here?"

"My parents are super mad at me," I said. "I shouldn't."

"Why?"

I mumbled something unintelligible. I didn't want to recount any of it, especially since he'd encouraged me to speak up in the first place. For some reason, I didn't want to disappoint him.

He didn't press. He just leaned in and grinned. It lit up the entire room. "Look, sitting here miserable is not going to help you work faster. Spend the day with me. I'll help you catch up later. I can be your sounding board. Maybe getting some sun will inspire you."

If getting some sun were all it took, my creative tank should've been overflowing. I couldn't even remember experiencing a day of rain so far, since we'd moved. The weather in California was like copy-paste into infinity. You didn't even need to check the weather app to know what tomorrow would be like. Another difference from Illinois, where sometimes in the summer, even if the app said clear skies in the morning, you could get caught in a thunderstorm in the afternoon.

I should've said no. If I did, I knew he would leave me alone. But all those good reasons fell by the wayside when I looked at his expectant face.

With him, I always found some way to say yes.

I didn't know at the time exactly what I was saying yes to, but once I did, I had to follow through with whatever Alan was planning as a "welcome tour" to the state of California.

That was how I ended up standing on a foam board, clutching an oar as though it could save me, in the middle of Santa Barbara Harbor in a last-minute bikini I'd bought an hour ago from a sandy beach shop with limited options.

Standing was, maybe, a generous description. I was mostly kneeling and occasionally rising to my feet, quickly to tumble back down hard into the water.

I sputtered as I fell for the ninth or tenth time and climbed back onto my board. This time, at least, I hadn't inhaled any water.

Alan watched me from his board. He was perfectly balanced. He seemed to exert as much effort as a person standing on dry land. "You stood for longer that time," he said, as a form of encouragement.

"Is this a welcome tour or some form of hazing?" I asked, trying to regain my bearings for a minute before rising again.

"Isn't this the best?" He was fully sincere and bursting with enthusiasm. "You would definitely not get to do this in Illinois."

"Lake Michigan exists."

"We didn't live near Lake Michigan. Besides, the entire ambiance is different. You're in the ocean. Look at the sun. It's February! Sure, it's unseasonably warm this year, but still! You're not dodging lake-effect snow."

He had brought his swim trunks on this trip. I wondered if this was part of living in California too. Being prepared to go in the water at any given moment if the occasion called for it. He had no self-consciousness at all. But why would he? He was an athlete. He physically looked great, which was something I would never openly admit to. He had a level of body awareness and poise that meant he wouldn't know how to be awkward, even if he tried.

I, on the other hand, felt like a flailing wet puppet. Too many limbs and no ability to control them. My hair was drenched and tangled around my shoulders. I was too pale and too angular. The bikini mostly fit, but it wasn't the cut I would've chosen. The gapping cups made me feel like a flat child, and although I didn't want to focus on this, I did anyway.

"I look ridiculous," I said.

"You don't," he said. "You are doing great. You haven't given up. I'm impressed you agreed, to be honest. It was brave to try something new. I had a backup activity if you didn't want to do this."

I hit the water in mock indignation. "You had a backup activity? Why didn't you offer that?"

"Because it was a backup."

"You tricked me."

"You had full freedom to decline. And I'm glad you didn't. You haven't gotten to swim in the ocean since moving here, have you?"

I shook my head, tendrils of hair slapping my skin wetly.

"I didn't think so. It's so refreshing. Don't you love the salt and the sound of the waves? I'll never get tired of it. Tell me you're not having fun. Even a little bit."

I put my hand up to my forehead to shield my eyes and peered up into the sky. The lightest wisp of cirrus floated around the periphery, skirting far enough away from the sun as if to reassure us that there would be no chance of cloudiness today. The air was lightly cool. A small distance away, a pelican bobbed on the waves, utterly unperturbed by our presence. He was busy fishing. Or maybe just enjoying being alive. Out here in the bay, we felt isolated from the rest of the world. And I felt, at least in some ways, free to be myself in a way that I rarely did.

"This is nice," I conceded finally, smiling at him.

"Good. I'm glad you like it. I wanted to do something you would enjoy."

"Oh, really? Are you sure you didn't just want to get us into swimsuits?" The second the words came out, I recoiled in horror so hard that my hand actually clapped over my mouth. I had meant it in the way of implying that he enjoyed being in the water too much, but it obviously had a second, sleazier meaning that was now the only thing the two of us could think about.

"I didn't mean— That wasn't what I was trying to say," I rushed out quickly. "This suit is terrible on me anyway." The follow-up was, possibly, worse than the initial line. I wanted to dive under the surface and hold the board over my head until all the water boiled off from the heat of my face.

"You look amazing," he said mildly, although he was flushing too. "You look good in everything." He coughed. "Not, you know, like my opinion is the one that matters."

I thought that we might fully combust from embarrassment, but mercifully, right then, there was a big spout of water from about fifty yards away. We both turned to look in that direction. A hulking dark shape breached the waves for a moment.

"A whale," I breathed. I swiveled toward Alan. "Right?"

In real life, it seemed so much larger than you'd expect from seeing pictures or watching a documentary. It brought our insignificance into sharp relief, and it was impossible not to feel threatened when placed next to something that could crush you with a flick of its tail. I felt a thud of real fear. The ocean was truly deep and unknowable, to be able to contain an animal such as this and much else, besides.

He was in awe too. "Looks like it. I've never seen one so close. But it is peak whale-watching season here."

"Should we get out of the water?"

His forehead crinkled in amusement. "No, it's fine. It's not a shark. Besides, I think it's headed away from us."

"What if it turns around and comes up right underneath us?"

"This is not a sea-creature horror movie. We should respect nature, but we don't need to be afraid."

He paddled to be closer to me, our boards touching. We watched in unison silently as it breached again—this time farther away—sending the seawater up in sparkles against the light. Then it headed back out toward the open ocean. People all around us, even far away on the beach, whooped and cheered, their sounds small and far away. It felt like we were all collectively together in this single precious slice of wonder.

I knew without a doubt that this was the best welcome tour anyone had ever gotten. I would remember this forever. "Beautiful, huh?" I said, staring out at the horizon in the direction of the whale.

Out of the corner of my eye, I could see him looking at me. "Yeah. Beautiful."

We finished our paddleboarding escapade and returned to the shoreline, where we baked out on the beach to dry for an indeterminate period. As long as it took, and then some. With nothing specific on our agenda, time felt like a luxury.

We wandered down the magnificent boardwalk, two happy

and sandy fleas. We stopped to pick up fried things to eat when we got hungry and ended up getting two very handsome ice cream cones to boot.

"So," I said. "What other skills, besides paddleboarding, have you picked up since moving out here?"

We licked our cones and meandered along the water. Every once in a while, I bent down to pick up an interesting-looking shell or a piece of blue-green sea glass. I put them in a canvas bag I bought at the same shop where I'd purchased the bikini. I didn't know what I'd do with them after this, but I had never stamped out the urge to collect things from when we were younger.

"I've already told you everything. The sports. The writing," he demurred. "I'm more interested in what happened to you after I left. What did you get into? I mean, other than journalism, which I already could've guessed."

I shrugged. At an age when a person's identity and worth could be measured in what extracurricular activities they did, I felt like the most uninteresting person in the world. Alan didn't want to tell people he wrote romance fanfic, but he did have that as a facet of his life, whether he shared it or not. I just didn't have any parts of myself to offer up.

"You know me. I mostly kept my head down and did just enough to get by."

What a sad summation of those years in Mount Pierce, where I made myself small and gray. I squinted toward a glare at the end of the boardwalk. "It was always Sam who was the one who did every extracurricular. He was good at everything. He was the Renaissance man under our roof."

"I remember that."

"He made it easy for me, you know. He was the oldest boy, the overachiever. I could never have done half the stuff he did, but it was okay because my parents at least had the one." My breath hitched slightly. I tried to hide it. I hadn't talked this much about Sam since he died. Not at home. Not with anybody. Some part of me was glad, having a release valve for all the pressure to go somewhere. But it also felt tender and tight, like my lungs were squashed together in the wrong place between my ribs. I still wasn't at the place where I could bring him up without feeling as though I were inviting people to dig through my private belongings.

Sam, before he had died, was a public fact of life. Sam, after, I wanted to keep to myself.

"Now it's just me," I said softly. "I'm an only child. I guess." I turned to him. "Like you."

"You'll always have a sibling. Just because he's gone, doesn't mean that he didn't exist."

I was grateful to him for saying that. "You're right. Of course you're right. But it feels different, for sure, without him there."

"It's a big adjustment."

"It's more like—" I scanned the horizon for the right way to say it. "My brother did all the things my parents ever could've asked for, and in an instant, they lost him. Then they realized there was only one kid left to meet all their expectations, and that kid isn't up to snuff. I feel like it's a double whammy for them."

"That's not what it is, Stella. They are definitely not thinking about it that way."

"That *is* what it is. And I've tried and tried and tried to make myself into what they want and not make waves, not make them have to worry about me. I'm splintering a bit on the inside. I think I'm losing it." I swallowed. "It's just, you weren't there after it happened. They were so messed up. Permanently broken, you know. I was sad too. We were all devastated. We didn't even know how to comfort each other or anything. I wanted to be perfect for them, so I wouldn't make them more wrecked."

"That can't be your burden."

It was dysfunctional. But I couldn't help how I felt. And since I had said so much ugly stuff already, I let the worst thought out. The one that I had sometimes when I could hear my parents sobbing in the bathroom at night or putting family pictures face down, ever so gently where they once stood.

"Sometimes, I think my parents would've picked me over him. If they had to lose one of us."

I was a hideous person for even imagining such a thing, but it was out there now. There was nothing a person could say in response to that.

I didn't dare look him in the face. I was afraid of what I might see there. "Anyway," I said, completely mortified at myself, "you always say I never tell you what I'm thinking. Probably wish you could take that back now. You can pretend like I didn't say anything."

I had made it clear how damaged I was. I expected him to run screaming in the opposite direction. He hadn't signed up for this when he agreed to go on this trip with me.

He shook his head. "Thank you for telling me." His voice was soft enough to land on a pile of snow and leave it pristine.

"I know you think I'm so messed up. I know that's a horrible thing to say. I even know that it's probably untrue, but my brain goes there anyway every now and again."

"I'm not judging you. It's impossible not to go there at times."

I tilted my chin up at last, gathering the courage to meet his eyes.

He looked thoughtful and sad. "You know, my parents wanted more children. It didn't happen for them. But I know what you mean about feeling like you have to be worth it for them because there's no one else."

A memory surfaced suddenly then. A dinner with Alan's family, where his father joked that between he and Baba, it was more like they had two daughters rather than two sons. He had had a little too much to drink, but it came out too sharp to be funny and too cruel to be accidental.

Alan and I had been sitting next to each other. His fingers reached out under the table for mine. We held each other tightly, in secret, until the moment had passed.

I remembered now, because his face reminded me of that

evening. Smooth and composed, but I could see how brittle he was underneath.

I reached for his hand because I needed it as much as he did, and he took it.

This time, not under the table, not fleeing into the shadowed streets, but in the daylight, where everyone could see.

How do people go from being friends to something more? Where is the tipping point when you look at the other person, who you've known for so long, and suddenly your heart goes, *Ah, yes*?

These were the questions I was asking myself as we walked beside each other that afternoon and laughed easily under the sun. I didn't know exactly when the transition happened, but I knew when I was on the other side.

Still, it was another question entirely when you suspected your feelings versus when you were able to take the leap of faith and see where you landed. It was the kind of gulf where you either had to make it across in one try, or drown. I was scared to ruin what we had, even as we were building it.

No matter how my pulse quickened as his thumb brushed my wrist, or how much I wanted to put my fingers through his hair, there was enough fear running through my veins that I stayed just on the right side of friendship without attempting to cross any lines.

I had no experience in this area anyway. I didn't know how

to start things, only how to screw them up. A fact that became abundantly clear from the debacle with Colin Greiner.

Colin had been nice to me during a tumultuous year, letting me borrow his notes when I struggled in class, and asking me how I was doing when other people were scared to look at me in those initial weeks after Sam's passing. I had been in no place to be contemplating serious relationships. I had barely noticed him before, but as he started popping up everywhere, I started to think—not that I liked him per se—but that it might be nice to have a distraction.

Which was how we ended up in my car in the back corner of a strip mall. He was the one who started everything, while I mostly went along with it. I had never kissed anyone before. Except that once he'd begun kissing me, his lips overly wet, I promptly began to cry out of nowhere. Uncontrollable, ugly sobbing. I couldn't explain why.

It was regrettable, but unsurprising, that he escaped out of there faster than if someone had told him the car was rigged to explode. He never talked to me again after that.

Even though it hardly should've mattered, I could still feel the vicious sting of rejection.

For that, and other reasons, going beyond friends with Alan seemed impossible.

Impossible, even as the late afternoon bled into an early evening and we didn't want to go back, suspended in this in-between day where no one asked anything of us and we had nowhere to go. We ate hot dogs with our legs dangling off the boardwalk. Our bare thighs pressed against one another, warm and familiar. Our hair was crunchy with salt. Our ankles were gritty with sand.

Impossible, even at the end of the night as he pointed at the temporary Ferris wheel put up for an expo, lighting up against the darkening sky, and said, "Let's go," and, as always, I followed. We squeezed against each other in the small creaky cage that made you wonder, just a little bit, whether a contraption like this was really safe. We rose up directly into the stars, and then fell backward toward the earth with the speed of a meteor.

Impossible, even as we looked down at the city, romantic as an oil painting with smears of light from the buildings below. The wind rushed around us. The world seemed to be passing us by. He pulled a strand of hair off my face as we flew upward, his face closer than I could ever remember. His hand brushed against my cheek. I saw that he was going to lean in. I felt the rapid and wild beating of wings in my rib cage. I wanted it.

But at the last moment, I had a fleeting thought, a blur of doubt.

The ride jerked to a stop. We snapped back in our seats, casting around for an explanation, as though we had broken the Ferris wheel ourselves.

After a minute, the man on the ground shouted that there was a technical glitch with the ride. They were going to manually crank the wheel around so the people in each car could get off.

Alan looked at me with a sheepish smile and shrug. "I guess we should go back, yeah? Getting late. Don't want to keep our hosts up."

I nodded.

He helped me out of the cage. Quietly, we went back down the boardwalk and toward the parking lot. I waited until my heart slowed down again. I tried not to think too hard about the uncertainty that anchored in my mind earlier.

At the last second, I had remembered the first time I saw him at Weston High and how he'd pretended not to see me at all.

He was lying, I was sure of it. And I still didn't know why.

nineteen

We drove back to the house. The road up to Viejo Pass was unlit. In the dark, the winding corners up to the top of the hill seemed way more treacherous.

Alan pulled the car up to the gravel driveway and killed the engine. The lights were off inside, although it was a bit early for people to be asleep. The clock on the center dashboard read 9:05, before it turned off.

We sat in the car quietly for what felt like an endless amount of time, nobody making a move to open the door. The air was inexplicably charged. Whatever was between us felt big and important, although I did not have a name for it. Neither of us were able to say anything. I shifted in my seat and peered up through the windshield. Tonight, the moon was a single bright eyelash.

"Well, that ended up being a long day," he said, breaking the silence. "Sorry I kept you out for so long. But you know, time flies—"

"When you're having fun."

"Did you enjoy today?" His voice was just a half step too eager, as always.

"I did. Thank you for the welcome tour. Even if you did distract me away from all the things I am supposed to be doing."

He looked at me, and we smiled at each other. His eyes were luminous, reflected in the silver glow. I wished fiercely, then, that things could've been easy. That we had no baggage and none of the hurts that had accumulated in the time since we'd previously known each other.

Maybe, just this once, I could go for it and sort out the rest later.

"Hey, Stella?" he said abruptly, as I was thinking about it and wishing.

"Mm?"

"There's something I—"

The light inside flicked on, startling us. The glow washed over the interior of the car, robbing us of the intimacy that darkness afforded.

"It's late," I said. "We should go inside."

"You're right. Got to drive tomorrow morning," he said softly.

I nodded. We got out of the car, and I followed behind him on the path to go inside. The front door was unlocked. We stepped in. Auntie Yang was on the far side of the room in the kitchen.

I patted my pockets suddenly, realizing that my phone was missing. "Oh," I said. "I left something in the car. I'll be right back."

Alan knelt down to untie his shoes, while I stepped back outside. The door clicked closed behind me.

I retraced my steps up the path. Just before turning the corner, the sound of rustling gravel rang out. A car door opened. I was about to walk onto the driveway, when I heard girlish giggling. Some innate self-preservation instinct stopped me from going ahead, although my curiosity peaked.

My view was obscured, because Alan's car was in between, but I could see the shape of a silver sedan on the other side, pulled several feet closer to the house.

I couldn't see everything. But I saw enough.

The car door closing on the passenger's side.

Uncle Ma rounding the front of the car and knocking sharply on the driver's side window.

A woman—Juliet—rolling it down, her mouth in an open smile, just before his head lowered to hers.

It felt like I was watching a slow-motion movie, like this could not have been happening in front of me in real life. My feet rooted to the ground. If I had the wherewithal to think faster, I would've retreated into the house as quickly and silently as possible, so I could pretend like none of this had happened. I could've at least given myself the option.

But I didn't think fast enough. Moments later, Uncle Ma was heading toward the front door.

Right in my direction.

He turned the corner, and his eyes met mine. He froze.

"Stella," he said, his voice too quiet. "What are you doing here?"

"I left my phone in the car. I was getting it. I was just on my way out. I saw your car." I was babbling, babbling. I hadn't prepared myself for a good answer. He had put me on the spot, and I wasn't good at keeping my cool. He could see through me in an instant. His face paled.

"You didn't see anything," he insisted. "I was at the lab late. Juliet dropped me off because we work together. She does it all the time. It's not a big deal."

I was silent. I wasn't sure what to say in response.

"You don't know what you saw." He was louder. "You're just a kid." He stalked toward me, and I stepped backward. He stopped immediately. He put up his hands. "Whoa. Don't freak out." He swallowed. I could see his Adam's apple bobbing in his thin neck.

I didn't want to talk to him. I wanted to go inside and lock myself in the guest room.

"Hey, it's okay," he said. "I'm not mad at you. I'm not mad. I just want to set the record straight so you don't draw the wrong conclusions."

"I'm not drawing any conclusions." It was technically true. It's not like anything I saw was implied and required any conclusion drawing.

"Okay, good. Because I don't want you to assume anything. You don't really understand anything about my life with Molly. You don't know anything about our marriage. It's complicated. And we have a child, who doesn't deserve to get hurt. So we all have to be very careful about that."

He said *we*, but he meant in the royal sense. He was telling me that *I* had to be careful about that. That *I* needed to protect James.

I said nothing.

Uncle Ma seemed encouraged by that. "It's okay to be confused. Adulthood is confusing. I think the best thing to do is for us just to go inside and go to bed. I'm here for you if you want to talk about it tomorrow."

In the shadowed light, his skin gleamed with a strained desperation. He was my parents' age, but it felt hard to believe that he was their peer. My parents had never seemed so flighty.

"Things said—they're hard to take back. Let's just keep it between us," he said. "Don't make anybody worry."

Don't tell anybody. Don't make anybody worry.

The words struck me wrongly. I had heard them before, from Sam, months before he died. I didn't think I'd hear them again like this.

The secret settled on me like an ugly coat I couldn't take off. He put his hand on my shoulders and steered me toward the door. Now, I didn't want to go inside. Now, I wanted to run into the darkness.

But it was too late. The light burst onto us as we opened the door. Auntie Yang and Alan turned toward us, their faces animated from chatting.

"Oh, you're home," Auntie Yang said to her husband.

"Yes," he replied. "I caught Stella outside. It's late, isn't it?"

I couldn't look at him. Everything was too bright, too disorienting. Uncle Ma had ditched me at the door, thankfully, and swept over to his wife. His voice was undisturbed, and he cracked some joke that left the two of them laughing over the counter.

I wished I could burn a hole into the ground and disappear into it. The same litany of protections I'd gotten used to telling myself came flooding back. I didn't have to say anything, of course. I knew all the reasons why I shouldn't.

This was different from before, wasn't it? No life or death this time, no mistakes that would haunt me forever. Only a domestic matter, one that didn't have to involve me.

But I couldn't get those words out of my head. The plea. The secret I didn't ask to keep. I felt like I was going to be sick.

All I could think about was what had happened the last time I kept something to myself. You had to be ready for the consequences of doing nothing too.

I wondered what Alan would do. Then, I realized it didn't matter. I was alone. I could say nothing, and he'd never know better.

He had turned toward me, and his expression sharpened, alert and concerned. He could sense that something was wrong.

"Stella? You okay over there?" Auntie Yang asked.

"She's fine," Uncle Ma said. "She told me she was feeling tired, so she probably doesn't want to stay up with us." He was dismissing me. He was going to stay out here, so I wouldn't be alone with anybody.

But Auntie Yang was still waiting for me to answer. She hadn't looked away. She seemed to stare straight into my soul. We didn't know each other very well. I didn't have to feel like I owed her anything. Still, I couldn't stop thinking about last night. She was the first adult who seemed as lonely as I was. When we talked to each other, I couldn't help but feel some kind of tenuous connection with a version of my mother that I had never been able to access.

You don't have to keep lying for everyone, I thought.

I looked across the room. And I told her the truth of what I had seen.

Later, Alan and I sat alone in our rooms as shouted whispers seeped under our doors from another part of the house. We were sent off by our hosts to give some privacy. We didn't talk to each other before we went our separate ways. Somewhere outside, three people's lives were shifting into a new tectonic formation.

I wondered what my mother would say when she found out what I had done.

There was no way to sleep, even if I didn't have insomnia. How could anyone sleep under this roof with all that was going on? I was afraid to make any noise, as it seemed disrespectful to disrupt from the core devastation that was happening. I didn't even change or go to the bathroom to brush my teeth. I had pulled the pin, dropped the grenade, and now, I wanted to make myself small. I sat, fully dressed, on my bed, waiting—waiting for what?

But eventually, my wait did come to an end. It only took about thirty minutes, a shorter time than I would've imagined.

Auntie Yang knocked gently on my door and then let herself in.

"I'm sorry about all this," she said.

"It's my fault."

"No." She shook her head vigorously. "None of this is your fault. It can't be your fault for saying things that happened."

I wanted to ask if it was over, but it was not my place. Maybe she wasn't even sure yet. Maybe she'd see James in the morning and feel differently.

She seemed pained, the conflict radiating from her face. And then she sighed. "I want you to know what I'm about to tell you is also not your fault. This is all wrong. But I have to ask you to leave."

I stared at her. I did not expect this. "Leave? Like, leave this house? Right now?"

"Yes. Uncle Ma and I have a lot to talk about tonight."

I noticed that she did not call him Peter.

"He doesn't want either of you here. And while I don't think it's fair, I also don't know that we'll get to a better resolution in the next hour. It's getting late. And you need a place to sleep tonight."

I was stunned. This was wildly out of step with Chinese etiquette. My parents would've rather died than put anyone out of their home. But that was how I knew it was serious. I had wrecked these people's lives.

She reached into her pocket and palmed a wad of cash into my hands. I looked down. It was two hundred-dollar bills and a bunch of twenties. "It should be enough for a night somewhere nice. I know we're being the worst kind of hosts, so at least we should cover a quality alternative." She gave me a wry half smile then. "You might find this preferable to staying here anyway. The atmosphere tonight is not particularly inviting."

I put the money into my purse, because it seemed like there was nothing else to do. "Are you going to be okay?"

She shrugged. "Who knows? It could all be fine. Or it could be devastation. But it is not for you to worry about. These are my problems, not yours. Oh, Stella, xiao jie, life can be so unexpected. Yesterday I was thinking about these beautiful windows we have and how lucky we are. Today, this. You know it better than anyone, I suppose."

She leaned in for a final hug. I squeezed her tight for an instant.

"I feel as though I should send you out the door with some kernel of wisdom, and not all this wreckage." Her sigh rustled like a disappointed autumn breeze. "If I can summon up anything, perhaps it is that you should never believe a man who tells you he has changed. I hope I'll have something more profound for you the next time we meet, whenever that may be."

She swept back up on her feet, giving me one last soft look, and then she was gone.

It was surreal, Alan and I leaving the house like thieves, getting into the car, and pulling away back down the dark path to the lights in the city.

We didn't say anything to each other. Just drove along the winding road. I thought we would find a place in Santa Barbara for the night, since it was already around eleven, but he turned onto the highway. For a moment, I feared he was going to drive us all the way home and end this trip right then and there. But no. We were heading north, toward San Francisco.

"Where are you going?" I ventured to ask.

"Away," he said. "I just don't want to stay in town. Want to get farther out."

It seemed I didn't really have a choice in the matter, so I sat back and looked out the window into the night.

We didn't go far, maybe forty minutes or so. We pulled off in a town called Los Alamos. The blue Lodging sign had plenty of hotels listed. He turned into the parking lot of a place with a sign that read Inn at Arroyo Verde. It was a single-story long house with stone walls and lamps lit all around the perimeter.

I handed him the three hundred dollars in cash silently before we got out of the car. The inn was $250 a night, so we got a room with two full beds.

It was only after we brought all our things into the room—a cozy, tasteful little space with tall wooden headboards and warm linen sheets—that he turned to me at last and said something. "Well, that happened."

I sat down on one of the beds. I was exhausted. Bone-tired.

The past two hours had felt like several days. "You think maybe they just won't mention it to our parents? Like Uncle Wang?"

"Yeah, I'm doubtful about that one. I don't think they can send us off without supervision into the night without saying anything." He checked his phone. "Shit. My dad is calling."

"Right now?"

He showed me the screen. "Literally right now."

"What are you going to say?"

We stared at each other, stricken. It was exactly like when we were young, when we knew we were about to get in trouble.

He let the call ring out without answering. We watched it go to voicemail. The silence in the room was smothering. Gently, so gently, he put his phone on the bedside table with the screen facing down, so we could only imagine the livid calls lighting it up but couldn't see them.

"I'm not saying anything. Not tonight anyway." He turned to me with a crooked smile. "What's he going to do? Find us out here in Los Alamos? He doesn't have location tracking on his phone. He'll have to wait." He was trying to make light of the situation, but I could tell he was terrified of the hell to pay later.

"You can tell him that I did it," I said automatically. "I ruined everything. He doesn't have to like me."

"No way. I'm not putting that on you."

"It's not throwing me under the bus. It literally was me."

"Still."

My parents hadn't called me, even though right now, it must've been the middle of the day in China. There was that familiar sting of neglect. They were avoiding me. I felt the low burn of fury rising. Worse than them being angry was the complete ice out. At least Alan's dad was keeping tabs on him. At least he was seen. It was as though I wasn't even worth my parents' time.

I would call them in the morning, I decided. I would make them face me.

"Why'd you do it, Stella?" he asked me. "I mean, it's not that I'm questioning your decision. It's just that you could have said nothing. You could've avoided all of this."

I turned inward, replaying the scene on the gravel path in my head. Uncle Ma's wheedling plea in the shadows, asking me not to say anything. It was a domino that tipped. Everything after that felt like a blur.

I thought about Sam's last request to me.

Alan waited expectantly. His eyes were darkly expressive, even behind his glasses.

There was so much I hadn't ever told him. I wanted to keep him from having too much power over me. To know another person's secrets was to be able to hurt them, and I was always too afraid of this.

I knew the danger of secrets from a young age, and so I was well practiced in keeping it all to myself. I didn't tell Alan anything, but somehow, he'd always managed to figure me out anyway. He was the only person who really saw me, but maybe it was because he was the only person who knew how to look. A magician knew that you could unlock every trick by watching for the sleight of hand. He had gotten used to watching for mine. He still knew how, even after all these years.

The way he was looking at me now seemed to go right into my soul. I couldn't remember the last time anyone had stared at me like that.

"Something happened to you. It's okay," he said softly. "Do you want to tell me?"

Nobody had asked me that before.

Even after we got the news from Sam, the toxicology results, the mystery at the core of it all, I both feared and hoped my parents would turn to me and ask, mei mei, did you know about this? What did you know? I would have to confess the truth, but at least, then, it would be out there, and it would no longer be just mine. But of course, they never did. They never thought to ask. They simply stopped talking about him. And they stopped calling me mei mei, because by then, I was no longer a little sister.

But here we were, in a hotel room in the middle of nowhere, California. At the end of the day, it was me and Alan—it was always me and Alan. It somehow felt like it would be us, together, even if it were the end of the world. There was no one who knew me better, and there was no one else I would have told.

I could feel the tears coming. "It's my fault that Sam died," I said at last.

He shook his head. "That's not true."

"It is. I knew he was using. I found out months before. I

knew he didn't have prescriptions. I should've told somebody. I could've saved him. But I didn't, and then he died."

I was sobbing, full snot and everything. It was ridiculous, but all I could think about was Colin Greiner, and how much of a mess I'd made on his shirt when we were in the back of my car. I couldn't blame him for bailing on me. I was wretched; I was volatile. No teenage boy would want anything to do with that.

I thought Alan was probably regretting asking. Any second now, he would pull back from this. He would probably find a reason to step out, give me a moment to collect myself, and then never talk about this again.

There was a space between the two beds, where I sat on one and he sat on the other. It was enough of a buffer to keep anything complicated at a comfortable distance.

But it only took an instant for him to cross it and pull me close.

We fit like a jigsaw puzzle, my cheek against his chest, his arms around my shoulders. I felt a crushing, immediate sense of relief that for the first time in a long, long time, at last, I was not alone.

"It was not your fault," he said. He repeated it again and again. I didn't know until then that I needed to hear it from someone, just like I didn't know that I needed someone to ask me what had happened. But all this time, I had needed these things.

I could feel everything through our heartbeats, going in perfect synchronization, and through the warmth of his fingers against my back. As he held me, I was flooded with a distinct sense of faint dread, an undeniable realization that I did not want him to let go. Not now. Not ever. It turned out that no matter how much I didn't want to say it out loud or admit it to myself, I loved him. Maybe I had loved him from the very beginning, from when he smiled at me and told me I could be his friend, but I didn't know the word for it. I definitely knew it now. But I couldn't say it, not in this context, not all mixed in with my grief, all my guilt and regret.

I should have let him go, gently. I should've coaxed us both to go to sleep in our separate beds, and talked about it in the morning when I wasn't shaking with emotions. If I had any self-control, I would've. But it felt too good to be held by him, too good to give up. I was going to accept this scrap, even if it meant nothing. And anyway, he didn't push me away.

He held me, until slowly, eventually, I calmed down.

It took a long time, but I fell asleep just like that, curled in his arms.

twenty

FIRST COLLEGE VISIT

When you pick me up from Logan airport, you are thinner than I remember.

It is after Thanksgiving break of your freshman year. You had told us you weren't coming home that year. Lots of work. Finals. Everything was harder than you expected and you needed the time. The short trip wasn't necessary, you said. You'd be home in a few weeks for Christmas.

Instead, our parents decide that I should come out and see you for a weekend. Get a feel for Harvard and college life, as though that will inspire me to become more like you.

I wonder if they would've changed their mind if they saw you now, looking exhausted and stretched out. You do not look like an advertisement for college. You look like an advertisement for a gap year.

You give me a hug, and I can feel the bones of your arms like the branches of trees around me. It's brief.

"Good flight?" you ask.

"Only a short delay."

"Do we need to go to baggage claim?"

I shake my head. I have a single duffel bag and a backpack as my carry-ons. I'm only staying two and a half days. I took an early Friday flight, so it's still midmorning here in Boston. I'll be leaving Sunday afternoon.

"Did you sleep on the flight?"

"A little." I glance at him up and down. "Did *you* sleep last night?"

You give me a ghost of a smile. "Mostly." You take the bag from me. "Let's get going. Have to get to the dining hall for breakfast before it closes."

I frown. "You're not even going to take me out to a nice restaurant in Cambridge? I've never been out here before."

"This is supposed to be an educational visit, Stella," you say.

"Whatever."

You sigh. "We can go somewhere else for lunch."

I grin at him. We exit the airport. I clutch my wool coat tight around me against the burst of chilly air. There is a flurry of snowflakes coming down. I stop in my tracks for a second and watch them drift down in whorls, landing on my cheeks, my eyelashes, my lips. My breath puffs out in a light fog.

"Come on," you say from out in front. I hoist my backpack straps up on my shoulders so they're not slipping off and hurry to catch up with you.

Each dorm has its own dining hall, and yours is pretty nice. The vaulted ceiling has exposed wood beams and the warm redbrick walls give the room a sense of coziness.

There's eggs and other breakfast food assortments, but also Thanksgiving-leftover-themed dishes. I pile my plate high with turkey, two kinds of cranberry sauce, and roasted sweet potatoes with brown sugar and plenty of butter.

Thanksgiving is the one holiday where my parents insist on cooking "American" food at home. But cooking American food isn't really their forte, so the turkey is always dry and the mashed potatoes under-seasoned.

I'm famished from my early dinner and foodless flight. I'm shoving my face. I notice that you have a tiny portion of eggs that you keep pushing around the plate and a big mug of coffee.

"Is that all you're going to eat?" I ask.

"I ate a bit earlier. Not hungry."

I don't believe you, but I don't press it. I can't make you eat. I'm not your mother.

"Any fun shows you're watching lately?" I ask to try to generate conversation.

You shrug with one shoulder. "Not really. I've had a lot on my plate."

You don't say anything else, and I can't think of anything to talk about either. I can't remember the last serious conversation I had with you. It must have been years ago.

We're sitting at a long table with benches. Students filter in and out of the room, most in their pajamas. I watch them go by as I eat. Nobody stops by to say hello. My silverware scrapes against the plate loudly. I am self-conscious about how long I'm taking, when you're just sitting there, sipping out of your mug, waiting for me.

After I'm done, you take my tray to the conveyor belt, and we head up to your dorm room. We go up a long staircase to the second floor. Your dorm is coed, so men and women mill about the hallways. We go into a room with a common area. Most of the housing accommodations involve sharing a suite with multiple people.

"Home sweet home," you say.

The suite is empty, and we go to your room.

There are two beds, but your roommate isn't here this week. "He's visiting his boyfriend back home in Connecticut," you say. "You can have his bed. He washed the sheets before."

The roommate has some posters up on his wall and a corkboard with a bunch of photos of his family and multiple with a guy who I assume might be the boyfriend.

"Do you like him?" I ask.

"He's fine. Nice. Goes home a lot of weekends. We mostly keep out of each other's way."

"What about the other guys in the suite?" There seems to be two other bedrooms leading to the common room.

"We all hang out every once in a while, but we're not that close. They're all in really time-consuming clubs, I think. So it's very in-and-out. I, uh—" You stop, as though you're not sure what to say. You scratch your neck.

"What?"

"It's only been a few months," you say. "It's just not been as easy to find my group as I thought." You shake it off and give me a smile. "What am I telling you? College is great, Stella. Get out of the house. Be free."

I laugh.

"I'm glad you came out." Your shoulders and cheeks relax, and suddenly, it seems like you are back to the person I remember. I am relieved.

I plop onto the roommate's bedspread. "So what's the plan?"

"I thought I might take you around campus and see my favorite places. Maybe check out some weekend events at the school that you might be interested in. I wish I knew somebody who worked at *The Harvard Crimson*, so you could meet them."

I sigh and crinkle my nose. "Let's be real, Sam. I'm not going to Harvard."

"You don't know that."

I look at him and roll my eyes. "I appreciate the optimism. But we know. Can't we do something fun? I haven't seen you in ages. Let's go to Boston. Let's get out of here."

For a moment, you appear to be fighting your impulse to push the weekend that we're supposed to have. But you give up. "All right. You win."

We take the T into Boston and spend the rest of the day sightseeing. We go along the Freedom Trail, take a duck boat tour into the Charles River, window-shop down the cobblestone road on

Newbury Street. When it gets dark, we go to the North End and splurge on Italian food. You use a fake to get us a bottle of wine, even. We get gelato and wander through the neighborhood under twinkly dinner lights.

I feel almost close to you, like maybe this is a new start. Our transition into the kind of sibling relationship people have as adults. As equals.

By the time we get back to your dorm, it's time for bed. Even with the one-hour advantage of Midwestern jet lag, I am wiped from the day. I say hello to your two suitemates, who are playing video games in the common area, and retreat to your roommate's bed. You use the bathroom after me. I mean to tell you about the new superhero movie coming out and ask whether we can go see it tomorrow, but as I'm waiting, I pass out.

The next time I wake up, it's dark.

There's a sliver of light coming through the sides of the shades. I blink at the big digital clock on your desk. It's 4:43 a.m. I notice that your bed is empty. I feel wide-awake for some reason. I lie in bed, waiting for you to return. Ten minutes pass, then fifteen, and you don't return to the room. I hoist myself up on my elbow and check my phone. I don't have any messages from you.

I feel a small bubble of panic. Alone in the darkness, outlandish ideas begin to run through my head about where you are. Maybe you got kidnapped or somebody stabbed you dead in the common room. I consider calling the police, but I'm afraid it's an overreaction. I lie there with a mounting dread for what feels like hours.

Eventually, the door opens and you come back in. I turn to my side, facing away from you so that you can't see I'm awake. You rustle around the blankets on your bed and then fall still. I am troubled, but I close my eyes.

By the time I wake up again, it's actually morning.

I sit up, disoriented. You're sitting at your desk, typing.

"Good morning," you say after you turn to see me.

"Good morning," I croak. My throat is dry.

You hand me a bottle of water from your mini fridge.

"Thanks." I take a few gulps and wash down the taste of stale sleep. "Where were you last night?"

You blink. "What are you talking about?"

"I woke up in the middle of the night, and you weren't there."

"I was just in the bathroom."

You are lying. I'm taken by surprise. You and I, we never lie to each other. To our parents, sure. But there was no reason for you to lie to me before. You are trying to protect me, I realize. From what?

"I was awake for an hour and a half," I say flatly. "You weren't in the bathroom. I heard you come into the suite from outside."

"Oh." You sound uncomfortable. "Yeah, I was walking around outside."

"Why?"

"I have trouble sleeping sometimes." You are hesitant, your explanation reluctant. Your eyes dart briefly toward the bottom drawer of your desk. You see me notice. Immediately, I know that you are hiding something.

I swing my legs out from the bed and come closer. I kneel down. You don't stop me.

I open the bottom drawer of your desk. You were always so organized. Everything in the same spot. The drawer is full of pills. My stomach drops.

"What are you taking?" I ask.

You push the drawer closed. "It's not that bad," you say. "I told you I'm having trouble sleeping. I just got some Xanax and stuff." You don't elaborate on the "stuff."

"Sam . . . are you getting these from a doctor?"

"I can't go to a doctor. I'm still on Baba's health insurance. You know that'll freak them out, and they'll think there's something wrong."

"Maybe there *is* something wrong," I say timidly.

"It's not a big deal. They're all prescription drugs. It's not like I'm doing cocaine. It's not like I'm shooting heroin," you joke.

I don't laugh.

You sigh. "College has just been a bit stressful this semester. I was taking some uppers to help me out. Had trouble sleeping. Needed to get some stuff to help me go down so I wouldn't be a zombie the next day. I try not to take them most of the time. It's really the least of my problems."

I wonder what all your problems are, if this is the least of them. You look exhausted this morning. I wonder if you slept at all last night.

"I think you should see someone," I tell you. I'm scared. You are unbalanced, and I've never seen you like this before. "Who cares if Baba and Mama see? You need help."

You shake your head. "I'll be fine. Don't worry about me." And then you say the thing that I think about for months after. After you're gone. The thing that haunts me when I lie in bed at night. "Don't tell anyone. Especially Mama and Baba. Please. It'll only make them worry."

It is the one time I consider saying no. Or telling my parents anyway. Because I'm just a kid, after all, and this secret feels too big to keep.

You look at me with desperate eyes, so I say okay. You look relieved, oh so relieved. "We got each other's backs, right?" you say.

I trust you. I trust you to be right about this, because no matter how far apart we've grown and how little I know about you now, you're still my ge ge, my older brother, and you've never been wrong before. "Right," I say.

We grin at each other, teeth bared, like wild animals in a hunter's trap, waiting for the end.

twenty-one

I WOKE UP in the morning with no concept of time, day, or place. I was still wearing my clothes from yesterday. On one side, the searing light from outside was bleeding over the edges of the curtains in the window. It could've been 7:00 a.m. It could've been noon. The digital clock at the bedside table said it was 8:20.

The previous night was coming into sharper relief. The sadness I had been carrying was still there, but I felt a sense of peace. The kind you could only get after a long, good cry, which I'd finally had.

I shifted in my spot to turn around. I was staring at a blue T-shirt across an expanse of chest. I tilted my gaze upward. Alan was still deep in slumber. His arm was still draped over my waist. It was warm. It was dark in the room from the blackout curtains, but now that it was daytime, I could see his face clearly. He had taken off his glasses at some point. With them off, he looked more like the little kid I remembered. My heart went soft.

How had we ended up here? It felt like a strange accident of fate, and yet entirely inevitable at the same time. We were always finding our way back to each other.

I didn't know what the rest of the day would bring, but I wanted to stay here forever. Just nestled in this small universe of the two of us, in a place where no one knew we were.

Of course, that was wishful thinking. Nothing good ever lasted. Minutes later, Alan began to stir. I thought he might move away, in case it was all too intimate for the raw light of morning. Nighttime invited closeness that daytime made uncomfortable.

But all he did was blink slowly and smile down at me. "Good morning," he said, yawning. "I hope you slept okay."

I nodded. "I slept great." In fact, despite the intensity of the evening, it was the best sleep I'd had in months.

We lapsed into silence, seemingly not knowing exactly what to say next. I noticed that neither of us had made to move from where we were. It dawned on me that this was the first time I had ever spent the night with a guy. We hadn't *done* anything, but still. What was I supposed to make of our relationship now? Did it mean something to me that it didn't mean to him? Someone had to take the first step toward the other person, and I was too deathly afraid of it being me.

My thoughts were beginning to snowball rapidly. But before I could do anything impulsive, like blurt out a question, or confess my feelings in the least artful way possible, his fingers tightened around me.

"Stella," he said, his voice gentle. Now here it came. I wanted him to kiss me, and he was going to—

He paused and made a face. "Blech. Sorry, I'm rocking some really aggressive morning breath right now."

I cracked up laughing. Seeing me lose it, he did too.

We sat up, the sheets falling around us. The critical moment had passed, but it was okay. The tension had been broken. There would be time to talk about everything.

After, maybe, we brushed our teeth.

We stood side by side in the bathroom at the double vanity, washing our faces, and brushing our teeth. It was weirdly domestic and comforting. Every once in a while, we'd catch each other's eyes in the mirror and grin.

We changed separately.

When I came out of the bathroom, he was fully dressed in a new outfit and staring down at his phone with a solemn expression. He looked up at me. "I have to call my dad now. Probably not wise to keep pushing it off. I have eleven missed calls." He let out a sigh.

I went and took my phone off its charger. Zero missed calls. Nobody had even tried. Helping with Xiao Xiao's wedding was apparently so all-encompassing that even the mess I'd gotten myself into didn't crack into my parents' top tier of concerns.

"Yeah, me too," I lied. There was a ringing in my ears, and

a sort of white-hot nothingness spreading inside me. Was it resigned disappointment? Or was it anger?

"This might take a while. My parents are probably pretty pissed."

"Sure."

"I'm going to go hang out in some corner of the courtyard. Let's meet back in the room when we're done."

We went our respective ways to different parts of the hotel outside. I could see in the daytime that the hotel was indeed quite nice. It would've been a great place to stay, if not for the reason we were there. I went by a carved stone fountain in the back. The bottom of the pool was coppery bright with pennies.

With the backdrop of the water burbling behind me, I tried to imagine what I'd say to my parents, since I was sure they must've known what had happened. I tried to imagine my mother's reaction to me being the linchpin to the crumbling of her best friend's marriage, but found that I could not conjure it up. I had no idea what she would think. The truth was, I couldn't imagine her reaction because I couldn't imagine my mother more broadly than her relationship with me.

I pulled up WeChat and dialed her number. It rang and rang, but nobody answered. I dialed again. And then, when no one answered, I dialed Baba. He also didn't pick up.

Finally, a message came through on chat from Mama. *We will call you later*, it read. I read it several times, feeling hotter by the second, as though I were sitting directly below a heat lamp.

I had done my best since Sam had died to work on autopilot so my parents wouldn't have to pause from their grief to worry about me. Don't cause trouble, do what you're supposed to, be good, be good, be good. I had been so convincing that they evidently felt that I was doing totally fine. I could be left alone. I could be fully ignored.

"No," I said out loud. "This is bullshit."

Pick up NOW, I typed back.

For a whole minute, I thought they were going to leave me on read. Then, Mama's call came through at last.

By the time I picked up, my face was red in the reflected screen.

"Hello?" Mama said. She seemed harried, as if I had caught her in the middle of something. "Is everything okay?"

It seemed ludicrous that she was asking. "Did Auntie Yang call you?" I demanded.

"Yes. I heard what happened. It was regrettable."

I had never heard anyone sound more businesslike about someone getting a divorce. She sounded as though she were their divorce lawyer. It was regrettable? That was it? I could hardly believe it.

"Did you get a hotel?"

"Clearly. I am alive. Thanks for asking."

My parents had never been great at picking up sarcasm, but this one didn't need much translation.

She frowned mightily, the lines in her brow going deep. "I am glad to see you are safe. We have a lot to talk about. But later. This is not a good time."

"You said that last time. Are you going to hang up on me?" I asked in disbelief.

It was only then that I noticed the background of the call. I didn't recognize it. It was blank and white. Sterile-looking. Nai Nai's walls in the city apartment were a pale yellow, and there were pictures everywhere. I realized when I listened closely that I could hear the sounds of shuffling and low voices. There were other people around, passing by. Mama was clearly not at the apartment. "Where are you? Where is Baba?"

She hesitated. Her eyes flicked off-screen to somewhere past me, and she mouthed something I couldn't read. A moment later, Baba scooted into the frame. They both sat against the wall. He had bags under his eyes, as though he hadn't slept in days.

They were hiding something from me. It was obvious now. They were clearly going to hide it the entire time, but I had blown their cover by derailing my schedule and forcing them to call me. I couldn't believe I hadn't realized before.

Baba sighed in a way that sounded like the air was coming out of the bottom of his lungs, like he was deliberately banishing every cubic ounce of oxygen from his body.

"Will you tell me now?" I said quietly.

Even before he told me, I already knew.

"Nai Nai is sick," he said.

I sat up, my heart pounding painfully in the hollow of my chest. "What's wrong with her?"

"The doctors think it's cancer."

"How bad is it? Are they going to treat her?" It hit me that for once, I did not have the words for this in Chinese, and I would not understand Baba even if he laid it out. Stages of disease, medical terms for treatment. It was not vocabulary that I traded in on day-to-day. It was odd to realize only now how much I'd changed. The distance from me to Nai Nai was vast, not merely in miles. I no longer fit so neatly in her world as I used to. This hurt, almost more than anything else.

"At this stage, they are not recommending much treatment."

I didn't need to hear him say the rest. They were at the hospital. Nai Nai was dying. I was breathless, desperate.

"I have to go home." The words in Chinese for returning—*hui guo*—an assumption in them that no matter where you went or who you'd become, going to China always meant returning home.

Mama looked at Baba, helpless, while he nodded like an agreeable bobblehead. "Of course. Yes. You will."

I had already moved on to plans. "Can I fly out of SFO?" My mind went to how much I had packed, the logistics of whether I could go direct in the next few days. "No, I need my passport," I said out loud. "I have to go back to San Diego. We'll drive today."

"No, no," Baba said. "You won't travel immediately. You have to finish your trip. You have college applications due soon. Are you all done? Have you turned them in?"

I gaped at the screen. I understood his words in total, but they still somehow seemed as though they were in a foreign language I'd never heard before. The context was all wrong. Why were we talking about college when Nai Nai was dying? How could anyone care about that?

I was short-circuiting. I didn't know what to say in response.

He took my pause as confirmation. "We will buy you tickets for after the application deadline, so you are not rushed. It will be okay. Nai Nai is resting and stable. The doctors think she has several months."

So that was the measure of time now. Months rather than years. It suddenly seemed ludicrous that I had never even thought about this possibility before. Everyone died. Humans did not live forever. All my other grandparents were deceased. Nai Nai was old. But it was interesting how mortality could feel so different from one moment to the next, just because a doctor told you a microscopic change about your body.

"I can't wait," I whispered.

"You can." His mouth was set in a firm line. His jaw clenched. I could tell when my father had staked out a position from which he would not be moved. This was one of them.

Mama leaned into the screen. Her face was gentler and immeasurably sad. "This year has been hard enough. We did not want you to find out this way."

It all clicked together then. This was not new information. Nai Nai had gone to the hospital before. This was why my parents had gone back to China in the first instance. The thing about Xiao Xiao's wedding, his mother's broken leg—it had all been a lie from the very beginning.

My world cracked open, fierce and searing white.

"How long have you known?" I asked, going straight to the point.

She hesitated again, looking at Baba. Guilt did not strain his features. "Three weeks," he said matter-of-factly.

"You didn't tell me when you left."

"No. There was no reason to. We had to go back to help my sisters put affairs in order. You just transferred schools and had so much to do on the applications. We feel terrible that we could not go on the trip with you, but it would not have been helpful if you were worrying the entire time about Nai Nai. Trust that we are taking good care of her. We were going to tell you after."

To my parents, it was a decision that required little contemplation.

It was ironic, really. I had agonized about keeping my secret about Sam from them for so long, and yet, I had forgotten that secrets were the only currency we knew in this family. The bitterness curdled inside me. "What is Nai Nai going to think when I come out and Sam doesn't?"

"She'll think what she always does. Sam is at Harvard. He needs to stay on top of his coursework."

The use of present tense crushed me. He wasn't at Harvard. He was in a box in my parents' room, since we still hadn't decided what we wanted to do with his final remains.

But the thing was, they were right. Nai Nai probably wouldn't question his absence. Our values were always very clear. She wouldn't begrudge him not coming at all. She wouldn't have blamed me if I didn't fly out either, but of course I had to. With Sam gone, there was no one left to remember us as we were.

I blinked back tears. "Can I talk to her?"

"She's not awake," Baba said. "It is important that we let her rest."

"I want to go back now," I said softly.

"One more week," said Mama. "You will be here before you know it."

I was powerless to do anything else. I couldn't buy my own tickets. I had nothing to do but wait. It was the most wretched feeling I knew, this waiting.

Mama tried to soothe me. "It will be okay."

"How can you say that?" I blurted out. "Sam is gone. Nai Nai is going."

She looked at me helplessly. "But we will still have each other. We will still be a family." Her voice wavered.

The two of them seated there, leaning toward each other to fit in the rectangle of the screen. I wanted to hate them for lying to me, but I couldn't, because I understood. It was one of the very few things I understood about them.

I scanned their faces, sagging with exhaustion and wild with desperation. I had so rarely sought them out for help or comfort of any kind. I tried to think of a time when I did and came up totally empty. They were my parents, my closest kin, and yet, I'd spent less than half my life with them. I tried to imagine them as full individuals, but I really couldn't, not in any meaningful way. I knew now that Baba was a great singer; Mama was the kind of person who was sentimental enough to make a memory box but not sentimental enough to actually give it away. But I hadn't even learned these things from them directly.

In another six months, I'd be gone again. I'd come home for the holidays, some of them, maybe. I'd sit at the dinner table, and we'd have nothing to say to each other. I imagined us getting further and further apart. Family by blood, but strangers in reality.

And yet there were so many things I wanted to tell them. Sam's secret, which I had kept. How I still didn't feel right lying to Nai Nai all the way to the bitter end and I wasn't sure how I was going to keep it up when I saw her face-to-face.

How I missed them and wished they were here.

The particular sadness of frogs.

The inexplicable magic of whales.

Whatever connection people exercised to open a dialogue on difficult topics, we seemed to lack it, my parents and I. It was as if we had one of those kids' contraptions with two cups and a string in the middle, except my parents were holding one cup and I was holding the other, and the string between us had been cut. I did not know how to reach them. I did not know where to start.

I wondered then if it was too late for us. If you'd let the connection wither and decay, if it was impossible to ever get it back.

By the time I got back to the room, Alan was already there.

"There you are," he said. He had packed his things. His

suitcase was sitting neatly at the foot of the bed. I noticed that he had made the bed too, even though housekeeping would come later to reorder everything. The indent where we slept had been fully erased.

I was shaky, still reeling from the conversation with my parents. My skull seemed to vibrate with a dull buzzing. But it was clear that he was agitated too, and he dove in without me needing to say anything.

"God, he is so arrogant, my father. He had to make everything about himself, as usual. He doesn't even think of me as a separate person. Just an extension of how I reflect upon him. Like, he can't even fathom me doing things removed from how they might impact him. I can't stand him sometimes, I really can't."

"Is he mad?" I asked quietly.

"Understatement. Uncle Ma told him directly, and he's angry about that, obviously. But he's also apoplectic that I didn't call him back last night. Not because he was worried something happened to me but mostly just because I wasn't at his beck and call. Fuck him, honestly."

He ranted with complete conviction, but it was easy to bluster while he wasn't facing his father. It was less clear if he had said any of this directly on the call.

"But I was the one who said something, not you," I said.

"I told him it was me." He shrugged.

"Why? Uncle Ma and Auntie Yang were there. I'm sure he'll find out what really happened, if he hasn't already."

"It doesn't really matter. If he does, he'll make it about me not having stopped you. I'm supposed to be the responsible one. Or he'll find ten other reasons why I've fallen short against the infinite yardstick he's measuring me against." He took a deep breath. "But whatever. I don't have to see him for another couple of days at least. I can deal with it then. What happened with you?"

I wasn't ready for the question. It stuck in the air, hovering. I stood there, hardly realizing that I was expected to respond.

"You okay? Did your parents know already too?"

"Oh. We didn't really talk about that."

"You didn't?"

I closed my eyes for a brief moment before opening them again. "My grandmother," I said. It sounded like it was coming from a completely unknown part of my body, deep inside.

His expression immediately sharpened. "How is she doing?"

Something about his tone struck me the wrong way. The even-keeled acceptance of it. The lack of surprise.

In that moment, I knew the trip was over.

"I found out she's dying. Just now," I said slowly

He looked at me, his face like a scroll opening. It was clear that this was not new information to him.

"You knew." A short sentence. A permanent condemnation. I felt a thunderstorm rolling into my chest—intense, wild, and enormous. Two revelations in one day. How could he know and yet I didn't? I sat heavily onto the bed, lights pulsing before my vision.

"You didn't?" he asked.

I shook my head. "But my parents told you."

"I heard it from my parents," he corrected, "as the reason your parents were going to China."

"You hid it from me."

He leaned forward earnestly. I pulled back before any part of him could reach me.

"No, Stella. No. I didn't hide it from you. Nobody asked me to, and I would never do that to you."

He was plaintive and urgent. He wanted me to believe him; that much was evident. But I knew how persuasive he could be, how utterly magnetic. And the doubt that had settled inside me like a hidden seed over the past few days burst into full bloom.

"Why would I lie to you about that?" he pressed. "What reason would I have?"

The narrative was coming together now. My parents asked him to hide it from me, just as we had all conspired to hide Sam's death from Nai Nai. They told him it would be for my own good, and he did it, because of course he would. He'd spent all these days humoring me, distracting me, making me think, even, that he could've possibly had feelings for me. It was all a ruse. He didn't need to go on college tours, after all. He wasn't the one stumbling through indecision. His future was already baked. For him, this was just a vaguely amusing diversion until we returned to our real lives back at Weston High, where he was a stratosphere above me and I was just some new girl he'd never talk to again.

I was so gullible. So unfathomably naive. I'd already gone through this all once before, and I had let him do it to me again. Never believe a man who tells you he has changed, Auntie Yang had said. I shouldn't have needed a second time to learn the lesson.

"I don't know. Why did you pretend not to see me on the first day of school? If you were really sorry about how it all went down back in Mount Pierce?"

There was a silence. "What are you talking about?" His forehead crinkled, but just like he could read me, I could do the same with him. He knew exactly what I was talking about. I could see it in the flutter of his eyelashes. The tightening in his jaw.

My eyes narrowed. "Don't make me ask again."

"What does that have to do with this?" he said eventually.

My gaze shifted around the room, landing on random details I hadn't noticed the night before when all I was paying attention to was him. The dainty little succulents in small white pots all along the windowsill. The paintings of bleached skulls in the desert framed in dark wood on the wall. It was incredible what you could make yourself focus on, instead of your heart breaking.

"You're always lying to me." My voice went small. "Why did you even agree to do this trip? Why did you pick me to be the one person who you can't leave alone?"

He flinched. That seemed to really wound him, more than anything else I'd seen. He took a moment to gather himself.

"Look, let's just get in the car, get on the road, and I can explain about the first day."

"I don't think we should keep going."

"What?"

"I want to go home. I'm done with this."

"Stella, I didn't lie to you about your grandmother. I swear about that. I really thought you knew already."

"Why didn't you ever bring it up, then?"

"Because I assumed you didn't want to talk about it!"

"Why would you assume that?"

He stared at me hard, like he was contemplating whether he should say the thing he was thinking.

"Spit it out," I said.

"Until last night, you've never told me anything important about your life. Why would I think you'd want to talk about something that personal?"

The blood rushed loudly in my ears. "Are you seriously making this my fault right now?" A cavern seemed to open up inside me, because even as I dismissed him, I knew that he was getting at something true.

"No! I'm not blaming you for being upset, especially after what you found out from your parents. I'm just saying that you could understand how I *might* have reasonably made the wrong assumption here."

I was quivering. He had never confronted me with this before. I didn't want to accept it, so I spat back. "You're full of shit.

I tell you things. And besides, it's not like you've ever given me a reason to trust you."

"Maybe not. I've said already, I've made mistakes. And I've apologized. But even before all that, you've never told me one single thing that mattered. You're like a black box. It was always me doing the talking."

All I really wanted right then was to hurt him as much as he'd hurt me. "Yeah, well maybe you talk too much. It's not like I asked for all that information about you."

The world seemed to drop silent.

At last, he took a deep breath. "Okay. Okay. You're right. I should've taken the hint a long time ago. I get it. You don't want me around. I'll stop bothering you." He sounded like something inside him had broken. The silence between us was dark and uncrossable.

I shouldn't have cared. He had betrayed me before, and he was probably lying to me now. Yet hearing those words were more painful than anything else. I knew then that I really did love him, and it wasn't so easy to stop loving someone, no matter what they had done.

But it was too late, because I'd already let him go. This time, I didn't think he'd ever come back.

twenty-two

WE DROVE ALL the way back to San Diego, stopping only once in between.

We didn't talk.

Just as he'd promised, he left me alone.

twenty-three

AFTERLIFE

NAI NAI USED to take us to church on Sundays, where we would learn about God and hell and what we were supposed to be doing on this earth. Mama and Baba weren't religious, so we didn't go once we moved to the United States. What I remember was a sprinkle of biblical stories, a blurry notion of Jesus and the trinity, and a general fear of judgment after we die.

So my understanding of spirituality and higher powers is a blend of Sunday school and Chinese myths about the ruler of heaven. I don't think too hard about it. Death is very far away. Ye Ye was long gone by the time we were born, and our other set of grandparents had also passed away when I was one.

I remember, once, as a child coming out of church with Nai Nai, I thought that heaven was in the sky behind the clouds and hell was underground, literally. Purgatory had been mentioned as a place in between, so I believed that's what people did when they went on a plane—they were going to purgatory. The idea of flying to Illinois, where Nai Nai told us we were going one day, was fantastical and terrifying. I wondered ceaselessly what purgatory would be like. I thought that to go from China to the United States, you had to die and then come back to life.

Your last day starts out ordinary for me. It's a sunny and clear spring day. Unseasonably warm. A Tuesday.

I go to school. I sit through all my regular classes. I stare out the window while Mr. Karlsson monotones about Ohm's law. I keep thinking about how *Ohm* sounds like the yoga chant, which is supposedly the sound of the universe. Mr. Karlsson says *Ohm* enough times that it sends me into a daze, and I almost fall asleep. The sky blazes blue outside. I blink repeatedly to keep myself from crashing into my desk.

I'm dealing with drama at the school newspaper. The features editor has dropped out. The two assistants I'm considering to replace her do not get along at all, and the tension between them is splintering the staff. One of the assistants is clearly better but is a graduating senior. The other is a junior and will probably be impossible to work with all next year if she's passed over. I worry about staffing next year.

These petty squabbles in this small place. Sometimes I wonder if I'll ever escape these cornfields.

I come home at the end of the day. Mama makes jiu cai dumplings for dinner. We eat while watching TV. Our parents discuss where we might go for vacation when you come home from the school year. I don't remember any of the options, after, because of course we don't go anywhere that summer.

After I help clean up, I go upstairs. There's a quietness at night that triggers a specific loneliness I mostly don't feel during the day, surrounded by people at school. I scroll social media for a while but don't post anything or leave any comments. I wish I had someone to talk to, but I can't think of a single person I'd call.

This is my life. Steady but unremarkable. The surface of an undisturbed pond. I could never have expected the stillness to be shattered with such force. I could never have prepared for the undulating ripples after the splash.

On the far side of the country, it's raining steadily. It comes down soft but unrelenting, soaking everything. It gathers in puddles along the curb and muddies the side of the path. It pools under desks in classrooms where people lay their umbrellas.

You wake up exhausted from the two hours of sleep last night. You have a quiz today too, and you're not sure you'll be able to get through the day without copious amounts of caffeine, a little something else. You take one pill just to give you a bump and get you through the morning.

You go to class as you normally do. Sit three rows back from the front—not too close to be weird, but close enough to be able to see everything on the board. Your vision is getting worse. You make a note to set up an appointment for an eye doctor. Another thing on a long list of to-dos that never seems to get shorter. You're twitchy. Your eyes don't seem to blink unless you remind yourself to do it. They feel dry.

Tuesday is the day you have the most classes. I know this only because we recover your schedule pinned up from a corkboard on your desk later. You have two classes in the morning and three in the afternoon. Your day concludes at five, which is a late finish for you. The other four days of the week, you're done by three.

At five, it is dark outside. The rain continues to fall. By the time you make it back to your dorm room, your boots are drenched. Everything feels vaguely damp. Your bones ache from the chill. You peel everything off and change into dry sweats. You glance out your window, where people rush past each other in the courtyard outside. A couple is kissing with abandon under an awning, the rain pouring down from the roof in front of them. You feel strange watching them, a curious longing in your heart for—what? You turn away.

You get a roll and one apple from the dining hall and eat it at your desk while you do your reading for tomorrow. Your roommate is not there. The common room has no one in it. The rain has finally emptied the path beneath your window.

You are tired. So tired. You have not slept well for an entire week, and it's starting to make your brain do weird, hallucinatory things. You swear you can hear people talking in the other room, even though nobody is there.

Maybe going to bed early tonight would help. You take a pill. You get ready for bed and lie down, the blankets tucked up to your chin against the chill. It should feel cozy. It should induce sleep. But as usual, it doesn't. Eyes open. Eyes closed. Sleep is elusive. Sleep is nowhere to be found. Sleep is an island that has sunk beneath the waves into the ocean.

Your brain won't stop thinking about everything for the rest of the week. And then the week after that. And soon the semester will be over. And then you'll come back in the fall for more. It all goes into an inescapable spiral that never ends. Your roommate is asleep in bed at this point. You stare at him for a few moments, jealous. He sleeps easily, like a bear entering hibernation.

If you do not sleep tonight, you won't be able to make it through the week. You must sleep. You get up and ruthlessly dump more pills into your palm. It's nothing bad, you tell yourself. You can wean off them later. You will go to a real doctor after this semester. You promise yourself. Right now, you just need a little help for the week. You need to sleep. You chase them down with a glass of water.

You get into bed.

You never get up.

Or something like that? I don't know. It's impossible to know, because I'm not there. Mama and Baba aren't there. Nobody is there, save for your roommate, who finds you the next day after you don't move in the morning, or at noon, or hours later.

I can only speculate, after, what your last day was like and what you were thinking. I go through all different kinds of scenarios. One where it is an accident. One where you did it with intention. We look for clues in all your things. Your planner, with notes jotted in for events weeks later. Your belongings, carefully labeled and organized for us to categorize and pack after you're gone.

But there is no way to ask you. You are horribly, irreversibly gone. Like that. The shock of it is complete. And the guilt. It's so surreal that there doesn't seem to be room for tears. We rarely cry. We mostly just move through each day, stunned, as though permanently struck with a post-viral brain fog.

Life seems less like a miracle, more like a biological process. Materials in, energy out. You must balance the equation to stay alive. If not, if you have a simple slip, then your time on this earth is over.

And what happens after? Will we be together again, like the pastor at Nai Nai's church used to say? It takes more conviction than I have to know.

Chinese people believe that the dead stick around for forty-nine days before they depart. Forty-nine is a special number. It is always said as part of an equation. Qi qi si shi jiu, seven times seven equals forty-nine. In *Journey to the West*, the Monkey King tries to rebel against the gods and become the emperor of heaven. The gods capture him and toss him into the great sage Laozi's sacred furnace. They lock him in the furnace for qi qi si shi jiu days. At the end of that time, they check to see if he has dissolved into ashes. To their surprise, he emerges from the furnace, triumphant, with flashing gold eyes and more powerful than ever. Reborn.

The forty-nine days after your death are a blur, except for the one thing I feel in my soul: that you are not here. I do not feel your presence. I do not see a flicker of you in the lights at home. I do not dream of you. I look for you all over, as your spirit is supposed to linger, but I find nothing. People always talk about how they see loved ones in cardinals, in butterflies. I wonder, Is there something wrong with me? Am I not looking hard enough?

Or worse: Are you just not there? Is there nothing to look for?

Because you never appear to me during the seven weeks of mourning, I know you are not drifting around. Not on this earth anyway. I know I am not speaking to you, not for real. But I think of you all the time. I tell you all the things I couldn't say when you were alive, when it was harder to do.

I tell you that we are the only two people in the world who have lived the same lives. The same memories growing up. The same arc. We flew over the sea together, you and I. I think this must mean that even though you are gone, I carry the parts of you onward.

I tell you that I will remember everything about us.

I tell you that I wish you were here.

twenty-four

THE HOUSE I returned to was lonely.

I watched Alan drive off from the entryway. This was the end of us, I thought. It would hurt whenever I'd see him at school. Maybe it would never stop hurting.

I went inside. It was exactly as I'd left it. Clean and a little bare, because we still hadn't finished unpacking. It was a place we hadn't made our own yet. I felt like a guest in my own home.

For a while, I meandered around, watched some mindless TV, even wiped down some dusty areas. It was mostly because I was suspended in a state of numb stupor after everything that had happened. But I'd have to shake myself out of it soon, because at last, time was running out on me.

This was it. The application deadline for the UCs was tomorrow night. Soon after, it would be Monday again. I'd have to go back to school. And then four days later was the flight to China.

All these hours, days, trickling together. My world was

closing in. And, as always, in my most critical moments: I was all alone.

Eventually, I made some stovetop ramen, adding an egg for protein, and ate at the counter of our silent cavernous kitchen. The entire time, I stared at the picture in the kitchen of the four of us when Sam and I first came over. I had a subtle gap between my teeth, which looked too large in front before braces. Sam's arms were wrapped around Mama's waist. He was wearing a dark green polo. It was the only picture my parents had hung in the house.

I wondered where the rest of our pictures were stashed away.

I cleaned up after dinner, and there was nothing left to do but get ready for nighttime.

I took my suitcase upstairs, walking carefully past the room with the closed door, where all of Sam's things were, still in boxes.

I left everything in my room without unpacking, got into a pair of pajamas, and crawled into bed early, breathing in the scent of my unwashed sheets. The familiarity enveloped me in its softness. I lay there for a long time, unable to sleep, but I breathed deeply in and out, in and out.

I woke up the next morning to the gentle pattern of rain, soothing as a mother's lullaby.

Outside, it was gray, and the downpour was light but steady. I stood by the back door and drank my coffee, watching with some wonderment since I couldn't remember the last time I had seen rain. It had been a dry month since we'd moved.

California felt less fantastical in the rain. It was finally a real place. One in which I now lived, no different from where we lived before. It had bad days too, and that was reassuring in a way.

I checked messages from my parents. I let them know I had made it home. They sent me a heart emoji and a jia you emoji for the application deadline today.

The rain was meditative. It made me think of those summer thunderstorms we used to have in the Midwest, the kind that washed the pavement clean and left the world smelling fresh.

When we first came over, my parents were so busy working all the time. They didn't seem to know how to have children, or what they were supposed to do with us. Most of the time, Sam and I were left to our own devices. Just us two, we chafed at each other's company, both of us wondering, perhaps secretly, whether we were enough for the people who had brought us into this world yet seemed like strangers.

Still, when the weather was a washout, my parents used to stay in with us, playing games that we were way too old for, but with no one watching, we'd participate gleefully without judgment. Mama would make paper masks, coloring them beautifully and cutting out holes for eyes and mouths, and Baba would chase us around the house wearing them until we squealed with laughter. Those memories lived brightly in my mind, like rare gems I had hoarded over the years.

Now, the rain reminded me of them. How delicate those days were. How fond. It had never occurred to me, but Mama had a real talent for drawing and an eye for art. Did she used to draw when she was younger? Why did she stop? How had I not asked her about that before?

I decided to get out of the house. I drove to a local café, one that I hadn't gone to before. The inside had a lot of plants and squashy armchairs. It wasn't too crowded. The music was at a low hum, the way I liked it. I ordered an oat cappuccino, and it tasted perfect. I knew I would come back here again. Maybe this would be my new go-to coffee shop—a tentative, hopeful root to put down, because I lived here now.

I sat next to a window so I could watch the raindrops slide down the glass, my laptop open to my college applications. I had started my essay on the trip, but it was terrible, all wrong. I deleted it entirely and took myself back to a blank page.

Alan might've no longer had a place in my life, but he was right about a lot of things. I *did* want to study journalism, although it was something I hadn't ever seriously discussed with anyone out of caution. I *was* like a black box, even to myself sometimes. I was scared to dream, scared to try. It was a safe way to live, but a diminished one.

I watched people come in with friends or alone. I watched a girl with pink hair flirt with one of the baristas. I watched someone wheel in an old woman—her grandmother, perhaps—with tubes in her nose and the brightest grin on her face.

There were other ways to be. Life could be big and bold. It could be fearless. You could expect pain and disappointment, but you could expect a lot of other things too. You couldn't choose what to let in and what to keep out. You'd have to let it all in, everything all at once. Even if it felt like too much. A soul could stretch, though. I believed that.

I worked on the rest of the application all day. I ordered a panini for lunch and returned to the seat I should've been paying rent on for how long I'd claimed it. I wrote the essay about Kit and the all-American girl I wanted to be, the one that Alan said I should. I talked about moving across the ocean with my brother and not ever feeling like I really belonged. The one thing I was good at, where I seamlessly fit in, was finding other people's stories and telling them right.

It wasn't the unvarnished truth, of course. Not the way I would've told it to someone I knew. It was trite and imbued with an air of the dramatic. I had squashed the messiness of real life into the four corners of a college application essay. But it was what colleges liked to hear.

I packed up my stuff and went home. The rest of the evening seemed to go by slowly. At long last, I was done with my application entirely. I had read it three or four times for typos.

I could've hit Send at any point, but I held off on pushing that button. I had the seed of an idea, one that I hadn't explored before. It would not be my parents' first choice. Perhaps they would be angry or disappointed. Perhaps they would refuse to help me and want nothing to do with my plan. I had never done anything so brash, so irreversible before.

It was funny and kind of sad, but even now, I wondered what Sam would've thought. I would probably wonder for the rest of my life, but soon—very soon—I would be surpassing him in age. Eventually, I would have to stop talking to him in my mind, because the version of him I was keeping would stop being meaningfully him. He would be frozen at eighteen, and I would go on without him, making all new decisions, all new mistakes. Would it matter what eighteen-year-old Sam would think of thirty-year-old Stella? I would have to let him go.

The minutes ticked by on the clock. Undeniable. Inexorable. Still, I left that application page up, unsubmitted.

Until eventually, time ran out. The future we had planned for me at a UC next year disappeared for good.

I thought I might feel panicked that I let it all go right at the very end, but I didn't.

Mostly, the space inside my head was quiet. And I was tired.

Outside, it had stopped raining. Tomorrow, it would probably be sunny again.

I got into bed. I fell asleep easily.

As though after all this time, my body had finally remembered how.

Weston High had chugged easily onward without me for a week.

I slid back into my schedule with hardly anyone noticing my absence, even the teachers. I had left little of an impression, it seemed. It was a good reminder, though, that no matter what was going on in your own life, it was not that important in the grand scheme of the cosmos. Life would go on, no matter what.

Morgan was still there in US Government, her deadpan expression unaltered upon my return.

"Did I miss anything important?" I asked.

She shrugged with a fluid single-shoulder movement. "Not really." She gave me a thirty-second monotone rundown of the foundations of democracy. "We got A's on the two assignments," she said. "So thanks for doing your part, I guess."

"Oh. That's good."

She gave me a curious look. "How were the UC college tours?"

Her question surprised me. She always struck me as uninterested in wanting to engage much. "Fine. I didn't end up applying, though."

"That bad, huh?" she said, a glimmer of humor playing on the edge of her voice.

"Well, I just wasn't sure it was the right choice for me." I disliked how defensive I sounded, but I couldn't help it.

"Hey, it's fine. Who's judging? I'm not going."

"You're not?"

"No. I'm doing community college for a couple years and then transferring."

I straightened in my chair. "Like in town?"

"Yeah, I mean, that's why they call it *community* college, no? Lots of people do that. Unlike some of the people at this school, my family's not made of money, so I'll save a bunch and then graduate with the same degree they will four years later." She smirked. "It's like a life hack."

"That's what I'm doing too," I said. "Staying local."

Saying it for the first time made it sound right. Who would've thought? Me telling Morgan Park before anyone else.

"Oh yeah?" A genuine smile spread on her face. The first one I'd seen. "Nice. Maybe we can do our schedules together. Just saying, you know, if we have to do group projects, I'd prefer doing them with someone who can pull their own weight."

"I wouldn't mind that," I said.

At lunch, I did my customary scanning of the room for a half-occupied table. The trick was to find a long one that had people at one end so I could sit sort of nearby. It felt less humiliating that way, because a casual observer would think I was maybe sitting with people rather than sticking out at a completely empty table. It was like a game for me.

I was feeling relatively proud of myself about having found the perfect situation. A group of girls who looked like they *could've* been my friends, even if they weren't. They glanced at me every once in a while, as though considering introducing themselves, but nobody made the first move. That was okay. I was used to eating by myself. One day, maybe, I'd muster up enough courage to walk up and ask to sit next to them without fear of rejection, but I was fine with being in my comfort zone for a little bit longer.

Part of this routine involved making sure I didn't make too much eye contact with people nearby. So I was focused intently on my mediocre hamburger and didn't notice Alan coming up to me until he was sitting right across from me.

"Hi," he said. He was wearing a soccer jersey and khakis. His shoulders looked so good in that shirt. My traitorous heart did a lurch at the sight of him.

The girls at the table next to me fell into silence. They stared at us, glancing back and forth between him and me, unable to comprehend why the guy who everyone knew was deliberating sitting next to the girl no one had ever seen before. It must've appeared like some kind of pity play.

I was too surprised to say anything, and it gave him an entry. He cocked his head to the side. "You look familiar. Do I know you?"

"Ha ha. Very funny." I considered telling him to go away, but I didn't want to cause a scene in the cafeteria. I had just spent nearly a whole week with him; surely, I could handle another thirty minutes. "I didn't know you had lunch at this time. I haven't ever seen you before."

"I don't, actually. Mine is next period, but I ditched today."

"You? Ditching class?"

"The teacher likes me, and I've otherwise had a perfect attendance record. I think it'll be okay."

"Of course." God, this hamburger was so dry. It made me think of Monty's Good Burger, where the burgers had been so juicy. It made me think of the eagerness in his face as he watched me try something he liked, how transparent he was about wanting to share his delight with me.

"Did you finish everything in time?" he asked.

"I wrote the essay you told me to."

His face lit up. "Oh yeah? About Kit? And studying journalism?"

I nodded. "It was a good idea, so I took it and ran with it."

"I'll keep my fingers crossed for you. Any place would be lucky to have you."

"I didn't turn it in."

He looked confused. "Huh? The essay?"

"No, the applications. I didn't turn any of them in."

"Well, maybe you can get an extension or something? Extenuating circumstances. I'm sure they can do something like that. We can do some research. I mean a lot happened in the past few days. You found out about your grandmother. There has to be a way."

He was running on, so I stopped him.

"It's fine. I decided not to go. I think I'm going to hang around here for another year and try the community college. Stay home. You know, a baby step."

It shouldn't have mattered what he thought about this. I didn't want to go into it with him, all my reasons, which felt intensely personal and hard to explain. I tore my gaze away and focused on the grooves in the table instead. There was a pause where I thought he might ask a bunch of questions, like whether this was really a choice I'd thought through since I'd made it at the last minute, or what my parents thought. I wouldn't have been able to answer those questions.

But he didn't ask me anything.

"That's great," he said earnestly. "I'm happy for you. Really."

We looked at each other for a long while, because whatever this meant for me, it was obvious, at least, what it meant for us. It was almost inevitable, no matter what decisions I'd made, that we would end up in different places. But this made it more final.

I didn't want to dwell on it, not now, when it was all still very new. "So what are you doing here, actually?" I asked finally.

He cleared his throat. "I came to confess."

I wasn't sure what I was expecting, but it was not that. "Confess? So my parents did ask you to cover up my grandmother's illness?"

"Not that. I was telling you the truth on that one. But I spent the entire drive back to San Diego thinking about how you had no reason to believe me because I had lied to you about other things—going back all the way to the beginning. So I wanted to confess everything I've lied to you about. Then you'll know from now on that what I'm saying is real." He made it sound so simple, so matter-of-fact.

Now that we had changed topics to something much juicier, the girls at the table were all listening intently, without even a pretense of keeping up appearances. They were making me nervous, but I couldn't bail. "Why did you feel like you had to ditch class to do this during my lunch period?"

"Well, I could've gone to your house, I realize that. But I figured you needed some time to yourself, and I wasn't convinced you'd actually open the door. And it felt less stalkerish to find you here than sleep on your doorstep, waiting for you to leave the house."

I crossed my arms. "You're right. That would be super creepy. So what do you want to tell me?"

"The first time you saw me in the hallway. I did lie. I saw you right away. I would've recognized you, even after twenty years."

I colored. "This is a weak confession. I already called you out on it, remember?"

"Yeah, but don't you want to know why?"

"It's probably the same reason you tossed me under the bus back in Mount Pierce, which by the way, is another lie. Not sure if that was on your list of things to go through." My skin was prickly and warm.

He furrowed his brow. "Mount Pierce?"

"Everyone here thinks you came here directly from Shanghai." At this, I turned to our captive audience and addressed them directly. "Right?"

They all nodded in unison.

"It's like you pretended that entire part of your life didn't exist. You pretended like *I* didn't exist. It's the same reason. You don't need to explain that we weren't good enough for you, just because you've finally gotten over it and can sit next to me now."

"That's not it, Stella," he said softly.

"Okay, well, whatever. It's time for me to go back to class. Don't try to trap me outside Journalism II to hear the rest of this." I stood up to go.

"Wait. Do you still have the marble?"

That stopped me. "What?"

"The orange marble from my tiao qi set."

"You lost it back in Mount Pierce?"

"I didn't lose it. I left it at your house. Do you still have it?"

I stared straight ahead. My ears were beginning to ring. "You can have it back," I said at last. "I should've mailed it to you."

"So you kept it?" His voice was stained through with hope.

"I have to go. I'm going to be late for class," I said, even though there was plenty of time left.

"It's okay," he said. "I'll go. It's just— I wanted to know."

I watched him leave, knowing that whatever was between us, it wasn't over yet.

I stood there for a moment, feeling the sensation rush back to my limbs.

"Hey," one of the girls at the table piped up after a pause. "That was wild. Like a freaking K-drama. So how do you know Alan Zhao, exactly?"

twenty-five

WHAT WAS THE significance of an orange marble anyway?

After school, I went home and dug out my jewelry box. I knew exactly where it was, in one of my unpacked crates tucked in the closet. It was there with a bunch of other things that were important but not important enough to be taken out immediately. Easily relegated to later months, with much less urgency.

The box was carved walnut-colored wood with a painted panel on the lid. I had owned it for so long, I didn't remember where I had gotten it from. When I'd packed for the move, I had just wrapped a couple of rubber bands around it and put it in the crate without looking inside.

I peeled off the rubber bands now and opened the lid. Inside, there was a xiang bao, a good fortune–embroidered sachet with a strong musky scent; my gold and jade jewelry; a string of pearls Mama had given me; and the marble. I took it out and rolled it around between my finger and thumb. It felt cool against my skin. It was still vibrant as ever in the light.

I wasn't sure what I was going to do with it. I thought about returning it at school or mailing it to him. But I couldn't decide. I didn't understand why he had left it with me, or why he was bringing it up now.

I thought back to the night before school started and how nervous he was. That long hug at the end. And then I realized. He had been saying goodbye. All along, he had known what he was going to do.

I couldn't put off calling my parents any longer. The application deadline had come and gone—the whole reason they'd held off on buying my plane ticket back to China—and I had to let them in on what I'd decided.

This time, Mama picked up right away. She was in Nai Nai's apartment, and she was alone.

"Where's Baba?" I asked.

"At the hospital." She must've seen something tight in my expression. "She is no worse. He and your aunts are taking turns being there, just in case."

Just in case, hanging precariously in the air like three glass ornaments on a wire.

"Are you back in school? Are you eating okay?" she asked. "There are frozen bao zi in the freezer. Two containers of beef stock. You can buy some bok choi and make noodles for yourself."

I was comforted by this familiar territory. Mama pushing food, me reassuring her that I was eating enough, that things were going okay. I was good at placating her anxiety with continual promises of being the child she wanted me to be. It was almost enough for me to go along with. Not now, I thought. Tomorrow, maybe. In person, maybe. But I would have to do it eventually. I might as well do it now.

"I went back to school. I'm caught up."

"Good, good. Your baba and I, we just wanted to make sure you took care of everything before coming back here."

"But, Ma, I have something important to tell you."

She immediately pulled herself taut. "What is it?"

Even as there was no going back from my plan, even as I'd committed to talking to my mother, I found the words catching in my throat. Sam and I had fully internalized the task of pouring ourselves into premade molds. I had never once in my life told her anything difficult. Everything hard, it seemed, took practice.

"Remember what I told you and Baba before about not wanting to go to college?" I said.

"Oh," she said, her face clouding over. "We were all tired then. We had just taken Nai Nai to the hospital. Your baba should've been gentler, I know. He shouldn't have raised his voice."

"I didn't send in my applications."

There was a moment in which she seemed to be struggling to even process what I had said. Then her eyes fluttered closed. I could see the tumultuous turning in her mind, the way she was imagining a future destroyed. The crisp, bright fear reflected outward. "Why didn't you talk to us? Why didn't you tell us beforehand?"

"I tried. You didn't listen," I said. "And I don't know how to talk to you. I don't know how to talk about anything real."

"Mei mei," she said, so quietly I could barely hear her.

"You never call me that anymore. You stopped calling me that after ge ge died. It made me sad."

She was crying. My mother never cried openly. I'd heard of it only from Auntie Yang or muffled through the wood of double doors in their master suite.

"It made me sad too," she said.

"I miss him. We moved away. We put all his stuff in boxes. It's like he was never even here. I was never a little sister."

Mama hesitated, wiping her cheeks hastily. "It hurts too much. Your baba and I . . . maybe we did it wrong. But we didn't know how else to keep going." The words sounded awkward coming out of her mouth. I could tell she was uncomfortable even mentioning her grief.

I felt the same. I felt as though I wanted to climb out of my own skin. We were so bad at this.

I had told Alan that there was nothing to tell about my love life so far. It had been true, but I'd had little crushes here and there, people I'd wanted to know better. With each of them, whenever someone would get close to me, I'd find some way to put some distance between us. *Emotionally unavailable*, I'd read online when looking for an answer for my behavior. That was me. But how could I have learned to be any other way?

"Wait," she said. She put the phone down.

I stared at the white popcorn ceiling that the camera faced. I heard her blow her nose heavily.

She picked me back up. "Sometimes, I wonder if any of this was worth it," she confessed.

"What do you mean?"

Her eyes flickered back and forth. She couldn't quite look at me directly. "When you and your brother were young, still in China, our house was so quiet. I hated it. You can't understand what it's like to give birth to babies and then one day, hear nothing but silence at home. It's not natural. I told myself it would be okay in the end. Everyone said it would be. You would come here when you were older and we had money. We would be so happy together. But when you came, it wasn't anything like I thought it would be. I didn't know you at all. I assumed I would always know you, because I am your mother. I thought the love and connection would come automatically. And I did love you. Of course I loved you. But the rest of it—it was hard."

She said all of this almost in one long breath. Rapidly, as if she were trying to get it all out before she lost the words. I didn't want to interrupt her. This was the most I could remember her ever saying to me about herself. The conversation between us seemed like a gossamer web. If I moved too much or spoke too loudly, it would tear.

What she said drew a memory from a hollow, shameful place

within me that I had mostly filled in as I grew older. And her honesty finally made me feel as though I could admit my worst feelings too. "Sam and I used to think you weren't our real parents. You seemed so barely interested in knowing us that we thought you were fakers. We used to look for evidence around the house. In the drawers, in old photo albums. Thinking we might find something that gave us a clue to who our real parents were. We even once made plans to run away."

She looked at me, her eyes deep and glistening—the same eyes I had, with the same shape and placement on our faces. "I wish I had never let you go. Maybe none of this would have happened."

I realized that she was talking about Sam's overdose. That she felt, in some fundamental way, like her lack of mothering had left him adrift. That if she had raised us, maybe she could've saved him.

We were all shouldering that guilt. The undeniable specter haunting us about what we could've done. Maybe I was at fault, for not spilling his secret when it could've made a difference. Maybe Mama was at fault, for making him feel as though he couldn't tell anybody himself. We had failed him, all of us, in one way or another.

It was strange, but I had never felt as close to Mama as I did now.

She gave me a wistful look. "You know, sometimes I am jealous of Nai Nai. She was doing us a favor, but I couldn't help but feel like she was stealing you away. I was always afraid you loved her more than me."

These were things she could never say to me in front of Baba, since it was his family and not hers.

"That's not true." But even as I said it, I wondered if she was right. Those early days in the beginning, I always dreamed about returning to China. I missed Nai Nai so badly. It would be a lie to say I hadn't ever fantasized about trading my parents for her.

Nai Nai, who had held us while we slept as toddlers. Nai Nai, whose gentle wrinkled hands wrapped bandages around our cut knees and brushed my hair every night with her precious whalebone comb.

Mama didn't ask for more. Maybe she sensed that anything I might say would be more to make her feel better than the actual truth.

I didn't want to linger on it. "Auntie Yang told me that you had made boxes of mementos for Sam and me when we were still apart."

She was startled. "She told you that?"

"You never gave them to us. Why?"

She fiddled around with her hair. "I thought you wouldn't like them. It seemed like a silly idea once you were here. I realized I had mostly put them together for myself, to cope with not having my children. They were for me, not for you."

"I would've liked to see it," I said. "Do you still have them?"

"I've always kept them. I'll find them when I come home. I'll give them to you."

I knew the trip back to China would be a short one, since it was in the middle of the school year. I was already dreading having to return. But at least now I had something small to look forward to. "Okay," I said.

She smiled at me. Then sighed deeply. "Baba will be back soon. I have to tell him about your applications. What will you do now?"

I had already told Morgan, so it should've been easier to say it to Mama, but it was harder. I would have to keep practicing. "I am thinking about community college," I said gingerly. "I could stay home. Live with you for another year. I could transfer to another place later, maybe. When I'm ready."

"Are you still afraid of what might happen? After—your brother?"

I wanted to say no. "A little bit."

"I'm afraid too."

"Really?"

"I know there is no reason to fear. But that doesn't matter, does it?"

I shook my head.

"I will tell your father," she said, taking a burden off my shoulders.

"Thank you."

"Aiya, I should go. I have to make dinner for the family. Your aunts can't cook at all. I can't leave it to them. Oh—how is Alan? He is doing well?"

My jaw tightened. "He is fine."

"I'm glad." She paused. "He was a nice boy, wasn't he? You used to be very good friends. It's hard to find good friends like that. It was kind for him to drive you all last week."

"Yes."

"Take care of yourself while you are by yourself, okay?"

"Okay. Hey—Mama?"

She held the screen up closer. "Mm? What?"

"Did you talk to Alan about Nai Nai?"

She looked confused. "What are you talking about?"

"You didn't talk to him before the trip?"

"What a question. We just asked Uncle Zhao if his son wanted to drive. Why would we talk to Alan?"

"No reason," I said.

The room where the staff for the school newspaper, *The Standard*, met weekly was in a wing of Weston High I hadn't gone to before. I got lost twice before finding it, and by the time I did, I was ten minutes late.

It was a computer lab, with two rows of big silver desktops. A smattering of students were at the computers. Another group sat clustered in the corner by the whiteboard. I could tell that they were having a news conference, sketching out where different stories would go on which page.

I had found the ad for the newspaper and emailed the address. The editor in chief had emailed me back, telling me to come to the after-school meeting to see where I could slot in.

Everyone was heavily focused on their activity at hand.

Nobody seemed to be expecting me, and nobody looked in my direction. This was my worst nightmare, having to go up to someone and ask what I was supposed to be doing. I was about to do the most awkward thing possible and back out of the room, when someone in the corner finally noticed me standing by the door and waved me over.

"Hi. Are you Stella?" A girl with clipped short hair and big, beautiful eyebrows met me halfway.

I nodded.

"I'm Marie, the person who you were emailing with." She extended her hand, and I shook it. "You're new, huh?"

"Yeah."

"You ever worked on a school newspaper before?"

"I was the editor in chief at my old paper." I felt gross saying it, as though I were bragging, even though I was just stating a matter of fact. "I mean, I came from a small town. It was a really small school. It was nothing like this. We published, like, once a week, and had three staff writers."

"No, that's great. Well, I'm sorry that my job isn't available," she said cheekily, "but we have tons of other stuff that you can do. We need a beat writer on features, sports, and also—do you know how to use Adobe InDesign?"

"I'm not great at it, but I can use it."

"Fantastic. A designer quit, so even if you can do inside pages, that would be a big help. Whatever you want to do, we have room for you."

I surveyed the room. I was beginning to feel calmer, more in control of myself. This was familiar. It was a new space, and I'd have to learn how to work with new people. But I knew how to do this.

"Thanks. I'm happy to be here," I told her, and I meant it. "Put me to work."

She grinned. "Welcome to the staff."

I went to school as usual during the week and came home to my empty house. I kept mostly to myself.

Alan didn't try to corner me at lunch again. I thought about texting him to acknowledge that I had jumped on him unfairly for something he didn't do, but every time I tried, I didn't quite know how to start. His final accusation had been true, and all I could do was lash out so he wouldn't see the way it stung.

The orange marble sat on my desk now between two grooves of the wood slats, where it couldn't roll off. Was it a worse betrayal for him to have left it with me intentionally or was it better to have held on to something of his after all those years? I couldn't decide.

The one thing I couldn't deny was that I missed him. I had gotten used to talking every day over the past week. And if I boiled it down to the pure hard center of it, it was this: Being around him made me happy. It was why we had always been friends. I allowed him to escape from his overbearing father, and he allowed me to escape from being an outcast. We were good together, if only for a summer. I had never been able to recapture the feeling I had from being with him.

Not for the thousandth time, I wished we could start over to when there wasn't any baggage.

Since that was impossible, I tried to ignore this particular sadness.

There was too much else to be sad about already. I was stuck in limbo for many things over which I had no control.

I didn't know what it would be like to see Nai Nai, when I finally made the trip across the ocean. I didn't know what Baba would say about what I had done after Mama told him. I didn't know, after all of this, whether I would ever get to a place of openness and understanding with my parents.

I didn't know if I would ever stop feeling the gap that Sam had left behind.

Being in the house all by myself made his absence seem more pronounced. The fact that my parents had relegated his belongings into one room only made it impossible not to notice how the rest of the space was scrubbed free of any mementos.

Every time I passed the guest room, its door slightly ajar, I could see the cardboard boxes stacked high.

One afternoon, I came home, filled with a whirring tickle to take action. I couldn't just sit on the couch and stare at the blank four walls in our living room anymore. Or walk past the Room of Sam as though it were normal to have a black hole in your house that everyone ignored as if it didn't exist.

Tentatively, I pushed the door open. I half expected some cosmic force to stop me, but, of course, nothing happened.

It was just a room.

I sneezed. It was a little dark and dusty, since no one had been cleaning it. Motes of dust swirled through the air. I picked my way past everything and drew up the curtain to let in some light. I cracked the window to bring in fresh air.

The boxes were not arranged in any kind of thematic order, except that farthest away from the door, pushed up against the unused closet, were four boxes marked "Dorm." I had not gone with my parents to Cambridge to clean out his room after he died. I hardly remembered the first week of aftermath, but they had done a quick twenty-four-hour trip out there without me, put everything in boxes, and FedExed them to our house.

In the weeks after Sam died, I went back to school. I thought I came off as put together, but it must have been protocol in these situations to get a referral to the school psychologist. I found myself sitting in the squashy orange chair as she talked me through how to cope with loss. I told her I was okay and that I didn't need to be there. Mostly, I just wanted to be left alone. The attention made me feel simultaneously like I was underperforming my grief and like I should've been expecting a complete meltdown at any moment.

"Your feelings may come and go for a long time," the psychologist had said. "You may feel fine today but be unable to get out of bed a week from now. That's all part of it."

"Part of what?" I asked.

"The first year."

So that was what it was, I realized. An event momentous enough that everything in my life from then on would be measured by its distance from that point zero.

"Will it be better after that?"

"It will and it won't," she said. "But you'll have made it that far. That will feel like something."

It was the most anyone had talked to me about what to expect from the grieving process. My parents and I exchanged words only when we had to, as though each one cost us, and none of them had been about Sam dying.

We would be coming up on that full first year in a few months. I didn't know how long my parents intended on keeping the room untouched like this. Did they even have a plan for when they would eventually unpack everything? Or were they going to wait until it all crumbled to dust out of sight?

I took a pair of scissors and sliced open the tape on the box closest to the door. It felt forbidden, but once I did it, I was emboldened.

I took out his old clothes. Medals and trophies from the shelves in his room, always more numerous than the ones on mine. His bedsheets. I unpacked an entire box of shoes. Worn-out sneakers, dress shoes, beach sandals. I found an entire box of baby things that Nai Nai must've mailed over but my parents had kept.

I unearthed things that I barely even remembered he had. There was a dusty old kite from the back of his closet. Our parents had gotten it as a gift for him one birthday, but it was in truth a gift to both of us, since we flew it together most of the time.

Model airplanes, misshapen clay projects from school, little army men from two different sets, flash cards with his neat handwriting fading, notebooks, device chargers, board games, a pair of old headphones, a framed poem in Chinese calligraphy he had been gifted from our maternal uncle, a recorder from sixth grade, loose chess pieces, a stamp collection, a Nintendo Switch, a pair of brightly painted maracas, backpacks, sand everywhere from an exploded hourglass, a lamp shaped like a car, and books, so many books—

I kept unpacking, seemingly unable to stop. Everywhere, everywhere, looking for my brother among his possessions. They were piled on the floor around me; I surrounded myself with what was left of him.

My chest ached like someone had put expanders in my ribs. I thought about what Mama had said about it hurting too much, but it had hurt when we hid him away too. He was here now, in this house, with me, with my parents, with this new beginning from year zero. It felt like I had exhumed him. It felt like a resurrection.

I found our old pictures with Sam, still in their frames, and I lined them all up in the living room. I would hang them before leaving for China.

I knew then that the school psychologist was right. I was going to make it that first year. I would survive the earth's full revolution, all the way around the sun. I wouldn't feel better, not every day, but I would keep going.

It was only long after it got dark when I noticed the mail had come through the slot in the door. I went to pick it up and put it on the table. There was a copy of *The Standard* from this week. It had been dropped off, not mailed.

There was a little orange tab marking a page in the back.

I turned to the bookmarked spot, page 3. It was the opinions section. A personal essay at the top. Byline: Alan Zhao.

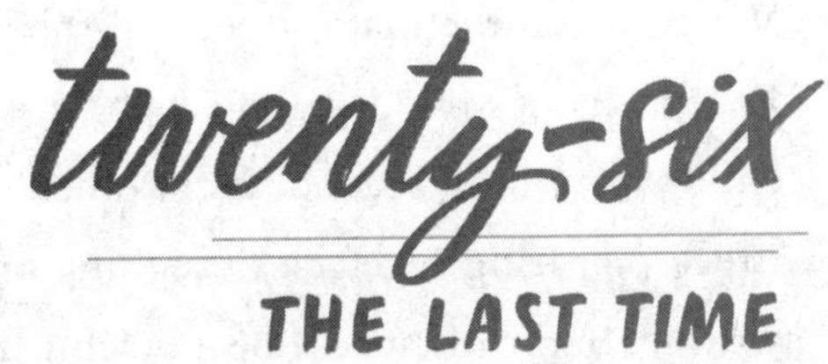

WE STEP OUT of the air-conditioned charter car onto the main road in front of Da Ji Cun. It's hot like I remember. The atmosphere smells faintly earthy and burnt. I can still recognize the brick wall, whitewashed, with the white paint fading back into pink from age, at the outer edge of the village.

But much is different now, as I was afraid of when we got on the plane to come back.

The final trip before the village disappears

The road is paved. The cement does not yield underneath my shoes, like the dirt used to. Heat reflects back up and roasts my ankles.

I'm wearing a light blue cotton dress and espadrilles. You're wearing a white shirt. We seem to realize at the same time that we're more well-dressed than we ever have been before, returning to this place. Although it has been several years since we've come back. It feels like many more than that.

The creek bed running alongside the main road is dry. It is now grassy and wild at the bottom, full of dandelions and other weeds.

We walk across the bridge over the creek that no longer runs. We go down the main street. All the houses are as I remember. Except that it's midday and yet there is no bustle of activity. No children running around. No women sitting on stools along the street, preparing vegetables, laughing loudly. The calmness is unsettling. In the distance, I hear machinery grinding. Construction in the works. It's coming closer. The sound is claustrophobic.

We round the corner to Nai Nai's house. My heart beats faster. I look over at you, and your jaw is clenched. I wonder if you, too, find this experience to be surreal. The place we grew up. The same and yet so, so different. It is just us for now. Mama and Baba are following in two weeks. They don't have a lot of vacation saved up, so we came first.

The double doors to Nai Nai's house—our old house—swing open. There she is. A little shorter and more stooped. But she is rosy and bright. She grins widely at us, and immediately, I'm in tears. We cross the courtyard. We embrace, a three-person pile much bigger than we used to be.

We used to be in her arms; now she is in ours.

Nai Nai has a huge spread for us waiting for lunch. She must've been cooking all morning, maybe even last night. We eat quietly. For the years of being away, there's so much to say that we don't know how to say it.

"It seems empty," I say as the plates in front of us become mostly clear.

"People are already moving out. There are only a few months left before the deadline," Nai Nai says. She sounds tired.

"Oh."

I look at you.

"Do you like the new apartment?" you ask.

She sniffs. "I've been there twice. It's fine. I'm on the twenty-second floor. So high up, you feel like God. It's unnatural. I like to be closer to the ground. But the building was filling up, and Gu Ma said this was a good place to be. Anyway, what does it matter? I only have so many years left. All the good ones were here."

I feel sorry for Nai Nai. When we were children, she seemed so in control, powerful. The matriarch of the family. But now, she is hunched over in her chair, her life being decided for her by others. She seems, in some ways, more like our equal than our elder.

"We should visit Ye Ye's gravesite," Nai Nai says. "It will be the last time you'll see it where it is today. He will be coming with me. The others . . . we haven't decided yet." She sounds distracted. "We have to . . ."

We get a knock on the doorframe. One of the neighbors from across the street comes in. Lao Zhou, an older man, a bit younger maybe than Nai Nai. His hair was always sparse, but now it is almost all gone, just wispy tendrils coming out of his temples. Makes him look like a bit of a mad scientist. His skin is tanned from the sun, liver spots popping out of his shiny bald head.

"They're finally here, eh?" he asks, grinning ear to ear. He pokes you in the shoulder. "Big strong man now. You used to be just a little boy. Going to Harvard? Making us proud."

You thank him and smile.

"And you, xiao jie." He cocks his head to the side. "You look different too. I wouldn't even recognize you from before, with all your fancy clothes and makeup. You like it better here or there?"

It's impossible to verbalize how it feels to come back. The things I miss here, but the sundry conveniences that I've grown accustomed to. I'm sweating profusely. My hair sticks to my neck. I wish I had air-conditioning. I wish I had a functional shower.

I hesitate for only a moment, but Lao Zhou clocks it immediately. He eyes me hard and then shouts a laugh. "So quick to become American."

His words are like a slap. My face flushes warmer than it already is from the temperature.

Nai Nai looks at me. Her eyes are dark and sad. She can see right through me. I wonder if she thinks it too.

At the end of the week, we go to Ye Ye's grave. It rained overnight, and the path there is caked with mud. Nai Nai leads the way, while you and I squish dutifully behind her.

The day is hazy, bright with glare. I gaze out toward the horizon. The foreground is still flat and broad with fields of low-slung wheat. The neatly sown rows stretch out in endless radiating lines. But in the distance, clouds of dust kick up against the outline of towers. You never used to be able to see tall buildings from this far out. The city has expanded, and it is coming closer every day.

The land here is going to be used—ironically—as a designed expat community, complete with an international school and housing complex. Soon, the developers will repossess the fields and raze all the homes to the ground. If I ever come back, everything will be gone. It will be unrecognizable. As though the places I once knew never existed at all.

I don't believe I will come back to see what replaces it. This will be my last time.

We pass the creek where, once, you and I went hunting with all the village kids for frogs. The summer has been dry. There is no sign of water, much less of wildlife. It feels like even Mother Nature must know that times have changed.

"Do you remember this place?" I ask you.

You nod. "That was a fun day."

We had come back numerous times after, of course, but it seems that first day is still what we'll always remember.

We thread our way through a patch of high grass that brushes our wrists as we pass, into a grove of trees. You rush ahead to pass Nai Nai and clear some of the overgrowth that is a tripping hazard for her.

"Not maintained," she mutters under her breath.

We step into a clearing within the pine trees. The plants are so thick here it is hard to notice at first that we are in a family plot, but as I look carefully, I see the gravestones, dusted in a coat of dirt and yellowed pine needles. They are lined up in the shade, one by one. The graves of our ancestors. Traces of charred paper linger from Qing Ming Jie earlier this year.

We stand in front of Ye Ye's headstone, side by side. Your shoulder is warm against mine. Nai Nai talks about how we are grown and how we have come to see him. Ye Ye passed away so long ago. You have a few faint memories of him. I have none. Still, I feel appropriately solemn and regretful as I stand there, listening to Nai Nai, the wind blowing through the branches.

"You will always be with us. We will bring you to the new apartment," Nai Nai says, tears catching in her voice. "Even if home is gone, wherever you are, we will be home."

I glance at her. Her words echo in my bones. I'm gripped with a wild need to grab her and not let go.

You shake your head very slightly at me.

So instead, I clutch your arm and stay rooted to my spot. We bow three times to the grandfather I cannot remember. I try very hard not to think about how one day, probably sooner rather than later, we will be bowing to Nai Nai too.

I compel time to slow down and freeze, but it doesn't. The last day comes upon us, inevitable, like the tide pulling in. I know this goodbye will not be the same as the ones before.

I will never come back here. I will never see these dirt roads again. Everyone is moving away. In the future, this will be an entirely new land, and I will be the foreigner.

If everyone departs a place, then can it still be your home? If someone were to ask me where I was from, would I tell them of a place that no longer exists?

This is all so strange, I think. For a land to just disappear, like Atlantis. Da Ji Cun may as well be sinking below the sea. If I were to drive back here, years later, I wouldn't even recognize the landscape. It might be beautiful. Overbuilt with gardens and new white buildings and wide roads. At night, it could have flashy neon displays and festivals with live music and delicious street foods. A subway line built directly out here, where people can come and enjoy the expanded greater city. They'll even call this area something else. Who would know that before, there was a village, with children who ran around barefoot and people who mattered? Who would know, except the people themselves, scattered to four corners, paid to fade away?

It is easy to be erased, I realize, when nobody is around to remember. The snap of a finger for a government bureaucrat. A decision from a person we'll never know, on high. We are being erased now, as we go, each of us. We are being erased today.

But everything is constantly changing, so maybe this is no different.

We eat breakfast quietly, all our separate thoughts, unshared.

It's difficult to tell what Baba thinks; this was his home too, after all. But his face is impassive, as always. I never know how he feels about anything. It's as though he believes his job is to keep it all inside.

You look sunken and tired, like you're just waiting to get this over with, the worst part.

Nai Nai is bright and hard. Chipper. Trying to paper over the tragedy of the day. She never liked to leave on a bad note. I watch her, bringing dishes out of the kitchen, and I try not to feel obligated to remember every outline of the kitchen. The chipped tile by the sink, the green plastic fringe across the doorway. I won't remember it perfectly, and soon, it will be gone.

I try not to think about it, but it's impossible not to. And then I feel silly for feeling nostalgic about a plastic curtain. Emotional over a squeaky faucet.

The clock hand on the big square analog clock hanging above the table keeps moving around the face. Time flows forward, each minute filtering through our fingers. Tiny grains of sand falling to the floor. I wish we could stop. Oh, I wish we could stop.

I'm trying to remember everything so hard that I forget most things. My brain stutters and impresses only snapshots as the morning wanes toward noon, when we have to leave.

Mama washing the dishes with Nai Nai after we're done.

The water droplets glinting off the swirled stone sink in the courtyard.

The sound of the neighbors' chickens clucking.

The dull resistance of the suitcases as we pull them out of the house for the very last time. Out the front door. Through the garden. Stepping over the main entrance and down the path toward the main road.

The pond in front of our house, green and clear and soon to be gone. I wonder if the frogs survived. I wonder if the frogs have descendants in that pond. I wonder where they will go.

Nai Nai's knuckles white as she clutches my hand as though she might never let go. Her fingers thin, too thin and brittle.

My eyes are dry. The glare of the overhead sun reflects off your white shirt ahead of me. My black hair absorbs the heat like a furnace.

The car waiting to escort us to the airport is waiting. The driver leans against the outside, pulls on a cigarette. The smoke wafts up.

We all hug, one by one. Then Baba is ushering us into the car, and the sound of the door slamming shut behind me shocks me. The window is tinted. Nai Nai stands alone outside the car. She looks tiny. I think—somebody should be here with her. We can't just drive away and leave her here by herself.

But, of course, we can and we will. We have always been leaving.

After, I don't remember much about that morning.

What I do remember: the last moment before we drive away. Nai Nai tentatively hobbles up to the car door. She places her hand on the window right in front of my face, and I put my hand on the window too, so our palms are together, through the glass. One old and one young. Our hands, finally, the same size.

We hold them there for as long as we can. A millisecond. An eon. And then, the car starts moving and she steps back.

You put your arm around me.

We drive away.

twenty-seven

ALAN'S PERSONAL ESSAY was tucked on the bottom half of the page, under an editorial about the rising cost of area housing. I started to read.

> When I first moved to Mount Pierce, Illinois, I thought that assimilation was the only way to live. I believed that you simply had to become the person who everyone wanted you to be in order to survive, that everyone was playing a version of themselves that was palatable to the world around them. Some of us were better at it, and others were worse. The people who didn't fit in, I assumed were just less adept at this crucial skill.
>
> I was born in Shanghai, a city whose strongest trait was its transformative ability. In China's early

days, it began as an important seaport for each of the various dynasties, a hub for trade with the outside world. As foreign powers began to encroach in the nineteenth and twentieth centuries, Shanghai was carved up into different pieces. Partly British, partly French, partly Japanese, and partly its former self, it became accustomed to adapting to the whims of world influences. Eventually, it would become a centerpiece of China's effort to institute economic reforms and modernize. In an astonishingly short period of time, its raised skyline would be indistinguishable from any major Western city.

Perhaps because of my birthplace, I was a product of this legacy. I attended an international school, mostly staffed with British teachers, with a healthy population of expat students. My family members were not expats. We were native Shanghainese. I spoke the dialect at home with my grandparents. I noticed that there was a clear tier of hierarchy at school. The students who were like me, who were native to the area, were on the lower rung, while the white kids who spoke perfect English, grew up with nannies, and had access to designer brands were at the top.

From the beginning, I saw what I needed to do to move up, so I did it. It never occurred to me to do anything else. I was a fast learner. I watched a lot of TV. I picked up the accent right away. I paid attention to how the most popular kids behaved. It was like a game, and I got very good at it. It became natural for me to code switch once I walked through those double doors. The expat students saw me as one of them, not one of the Shanghainese kids.

I had perfected my approach by the time my grandparents informed me I would be moving to the United States to join my parents in some small town called Mount Pierce in the middle of nowhere. Mount Pierce didn't even show up on world maps. It was as big a difference as there could be. I was going to have to figure out this new place from scratch.

When I arrived in this nowhere place, I had the chance to start over. I could shed the artifice, which could be heavy, and stop pretending to be someone I wasn't. Even if it meant being rejected by others. What is that quote? Better to be hated for what you are than to be loved for what you are not? It is a lovely sentiment but probably written by someone who was not a pimply immigrant preteen and desperately afraid to find out that nobody loved me. And old habits die hard.

Yet again, at the most critical juncture, when I had the opportunity to do something else, I chose acceptance over courage, assimilation over authenticity. I acted out of fear and rejected others, so that I myself would not be rejected.

I was lucky that soon after, we moved again. To here. I could only maintain this trick mirror of myself for so long, and every so often I'd have to reset. I've often wondered what would have happened to me if I had stayed in one place my whole life. Would I have made a misstep and eventually be forced from the identity I created for myself, since no facade can last forever? Or would I have fully become my disguise?

I have seven more months—give or take—before I move again to a new place, and the cycle will begin anew. I imagined that the persona I would take next would depend on where I ended up. I applied to colleges based on the person I thought I wanted to be. I think all of us do that, to some degree. We see ourselves Becoming, in the grander sense, where we go. We could become a Bear or a Titan, even a Bruin or a Leprechaun.

I applied early acceptance to Stanford, because I saw myself there, among the Romanesque sandstone and glass and red-tiled roofs. I thought going there would confirm who I always wanted to be: intellectual, but in a cool, effortless way; automatically interesting; worldly; socially adept. I would walk into the grown-up world a graduate of a place that needed no introduction. It would mean that when people met me, they would know about me just from finding out my alma mater. They would make all the right assumptions.

But I didn't get in.

I wasn't the first person for this to happen to, and I won't be close to the last. Many of you will probably have the same experience. When I got the rejection email, I saw pieces of myself floating away, like burnt-up remnants of paper. I felt like I'd reached a dead end.

Here's the thing about making and remaking yourself: Do it enough times and you begin to lose who you really are. You start to wonder if anyone actually likes you or just a constructed idea of you. You start to wonder if you actually even like yourself. You start to wonder if you are even real.

The truth is, a place does not decide who you are. The people around you do not decide who you are. I realized, when I opened the message and read those words—*we regret to inform you*—that I was tired of trying to be what I was not for everyone else. I'd been doing it for as long as I could remember, and all it had gotten me was an unhealthy dose of identity crisis. I couldn't fix that with the right college admission. Stanford wasn't a shortcut to Becoming. Stanford was just a place.

> Now, there is the hard work to do of Becoming, all on my own. We will all face this, as we leave Weston High. Who we are, and who we want to be. Maybe it is okay to try out various skins, but to do so in a way that doesn't compromise your core values or sense of self. We should all be loved for ourselves, because that is the only love that really matters.

I finished the piece. My thumb clutched the page, leaving an indent in the paper.

Before I could lose my nerve, I pulled out my phone and sent a text to Alan.

Hey. I read your essay. Can I see you sometime?

I figured we might find a time after school tomorrow, before I flew to China the day after.

It was late. I was about to go upstairs and go to bed, but almost immediately, there was a knock on the front door.

I opened it and was astonished to see Alan standing there.

"What the hell? Were you waiting outside the entire time?"

"Not right outside," he said sheepishly. "In my car."

"I thought you said it would be creepy for you to wait outside my house, and that's why you didn't do it before."

"Yeah, well, honestly? I thought you were going to text me earlier, so it would be less weird. I dropped off *The Standard*, like, two hours ago. I figured you'd read it right away, and I'd just happen to be on my way to the car. I wanted to be here for when you did get through it."

"That's an excessive amount of confidence. I mean, that you thought I'd definitely read it. And that I'd want to see you afterward."

He shrugged. "I was right, wasn't I? It was my Hail Mary pass at getting you to talk to me again. So what did you think?"

I had a whirl of thoughts about it. My tenderness at his childhood and fear of being ostracized. His admission that he had hurt people in Mount Pierce. I hadn't planned for what I was going to say. I hadn't expected him to be on my doorstep seconds after I'd texted him. "You didn't get into Stanford?" was what actually came out of my mouth first. "When did you find out?"

"The day after we got back."

"I'm sorry," I said.

"It's okay. It was sort of silly to even write about, because nobody's biggest life problem is that they didn't get into Stanford, you know? It'll be fine. I felt whiny even talking about it."

"I know you really wanted to go. It's their loss."

"Ugh. Please never say those three words again. It's what everyone says when they find out. I guess I'm glad that we didn't do the student visit there. Would've been a waste of time, with neither of us actually going."

"You're a good writer," I told him. "Maybe you should be the one majoring in journalism instead of me."

"It's all that practice from the *Neon Nights* fic."

"So you weren't bringing your whole self to the essay, because you definitely didn't share how you're writing *Neon Nights* romance on the side. What's your AO3 username? That's going to be one of your confessions, right?"

We were both smiling now.

"It wasn't, actually. A guy has to have *some* secrets. But I did have one more thing to tell you that didn't make the essay."

"And what's that?" I was expecting something silly, something funny.

"I didn't tell you the truth about what happened in Mount Pierce. I did know, the night before school, that we were going to stop being friends."

It cooled the room instantly.

"That you were going to dump me, you mean."

He winced. "Yes."

"I worked that out. You left me the marble on purpose. Like a strange goodbye, except that you couldn't tell me to my face."

"I didn't do it because I was afraid of the other kids in school," he said slowly. "I did it because I was afraid of you."

I swallowed. "Why were you afraid of me?"

"Can't you see? Because I loved you. I've always loved you, even when we were little. I remember when we met, and you liked my magic trick, and I don't know, I think that was it. You were so hopeful, so strong. Every time I looked at you, I couldn't believe you even wanted to hang out with me. I was so afraid that you would hurt me one day, I preferred for you to hate me. It was ridiculous. It hurt me anyway. I thought about you all the time. When I saw you again here, it just felt like—I had to fix it. I missed you too much."

I felt like I couldn't breathe. So many years ago, so many miles away, and yet here he was, at my door. He was saying these things to me, all the things I'd been waiting my whole life to hear.

"I loved you even when I hated you," I confessed. Once I said it, I knew it was true. "That's why I kept the marble. I just couldn't let it go."

I looked into his face, the curves and lines of it so startling yet familiar, and the way he was holding me with his gaze made me want to cry. He was the only person who ever saw me, all my weaknesses and brittle fears. He took a step into the house, tentatively, as if he was nervous.

"Can I?" he asked.

He seemed to be asking many different things. Can I come inside? Can I kiss you? Can we find each other again? Can we go back to the beginning? I couldn't parse all the questions, but it didn't matter because the answer to all of them was yes.

He leaned in. He brushed my temple. At long last, we had closed the gap between us. He kissed me as though we'd been waiting our whole lives for this, because we had.

In the darkness, I closed my eyes. It was nighttime, but all I could feel was the piercing brightness of a full orange sunrise.

twenty-eight

I ROLLED MY suitcase to the far corner of gate 15 and plugged my phone into an outlet. It was 6:30 a.m. I had an unappetizing greasy breakfast sandwich wrapped in foil and a teetering cup of coffee that I carefully set down in the empty seat next to me so it wouldn't spill. The sun was just starting to come up.

My flight was boarding at eight.

I had promised my parents I would call them before I got on the plane. I debated whether to dial Mama's phone or Baba's. I decided to call my father.

He picked up after two rings. Mama was at his side. It must have been fairly late. They were at the hospital together.

"At the airport?" Mama asked anxiously without introduction.

"Yes. Checked in. It should be on time. Is everything okay there?"

"Everything is the same. Not better, not worse. We will be leaving for the night soon." Baba repositioned the phone in his hand. “Gu Ma will come pick you up at the airport tomorrow. You can come straight here if you want, although maybe you will be tired.”

“I’ll sleep on the plane.”

“Good. You should get some rest. Everyone is very excited to see you. Nai Nai is asking for you.”

“And Sam?”

He looked uncomfortable. Baba had always been so certain of everything. Confident of all his decisions. For once, he seemed unsure.

“She still doesn’t know,” I said. I wasn’t asking. I was mainly confirming what I would be dealing with.

“She fades in and out,” he replied by way of explanation. “It is hard to get her to concentrate on a single thing. It’s not— She will be gone soon.”

“Right.” I still couldn’t quite swallow how wrong it seemed, but then, everyone had taken it out of my hands. I hadn’t talked to Nai Nai without supervision in a year. Baba was saying that it wouldn’t be long before our choices wouldn’t matter, one way or another.

We lapsed into silence. Mama’s eyes connected with mine nervously.

“Your mother told me about what you decided for next year.”

I waited, wondering whether he was going to yell at me or tell me I’d thrown everything away in one singular moment of weakness. Under his scintillating gaze, it was hard not to feel like I’d messed up.

"It could be good," he said.

I blinked, barely able to breathe.

Baba was one of those old-school fathers, the never-cry, chin-up, don't-show-emotion kind. Whenever something underneath was threatening, he'd cloak it through a rough cough or an artful face wipe. But he wasn't doing that. His lower lip was practically quivering. It hurt to see him like that, but I couldn't look away.

"I'm sorry you had to wait until afterward to tell us. We should have talked about it before."

A bubble of protest surged up inside me. I wanted to, but he didn't seem to hear it.

"Mei mei, am I bad to you?"

"What?"

"Do you think I am bad? Is that why you do not tell us things? Is that why Sam didn't tell us he was using drugs?"

I was at a loss for words. Baba wasn't like Alan's father. He wasn't cruel or harsh. He was impatient sometimes and had a rigid worldview, but he tried to love us, in his way. It was just that his love seemed hard to access. Distant. It wasn't as though I didn't want to talk to him. I wanted nothing more than to have family dinners where we could talk about everything, but for some reason, we never could.

Even now, I couldn't conceive of telling him that I knew about Sam's drug problem before the overdose. Maybe one day. But not today.

"I don't think you are bad, Baba," I said finally. "I don't know why we are like this."

"Your ma says, maybe we should talk to someone together."

"Talk to who?" I didn't understand.

He shook his head, seemingly embarrassed. He looked at my mother. "You know. Americans are always doing it."

"A therapist," Mama said in English.

"I don't know," Baba said helplessly, palms toward the sky. "Do these things help? I'm not sure. But maybe we can try."

I was amazed. I didn't know what my parents talked about, but I never imagined that they would suggest this.

"Anyway," he said, obviously looking to move on, "it's an idea. We can consider it."

"I think it's a good idea."

He blinked rapidly. "So we will have time to do it, with you staying close. I will be happy to have you around for another few years."

"Yes," I said.

I looked into their faces. Each of us, slightly cracked but still hopeful. It was not too late, maybe.

"You will have to go soon," said Baba, gathering himself. "I don't want to keep you. But first, since we are here, do you want to talk to Nai Nai? She is awake. We will leave you with her."

I could hardly believe it. "Really?" I asked, my voice leaking air.

But then: My parents were standing up and walking out of the seating area. Like a dream, I watched as we went down the hallway and into an elevator. The ping of the doors opening on another floor. We traveled down another two hallways, and then they paused in front of a room. I caught a flash of the number: 719. I heard the sound of a knock.

A million wingbeats rising and falling inside me.

We were in the room. For all that I'd hoped and wished, I was unprepared for what came next.

Nai Nai was in bed, sitting up and alert. She had an IV stand rolled up next to her, the tube taped against her wrist.

The screen kept shifting as Baba walked around the bed, the phone in his hand. "I can prop this up on the bed tray table," I heard him say in the background.

Nai Nai waved her hand dismissively. "I can hold it. It's a phone, not a brick."

I could've laughed, but nothing could come out.

Her face swam into clearer view as Baba handed the phone to her. "Mei mei?"

"Hi," I said.

"We'll be outside when you're done, Ma," Baba said to her. I heard him leave.

It was just the two of us. I drank in the sight of her. She was thin, but her eyes were still bright, and she was still herself. I was so grateful for that.

"How are you feeling?" I asked.

"Not as good as I could be." She squinted and cracked a smile. "Getting old. Everything falls apart."

The screen was like a window between time and space. Seeing her was seeing another slice of my life, one that I hadn't known for a long time.

"When are you coming, eh?"

"When you wake up again, I'll be there." *Hang on,* I wanted to say to her. *Don't drift off without saying goodbye.*

She closed one eye slyly. "You don't have to sound so worried, like I'll disappear before you can make it. I look weak, but I'm still strong." She made a fist. "I'll jump right out of this bed when you walk in the door. I have to conserve my energy until then."

"Are you eating okay?" I asked her, reversing the question that she had always asked me.

She grimaced. "Nothing here tastes good. I can't wait to go home. I used to think the bao mu's cooking was terrible, but then I came here." I knew she wasn't eating because she was nauseous, even though she didn't mention it. She was hiding the things that hurt from me, just as we were doing for her.

"What about Gu Gu and Gu Ma? Can't they bring you food?"

She lowered her voice, as though confiding a secret. "I don't want that. Don't tell your aunties, but their cooking has never been good." She sighed. "It's because I never made them cook growing up. They got too spoiled with my food."

"You cooked for me growing up."

"Yes, but you won't need to cook for anyone. It will be someone's privilege to cook for you."

"Only you think that."

"You're my granddaughter. Of course you are the best." She served up praise as a steady diet, the way my parents never did. That was the way of grandparents. What was it about skipping a generation that softened a person? Between us, there was never a wall.

She sniffed wistfully. "Since I had to move into that new building in the city, I've had the most terrible time. The air is bad, and it's unnatural to live so high up, like a stranded bird. I miss the water and the mimosa trees. But at least when I meet up with my neighbors, I can tell them about my American grandchildren and their success. I raised those children, I tell them. They are forging their own paths, moving through the world. They will be what we couldn't. They will make us proud."

She was so confident. She always put me in the exact same bucket as Sam, as though we were equals. But he went to Harvard and followed all the points along the path my parents had laid out. He was the one everyone meant when they talked about being proud. I felt that she included me out of pity—or a kind of unworthy generosity.

I suddenly felt a pang of fear. The one that was coming less lately but still lurked there in the background sometimes. It was the fear that everyone wished Sam were the one here instead of me.

"What if I'm not?" I blurted out. "What if I disappoint you? And Baba?"

She furrowed her brows. "What are you talking about, foolish girl?"

"Baba and Mama came to America so we could have the type of life they wanted. What if I waste their efforts?"

Nai Nai stared at me, her gaze never wavering. She could be

funny and wry, but she could pin you with a single look. That's why she was the matriarch. "Is that what you think? They went to America so you could have the type of life *you* want. As long as you are working toward that life, you are not wasting their efforts."

There was a tightness in my chest that seemed to grow until I was fairly sure I was going to burst and split open, but somehow, I stayed intact, holding it all in. I had a feeling like lying on the ground and staring into the sky until you were falling or flying but you couldn't tell which. All those years apart, and so much had changed, yet while all the love was distant and hard to access sometimes, it didn't go away. It would never go away.

She was so beautiful, I thought.

She lowered the phone. "Ah, my wrists are tired." The screen wobbled as she balanced the phone against the breakfast tray. "That's better." It left her image slightly askew. "Don't be worrying about these silly things. You worry too much, always. You are so young. Life is long."

Except when it wasn't. I had brought a book from Sam's college boxes with me to read on the plane. It would be with me, but he wouldn't.

"I'm lucky," she continued. "Lucky to have had all those years with you and your brother and sent you off to America to grow up. Your grandfather would've wished to see this." Her hands smoothed the sheets across her lap. "I am so happy you are coming, but I confess that I miss Chen Wei. It feels like it has been a long time," she said.

This was it. I knew I could tell her, if I wanted. We were alone. My parents had left me here. I could change everything. It was all spinning around in my head. Did she deserve to know? Was I a monster for keeping it from her, or would I be a monster for telling her when I could see for myself that she was waning?

"Nai Nai," I choked out, "Chen Wei would want to visit. He can't. It's because—"

Honestly, I did not know what I was going to say after that, even right up to the edge. It didn't matter, because she cut in before I could finish.

"You don't have to say it." She shook her head sharply.

I was silent. Surprised. The air itself seemed to hover breathless between us. Her jaw was tight and clenched. We didn't say anything for an extended period of time.

"It doesn't matter where he is," she said finally. "I know wherever it is, he wishes he could come. I know that."

I wiped my face, mildly damp, and quelled my hands from shaking. I didn't know what else I could say. Nai Nai settled farther back in her pillows, letting out a slow exhale. "When I go to sleep, I dream about when you were still babies, out in our village. Do you remember the hot summers?"

I nodded, not trusting myself to speak.

"The past can be a gift. I am grateful for the memories. They're good for me, an old woman. Future hopes are for the young."

"You still have a future."

She laughed and sounded like crackling autumn leaves. "You

are a flatterer, my granddaughter. I always thought you were the funny one. Can you do something for me?"

I sat up. "Yes."

The gate agent announced that the plane had arrived and was being cleaned out. Boarding would begin in fifteen minutes.

"Tell your brother that he's in my heart."

I looked and looked at her, searching for a sign of clarity, whether she really knew the truth or not. But all I could see was that she was sleepy and that our conversation was winding down to its end. She was waiting to drift off into her dreams, where she didn't live in that drab building in the city, where Da Ji Cun would always exist and the three of us were locked, perpetually, in a sun-drenched story, our shoes dusty with that familiar yellow dirt. And I was going to let her go there.

"I will," I said.

Her face softened, the lines around her lips going slack. "Thank you."

"I have to go now. We'll talk more when I get there. I'm about to get on the plane. I'll see you very soon. Tomorrow."

Her eyelids were drooping. "Yes," she said sleepily. Her breath evened out and turned into gentle snoring.

I watched her for a minute, sleeping peacefully, and ended the call. Then, I gathered all my bags, walked over to the line at the gate, and boarded, at last, the flight that would take me home to my family.

ACKNOWLEDGMENTS

THANK YOU FIRST and always to Wendi Gu, my absolutely brilliant agent, who is funny, levelheaded, and has flawless book recommendations. You are the only person who could ferry me through this maddening industry that breaks my heart and makes my dreams come true. You always believe in my words even when I do not.

This book had two editors who are the best in the business. Thanks to Alessandra Balzer for working through its conception and early messy drafts, tirelessly pushing me to find the emotional core of the story. And endless gratitude to Jen Ung, who reshaped the book into the truest, best version of itself. Jen, I could never have gotten here without you. You are an irrepressible ray of sunshine, and I'm so blessed that you adopted this book.

Thank you to every person at Quill Tree and HarperCollins who helped bring this book to readers, including Carter Wilken, Alexandra Rakaczki, Alison Klapthor, Allison Brown, Lisa

Calcasola, Jenny Lu, Patty Rosati, Mimi Rankin, Jen Wygand, Susan Yeager, Kathy Faber, Tom Pombo, Laura Raps, the schools and libraries team, and the sales team. It's truly an immense effort, and I appreciate every person who played a part. Special thanks to Jessie Gang and Hsiao-Ron Cheng for the cover of my dreams, and to Rosemary Brosnan for welcoming me to Quill Tree with such enthusiasm, generosity, and warmth.

Thanks to Afua Antwi and my UK team at Penguin for their efforts across the pond as well.

I'm so appreciative of my colleagues at YouTube and Google for their genuine interest in and support for my side gig.

Much gratitude to friends—Rosie Powers, Jill Disis, Kara Giacobazzi, Melissa Silverberg Meyer, Andy Maloney, Charlie Tan Lim, Hannah Meisel, and Laurie Feigenberg—for the emotional support now and always. The Daily Illini changed everything for me, and I'm lucky to have found you all through that. Thanks as well to Angela Kim and Andy Chon, who I continue to go to for everything, personal and professional. Still hoping one day we can move into a giant house together with our spouses and children.

A big thank-you to E. L. Shen for being a joyful resource, venting buddy, and friend in publishing.

Jas Hammonds, Anna Gracia, Maggie Horne: I was in a low place and really needed someone to talk to in Arizona. You brought me more comfort than you can ever know.

Thanks to Jessica Kokesh, my eternal fandom friend, irreplaceable writing partner, and life cheerleader. Here's to almost two decades of words together.

Thank you to my family—my parents, my brother, Stacy, my cousin Jane, Chang Zhao, and my extended group of perfect in-laws.

Finally, thanks to my two favorite people in the world. Chris, my husband, who does all the things that matter so I can live with my head in the clouds. I don't want your notes, but I want everything else with you. And Henry: There is only the time before and after you came into existence, and after will always be better.